SOMEONE IS AFTER LULU DUPREE

OTHER BOOKS BY JOSI S. KILPACK

THE SADIE HOFFMILLER CULINARY MYSTERIES

Lemon Tart
Tres Leches Cupcakes
English Trifle
Baked Alaska
Devil's Food Cake
Rocky Road
Key Lime Pie
Fortune Cookie
Blackberry Crumble
Wedding Cake
Pumpkin Roll
The Candy Cane Caper
Banana Split

PROPER ROMANCE

A Heart Revealed
Lord Fenton's Folly
The Vicar's Daughter
Miss Wilton's Waltz
The Valet's Secret
A Lady's Favor (eBook only)
Forever and Forever
The Lady of the Lakes
All That Makes Life Bright

The Mayfield Family Series
Promises and Primroses
Daisies and Devotion
Rakes and Roses
Love and Lavender

SOMEONE IS AFTER LULU DUPREE

JOSI S. KILPACK

SHADOW
MOUNTAIN
PUBLISHING

Photographs on pages 290 and 291 courtesy of the author.

© 2025 Josi S. Kilpack

All rights reserved. No part of this book may be reproduced in any form or by any means without permission in writing from the publisher, Shadow Mountain Publishing®, at permissions@shadowmountain.com. The views expressed herein are the responsibility of the author and do not necessarily represent the position of Shadow Mountain Publishing.

Visit us at shadowmountain.com

This is a work of fiction. Characters and events in this book are products of the author's imagination or are represented fictitiously.

Library of Congress Cataloging-in-Publication Data

Names: Kilpack, Josi S., 1974– author.
Title: Someone is after LuLu Dupree / Josi S. Kilpack.
Description: Salt Lake City : Shadow Mountain Publishing, 2025. | Series: LuLu Dupree mystery | Summary: "After a traumatic brain injury, LuLu's peaceful new life in Sedona shatters as deadly threats force her to confront her buried past and unravel a dangerous mystery"—Provided by publisher.
Identifiers: LCCN 2025003354 | ISBN 9781639934317 (trade paperback) | ISBN 9781649334664 (ebook)
Subjects: LCGFT: Detective and mystery fiction. | Novels.
Classification: LCC PS3611.I45276 S66 2025 | DDC 813/.6—dc23/eng/20250303
LC record available at https://lccn.loc.gov/2025003354

Printed in the United States of America
Publishers Printing

10 9 8 7 6 5 4 3 2 1

To Doug,
Waking every day to you is a gift.
I love you so much.

CHAPTER 1

I put the empty Snapple bottle on the desk with more force than necessary, and the thump startles me. *Careful, LuLu*, I tell myself. It's important I set the right tone for this meeting—both metaphorically *and* literally.

"Sorry." I lift the bottle to replace it more gently. The softer sound invites a better energy, I think.

Mr. Hernández—the attorney I hope will take my case—does not react. He stares at the Snapple a moment and then looks up at me with the same flat expression he's had on his face since I entered his office less than a minute ago. The black polo shirt he's wearing complements both his stoic presentation and the stark emptiness of his office, which has exactly one desk, two chairs, and one of those extra-wide filing cabinets—black, which matches his shirt, though I'm guessing that is a coincidence rather than planned coordination.

"I need to get this tested," I say when he doesn't say anything. "And I'm assuming you know people who can do that on the *low-down*." I make a pressing motion with my hand to emphasize the need for discretion.

His expression does not change. "Do you mean the down-low?"

I nod. I mix things up sometimes, but the meaning is usually still intact.

"Tested for what?" he asks.

"Poison."

His dark eyebrows lift slightly above the clear rims of his glasses. "Poison?"

"All kinds, though I suspect they would have used one of the undetectable kinds."

His eyebrows go back down. "You want me to test this empty bottle of Diet Peach Snapple for undetectable poison?"

"I mean undetectable after a person is dead, of course. Undetectable in the body." I wave my hand from my shoulders to my waist to further demonstrate. "Half-life and all that. The lid was still on when I pulled it out of the recycling, so the inside is undisturbed." I bend down to tap the outside of the plastic with my fingernail. I miss the glass bottles and the metal lids that popped when you opened them, but if there is anything I have learned, it's to accept change and get on with my life. "You can see the droplets of liquid, which should make for excellent testability."

Mr. Hernández straightens, and his chair squeaks in a way that makes my brain stutter. I send pink thoughts to my frontal lobe to reset everything back to the proper columns and lines in my head and tune into my senses to keep me present—the coolness of his office, the cushiony softness of the chair beneath me, the sound of the rather loud AC unit down the hall.

"Maybe you can start from the beginning," Mr. Hernández suggests.

"Excellent idea," I say with a nod, keeping my eyes on the bottle so as not to get distracted by anything else, like the water stain on the ceiling behind his head or the fact that he has a mint-green mouse for his computer. Despite our very limited acquaintance, he doesn't seem like a mint-green-mouse kind of guy. "On June fourth," I continue, "exactly one week ago, I retrieved this Diet Peach Snapple from the fridge at approximately 1:20 p.m. It was a Tuesday."

"Is that important—that it was a Tuesday?"

I shrug, feeling the bows of my sundress straps brush my ears when I do. The fourth best thing about living in Arizona is wearing lightweight dresses almost all the time. Today's dress, the pink linen, has straps that tie at the top of each shoulder. It's as cute as it is comfortable. "Anything could be important when we're talking about attempted murder."

He seems to consider this, then makes a *do-continue* gesture before leaning forward and clasping both of his hands on the desktop between us.

I continue. "I retrieved the bottle from the fridge and twisted off the cap while looking at the clock—I needed to leave the house by 1:30, which is why I'm pretty sure it was 1:20 when all of this happened—but the cap did not seem to be sealed. You know how when you open the cap on a plastic bottle there's a clicking sound?" I look at him expectantly, wanting to make sure he's following. He still looks slightly bored, which makes no sense because I am an excellent storyteller, and this particular story is very interesting.

"Yes," he says after a few seconds.

Truth. I would know if he were lying about this. Plus it would be weird if he didn't know what I was talking about.

"Well, on June fourth, it did not click even though the lid was on tight. I put the cap on the counter and was raising the bottle to my mouth when I realized that it did not smell right.

There was something . . . I don't know, *off* about it. Sort of nutty or cherry or something."

"It *is* a peach-flavored drink."

"Peach-*infused*," I clarify. "I drink a lot of Diet Peach Snapple, and this one didn't smell right. Anyway, I was in a hurry because I was taking Mrs. Larado to Rachel's Knoll, and I only had a few minutes to get on the road."

"Who is Mrs. Larado?"

"My Tuesday afternoon client."

"What does that mean? What kind of client?"

"I do home care for seniors," I explain. "I have two appointments a day, Monday through Thursday. Mrs. Larado is my Tuesday afternoon, and that day was an extended appointment because, like I said, Rachel's Knoll. She likes to visit the Peace Pole there once a month or so."

"Got it," he says with a nod. Clearly he'd been in Sedona long enough to not ask what a Peace Pole was or why an elderly woman would want to visit it once a month. Outsiders often find this sort of thing strange. I find it invigorating.

After getting nowhere with the police yesterday, I had debated whether it would be better to go to a private investigator or an attorney, but then Fiona reminded me about her nephew. Since attorneys surely know the best private investigators, it feels like a two-stones-one-bird sort of thing, and I do not have time to waste birds. I also do not take it lightly when Fiona makes a helpful suggestion.

"So, I had planned to take the Snapple with me, but because the cap hadn't clicked and it smelled funny, I poured it into my bamboo palm instead, replaced the lid, threw the bottle in the recycling, and grabbed a different Snapple that clicked the way it should and smelled the way it should. I didn't think much about it until a couple of days later when the leaves of the palm started to turn brown. By Sunday, it was more brown than green."

"Why didn't you pour the Snapple down the sink?" Mr. Hernández asks.

"We live in the second driest state in the country. I don't waste water." Second to Nevada, which receives even less rainfall than Arizona—a surprising fact, but a fact nonetheless.

"It wasn't water," Mr. Hernández says. "It was a diet drink full of engineered chemicals. I'm not the least bit surprised it killed your plant."

Truth. This ping of truthfulness is not as exciting as it might seem. When a person shares their own opinion, it only means they believe their belief. Still, it's better than when they share an opinion they *don't* believe in. That is all sorts of confusing.

I lean forward. "Then you agree it was poisoned?"

He lets out a huff of a breath. "Let me try this again—do you often pour chemically engineered diet drinks into your plants?"

"Yes."

He blinks and cocks his head slightly. "Really?"

"I mean, maybe not *often*, and I'm not sure I would define Diet Peach Snapple as chemically engineered—they use natural ingredients—but if I don't drink something, I pour it into a plant. Bamboo palms are known for hardiness; they can handle FDA-approved diet drinks. Like I said, I don't waste water."

"It's not—" He seems to stop himself. "Never mind. Okay, so we've established that it is usual practice for you to pour diet drinks into your planters, fair enough. And until now, it has never resulted in the demise of your plants?"

"Exactly."

"Which has led you to believe that the Diet Peach Snapple

had been tampered with for the intention of trying to poison you."

"Well, the death of the bamboo palm in addition to the lack of lid-cracking, the funny smell, *and* the attempt to burn down my house."

"The attempt to burn down your house?" he repeats with no change in his expression. What would it take to get an animated reaction, I wonder?

"I woke up Sunday night and couldn't fall back asleep. I went into the kitchen to make toast, which is when I saw—and smelled—the candle right there in the middle of the stove."

"You don't usually find candles on the stove at night?"

"Never," I say with an emphatic shake of my head. "It wasn't one of *my* candles—I make my own—and I would never light a candle during the summer. It was the Walmart brand. Someone put it there."

"And how do you figure a candle to be an attempt to burn down an entire house?"

"Well, all the gas burners were turned on."

Mr. Hernández straightens, and his eyebrows go up. "The gas burners were on?"

Oops.

I had left that out when I first talked to the police too. Since the accident several years ago, my brain sometimes skips over details, especially when I'm excited.

"All four knobs had been turned to high, though I didn't notice that particular detail until the next morning. That's when I *knew* that candle was nefarious."

"Didn't you smell the gas when you made toast?"

"I turn the gas off in the summers to reduce the unnecessary heat from pilot lights. But, yes, *if* my gas had been on, that candle could have blown up my house instead of just making everything smell like fake mulberry and fake plum."

I reach into my purse and withdraw the offending candle sealed in a gallon-sized Ziploc bag I'd blown into like a balloon. I place the ballooned-Ziploc on the desk. "Can you also have this tested for prints?"

Mr. Hernández's momentary interest disappears, and he settles back into his chair, making it squeak again, which shudders through my thoughts like shaking an Etch A Sketch.

What were we talking about?

This mixing up of my thoughts happens less now than it did in the beginning—thank goodness. The shifting is often triggered by sharp, unexpected noises or shocking information—like yesterday morning when I realized the implication of all the burners having been turned on. When this happens, visualizing a ball of pink light works like a magnet in my brain, sticking my thoughts back where they belong. Focusing on my external senses also helps, so I squeeze the arms of my chair and wiggle my toes while thinking over the last several seconds to remember where we are in the conversation.

"So, you think that someone has tried to kill you twice," Mr. Hernández says. "Once with poisoned Diet Peach Snapple and once with a mulberry-plum-scented candle from Walmart?"

My thoughts come together, and I am back in the game! "Yes."

"And it's someone who knows you well enough to know that you drink Diet Peach Snapple but not well enough to know that you turn off the gas to your house in the summertime."

I consider this a moment and smile widely as a triumphant wave of energy washes through me. "That is an excellent point! I just knew coming to you was the right decision, and I promise to let Fiona know you are not washed-up and lazy like she said. So, when do you think you can have these items tested?"

It's only when I stop talking and notice that Mr. Hernández's expression has gone even flatter that I realize I probably shouldn't have included Fiona's opinion of him.

Oops again.

In my defense, I'm sure she would say as much to his face. She probably has, which is why he doesn't stop by to see her very often.

"How do you know Aunt Fee again?" Mr. Hernández asks.

"You call her Aunt Fee?" I say, smiling at a sweet nickname for a woman who is not very sweet. "That's adorable."

He says nothing and simply holds my eyes, which prompts me to answer his question.

"She's my Monday morning appointment every week. That's how I got your information."

"She said I was washed-up and lazy?"

I wave my hand through the air to help move our energy past that little faux pas; sometimes I talk too much. "Oh, you know how she is." I nod toward the items I've put on the desk between us. "When can you get these items tested?"

He pauses, maybe debating whether to keep digging into Fiona's insult or move forward. I am relieved when he looks at the candle. "Testing for poison and running prints is more of a police detective thing."

Truth.

He is sitting up straighter in his chair than he was before, however. I'm pretty sure he's interested in my case.

"I agree. But I talked to them yesterday, and they did not take me seriously."

"You don't say."

Sarcasm is neither a truth nor a lie, nor is it very professional, but I ignore it. "I expected better from local law enforcement, too, but I had the distinct impression that the police detective had been laughing at me in his head."

I'd gone to my weekly appointment with Fiona yesterday feeling unsettled from that disappointing interview with the police. She called me out on it when I put dish soap in the mop bucket instead of floor cleaner. I ended up telling her all about it while dumping out the dish-soap water, rinsing the bucket, and preparing the correct mop bucket before mopping her floors. She monitors everything I do to make sure I don't miss anything. Loneliness makes people difficult sometimes.

Fiona had then reminded me about her nephew who had moved to Sedona a few months earlier after being run out of the DA's office in Phoenix—Jaime Hernández; his first name is pronounced *Hy-may*. She'd mentioned him to me before, but not with much warmth or recommendation.

The picture I had pulled up on my phone a minute later had apparently been an old one. In that photo, Mr. Hernández had short hair and had been wearing a suit and tie. In real life, his hair is almost to his shoulders, and he's wearing denim shorts and Birkenstocks. His teeth had also been terribly white in that photo. Not that they aren't white now, but they are just the right shade of white, as opposed to that super-bright white in the photo that made me think of elementary school glue. Which makes me think of his teeth being pasted together. I tap my teeth together, imagining them sticking.

I break into that unwelcome thought loop by imagining a flamingo standing on one leg at the top of the Stratosphere. Silly flamingos have proven to be very effective in preventing my thoughts from scampering off into the reeds. I have a dozen of these little brain-hacks I use depending on the situation.

With the help of the precarious flamingo and some pink

light, I sharpen my focus on my reason for this appointment. I need Mr. Hernández's help.

I am aware that sometimes I come across as aloof or weird. Most of the time what people think of me doesn't matter. Sometimes, however, I need people to see more than a ditzy, middle-aged, blonde woman in a cute sundress. I look at Mr. Hernández straight on and feel my energy slow from the frantic pace it's been at since I arrived.

"I really need some help, Mr. Hernández. My daughter is supposed to come out next week for the summer, but I can't have her here if someone's trying to kill me. I can pay whatever your hourly rate is—I'm not asking for a favor—but I need to know you're committed to helping me figure this out."

Mr. Hernández sizes me up from across the desk for a few more seconds, seeming in deep contemplation though his expression hasn't changed. Then he takes a breath that feels decisive and sits forward, returning his elbows to the desk and tenting his fingers. "I charge $350 an hour with a half hour billable minimum and will require a $10,000 retainer to get started, the balance of which I will show through monthly invoices. I also require a credit card on file should we go over the $10,000. If these terms don't work for you, then you have my best wishes."

I smile with relief and immediately begin fumbling in my purse which could double as a small suitcase if I ever went anywhere overnight. I named this purse Lisa after a particular episode of *Mad About You* when the sisters accidentally trade purses for the day. Brilliant television.

"I have $3,000 in cash and can write a check for the other $7,000." I pull out the envelope of cash I'd withdrawn on my way here and set it on the desk before pulling out my wallet.

He smiles for the first time, but it doesn't reach his eyes. "It will be a pleasure to do business with you, Mrs. Dupree."

"Ms.," I correct him. "Divorced. Please call me LuLu."

"Alright. Is LuLu short for something? I'll need your full legal name for the file." He starts tapping on the keyboard of his computer, the satisfying sort of clicks my brain likes.

"It's short for Catherine," I say as I open my checkbook. "Should I write the check to your law firm or you personally?"

CHAPTER 2

I am back at Mr. Hernández's office Friday morning after leaving two voicemails and sending three texts—none of which he responded to—since our first meeting on Tuesday morning. One of my personal rules is not to over-demand communication from people, but I paid him $10,000 so I think it's appropriate for me to be here when he didn't respond to my other attempts.

A paper with handwritten hours of 9:00 a.m. to 4:00 p.m. Tuesday–Friday covers the logo of the denture company that had been leasing the building before Mr. Hernández became the tenant. I used to bring one of my clients here before the company moved to a fancier office in uptown. Dentures are good business in Sedona, Arizona, where the median age is fifty-eight. So is lip filler. And rocks.

It's almost 9:30, and he's still not here. I text to let him know I'm waiting for him and that he's late per his posted office hours. I add a smiley face emoji so he knows I'm not mad.

I am sitting on a bench in the shade of a shade of a pinion, trimmed to accommodate the bench, waving the collapsible fan I keep in my everyday purse—named Kermit because of his particular shade of green—when a silver BMW pulls into the empty parking space next to George Flemming III—the name I have given my new-to-me Subaru. I like naming things.

Mr. Hernández steps out of his fancy car while I pick Kermit up from the bench beside me. Kermit is a cross-body purse, my purse-type of choice when I am not transporting cash and evidence, like I was on Tuesday.

"Good morning, Mr. Hernández," I call out as I hurry toward him, my flip-flops slapping the pavement in rhythm with my steps. When I leave the shade of the cottonwood tree, the heat shocks me, even though it's only in the mid-eighties right now. It will get hotter by the hour until it hits the mid-nineties this afternoon, then the whole city bakes for a few hours before it starts to cool down again. For a girl who grew up in Seattle and loved the rain and wearing sweaters six full months of the year, this climate still takes me off guard sometimes. And it's only June.

Mr. Hernández stops in front of the office door and turns to face me as I approach, his expression betraying nothing of how he feels to see me or what he's learned since we last met.

"Did you get my texts?" I ask when I reach him.

He pauses a moment. "I saw your text just a few minutes ago. I had a late breakfast meeting."

Truth. I'd sent three other texts in the last few days, however. He doesn't explain why he never responded to those.

"Well, good, then my being here isn't a total surprise. Do you have an update on my case?"

"The update will take about three seconds, Ms. Dupree," he says. "I don't have test results."

Truth. "I figured as much," I say, disappointed but understanding. Sophie's supposed to be here on Wednesday though—

that's five days from now. "How long will it take before the results are ready?"

He lets out a breath and wipes at his forehead already shiny with sweat. "Why don't you come inside for a few minutes?"

"That would be lovely. Thank you."

He unlocks the door and holds it open so that I can enter first. For a moment, I wonder if he might offer me a cold drink—I've already finished the Diet Peach Snapple I brought from home—but a glance at his perpetually frowning expression as he comes into the office makes me think that he's not the *offer-the-lady-a-cold-soda* sort of guy. He's wearing nearly the same outfit from Tuesday except that this polo shirt is navy blue with a swish in the upper left corner.

It's stuffy inside the reception area which boasts a fake ficus tree in one corner and a fake saguaro with rubber needles in another; I couldn't resist touching them last time and, thankfully, they just sprang back. Three chairs complete the furnishings of this room with dingy pink carpet and walking paths a shade darker than the rest. It still smells like the denture company—cloves and hot plastic.

Mr. Hernández mumbles an apology for the office being warm as he crosses to the thermostat; apparently it shuts off intermittently. He's been meaning to get it checked.

Truth.

Maybe I should give him Handy Manny's card. I keep a few in Kermit just for situations like this. Thinking of Manny, even just as a referral, makes my toes tingle, and I have to picture a flamingo with reflective sunglasses stepping out of a DeLorean to keep my thoughts on track.

I'm wearing my hair in a messy topknot today, and the first wisps of conditioned air catch the tendrils that have escaped, tickling my neck and making me shiver—which helps to keep me present. Mr. Hernández continues walking through the reception area toward his office in the back. When he reaches the doorway and turns around, he seems surprised that I'm right behind him.

I smile and step past him to slide into the same seat I'd occupied on Tuesday. I fluff the skirt of my dress around my legs. Today's dress has a stretchy bodice and then four tiers of complementary patterns of blue cotton, each a bit fuller than the tier above it. It's not ruffly, exactly, but a very nice A-line cut with a billowy skirt that hits me mid-calf.

It's hard to believe there was a time when I only ever wore black, tan, or white, and rarely in dress-form. That was Catherine's corporate uniform, but then she wore mostly black when she was casual too. Nowadays, colorful, loose-fitting dresses make up the bulk of my wardrobe with a few T-shirts and two pairs of leggings to round things out. Sometimes life requires pants—yoga, for instance, and probably skydiving—but not as often as most people think.

"So?" I ask eagerly once he's seated and we've gotten the first squeak of his chair out of the way. "What lab did you send the evidence to?"

He pulls open a desk drawer and removes the Snapple bottle and mulberry-plum-scented candle still in the zip-top bag.

My smile falls as I stare at the items he sets on the desktop between us. "I thought you'd sent them."

"I didn't need to send the bottle," he says. "All you have to do is swab the liquid and send that in. Testing can take up to six weeks. The facility does criminal testing as well as private, however, and criminal cases get priority. But I'm pretty sure I know what was in it."

"You do?"

"Paraquat."

Truth.

I feel my eyes go wide as I stare at the offensive bottle that may as well have been a guillotine for its intentions. "Is that a type of poison?"

"It's an herbicide—a weed killer that is as bad for people as it is for dandelions. I had first thought it was cyanide since you said it smelled like cherries, but cyanide doesn't kill plants. Paraquat, however, has been mistaken as a beverage before and proven fatal in several of those cases, which is why it's no longer available to the general public. It would kill your bamboo palm and would have a good chance of going undetected in an autopsy. There are only so many things the coroner automatically tests for."

I collapse back into the chair, and my body tingles in a very different way than it had when I thought about Manny. I had pulled three more dying leaves from my bamboo palm this morning.

Paraquat.

I think I remember it from that show *Yellowstone*, which is a show about a lot of horrible people doing horrible things that I can't seem to stop watching.

Suspecting that someone is trying to kill me is one thing, like considering the *idea* of skinny-dipping in a neighbor's pool on a hot day, which is something I'd never *actually* do. But to have the threat confirmed is something else entirely. This isn't a TV show. It's not random or accidental. Someone wants me dead in real life. Someone spiked my Snapple with actual poison.

"Paraquat," I say, feeling the terrible word roll over my tongue. It is a dark word. Spiky. "Para-quat."

Mr. Hernández leans forward in his chair, and the squeak sends my thoughts scattering for a full second before I manage to visualize enough pink light to pull them back together. It's essential that I stay present and engaged and as clearheaded as possible right now.

"And the candle?" I ask, gripping the arms of my chair tighter, needing to hold on to something.

"That's a bit trickier," he says, gesturing toward the plastic bag still housing the candle. "Fingerprints have to go through the official database, which is maintained by the FBI. The officer you approached last week logged your visit as a neighborhood complaint, so I need to figure out how to get someone else at the department to buy into this."

Truth.

I nod, then say "Paraquat" again under my breath. What if I'd brought Mrs. Larado a cold Diet Peach Snapple that day? The thought sets off popping noises in my head as my brain tries to shift away from this moment again.

Stay here, I tell myself as I picture a flamingo standing on its head. *Remain present.*

"So, who would want you dead?"

That helps keep me in this moment. I look up at Mr. Hernández and blink. "What?"

"Someone put poison in your Diet Snapple. Who wants you dead?"

"Someone" is actually some *one*. A person. I feel the heaviness of that throughout my body and blink back the sting of tears as I accept this fact.

Why would someone not want me to have this life I've worked so hard for? It has taken an incredible amount of physical, mental, and spiritual focus to recover from the injuries I sustained in a car accident five years ago that should have killed me. My life now is simple, small, and manageable. How would my death make someone else's life better?

I swallow a thickening in my throat at such a sad thought—one I can't ever un-think again.

Mr. Hernández lifts his thick eyebrows. "You have no idea?"

I shake my head.

"An ex-boyfriend? A landscaper you owe money to? A lover's wife? A rival for your daughter's cheerleading aspirations?"

I pull myself up straighter in my seat. "What kind of person do you think I am?"

He gives no reaction to my offense. "Poisoning a person's Diet Snapple isn't something done on a whim, Ms. Dupree. It takes some pretty intense motivation and planning to pull that off. Are you on the run from someone? Do you ever carry drugs over the border? Are you an undercover CIA agent? Have you been to Russia lately?"

I shake my head and take a deep breath. "The only things I'm running from are the weather patterns of the Pacific Northwest," I say. "I don't take drugs or go over the border—I don't even have a passport. I don't know any landscapers because I don't have a yard, I never finalized the CIA application, and I haven't been to Russia since 2006."

I stand up and shake out my skirts. I've done a good job of staying present and focused so far, but that tingling hasn't gone away, and I'm worried I'm going to lose my chill. I need to process what I've learned before I can continue this conversation. "Thank you for your time, Mr. Hernández. You've given me a lot to think about. I'll call you this afternoon."

He stands. "Wait, you applied for a job with the CIA?"

"No," I say, turning toward the door while remembering

that most people are murdered by someone they know. Faces flash on hyperspeed through my brain like a lineup. The trouble is that I don't actually know that many people anymore. A few dozen, maybe, and some of them are circumstantial—like the clerk at the grocery store and my clients' family members that I see when my appointment overlaps a visit.

That produce manager didn't appreciate my comments on the quality of the organic lemons a few weeks ago, and the lady who lives next door never waves back. Not once in more than two years. I took her some of my peppermint-scented Good LuLu Bathy Oil at Christmas in hopes of striking up a conversation, but she wouldn't answer her door even though I knew she was home. I left it on the porch. The oil wasn't there when I looked the next day, so I assume she took it inside, but she's still never talked to me. I've accepted her indifference—Jerry across the street says she's that way to everyone—but could it be *hatred* she feels toward me? Enough to want me dead?

"You just said you applied for a position with the CIA," Mr. Hernández says, drawing a portion of my attention back to him.

"I said I never finalized the application," I clarify. In my mind I see an animated dark figure with wispy edges sneaking into my house and opening a Snapple bottle from my fridge. Did they take a drink from the bottle so there would be room for the poison? When I drank from my parents' liquor cabinet as a teenager, I always added water so that the levels stayed the same. I look up at Mr. Hernández. "Can you also do a DNA test around the rim of the bottle in case they drank some first?"

"You were recruited by the CIA?" Mr. Hernández asks.

"I wish I had thought to put the Snapple bottle in a Ziploc bag in case it had prints too," I say out loud as the details bounce around in my brain. "I didn't even think about it, and now I've touched it, and you've touched it, and it touched all the other bottles that were in the recycling bin." I would make a terrible private investigator. "I bet any prints the killer left behind are completely corrupted."

Mr. Hernández waves me back toward my chair. "Ms. Dupree, why don't you sit back down so we can talk things through? Getting a bit more background would be helpful for me, so I know exactly how to handle this case."

Truth. Even though I came here for answers, I guess I wasn't really prepared for what those answers might be.

Paraquat.

"Can we talk later?" I ask as I adjust Kermit's strap across my chest so he hangs against my hip. I don't return to my seat. "I need some time to process all of this. I'll call you. Will you answer your phone when I do?"

"Let's process it together."

I shake my head. "I'm sorry, but I know my limitations, and I think I've reached them for the day." I smile so he won't notice how embarrassing it is to say that out loud. I'm an adult woman who has to give herself time-outs in order to function. In my defense, the acceptance that someone wants you dead is something I'm pretty sure most people would struggle with.

I head back through the reception area with Mr. Hernández right behind me. My thoughts are getting splintery, and I try to send pink light to them, but this might be bigger than even pink light. I picture a flamingo in Groucho Marx's glasses, but the broom-bristle mustache melts beneath my increasing anxiety.

Paraquat.

I feel a mourning for my bamboo palm . . . and then follow up with an intense wave of gratitude, which I always picture as golden liquid-light. If I hadn't poured the Snapple into my plant, I would never have known someone was trying to poison me. That palm very well may have saved my life.

I start planning how to best pull myself together as I make my way out of the office.

There are four energy vortexes in Sedona—points where it's believed that the energy of the earth spirals up in a concentrated form. Proximity to these vortexes affects individual energies when a person opens themselves up to them. My accident separated me from the world in a lot of ways, but the energy of the vortexes moves through me sort of like a radio wave—I feel it all the time when I'm in Sedona, a soft vibration like the patter of light rain on a tin roof. Sometimes it's necessary for me to finely tune into those frequencies, however. Now feels like one of those times.

I decide to stop at Posse Grounds Park on my way home. It's not a vortex, but it's powerful in its own way, and the trails there are easy to access. Plus, it's not a tourist stop, so I have a better chance of finding solitude. I'll stand barefoot in the dirt until I feel properly grounded to the core of the Earth. I used to need twenty minutes to feel that kind of grounding, but I can feel the benefits after only four minutes now. Perfect practice makes progress, and practiced progress is perfect.

I reach into Kermit hanging against my hip and wrap my hand around the large, rose agate I'd purchased when I first came to Sedona. I believe in an infinite God of love and possibility, and it feels absolutely probable that He endued that love into the minerals of the earth He created. Sometimes I pray and sometimes I meditate and always I seek peace anywhere I can find it—church, rocks, green grass, butterflies, vortexes. Rose agate supports emotional healing, and the stone itself, about the size of slightly flattened chicken's egg, fits perfectly in my hand and calms me when I need that little something extra.

I'm struggling to find peace right now, though, even with the rose agate in my hand and faith in my heart. The need to separate myself from this meeting with Mr. Hernández and connect with God through Mother Earth is incredibly strong.

"I'll call you this afternoon," I say as we reach the door that leads to the sidewalk. "I can't really think about this anymore right now." There's a slight buzz in my head, in fact. It will get louder until I can't hear anything else—a sort of shutting down and shutting out of my senses. It's happened before.

Mr. Hernández continues trying to talk me into staying as I push through the door. The heat surprises me again when I step onto the sidewalk. I blink against the sun, but also a glint of something hits me right in the eye and makes me drop the rose agate back into Kermit.

Everything happens so fast. The buzzing in my head stops. I hear a shout from Mr. Hernández, feel hands grab me by the shoulders, and then I am thrown toward the ground at the same time a burst of stone and dust explodes above me.

CHAPTER 3

I'm pretty sure Sergeant Rawlins is not laughing at me in his mind this time as I explain what happened while lying on a hospital gurney in the emergency department of the Verde Valley Hospital. In fact, he is listening quite intently as I end with the description of Mr. Hernández tackling me to the sidewalk, someone across the street screaming, and someone else yelling to call 911.

Mr. Hernández is in the ER, too, though I haven't seen him since all the flashing police lights sent my brain wheeling—the whole ambulance ride is a blur. I remember repeating the affirmation "Everything works out perfectly for me" over and over again. It's my favorite affirmation, reminding me that even when everything feels wrong, the outcome *will* be perfect for me.

I've also been visualizing pink light nonstop and tapping my meridian lines every time I'm left alone in my little curtained area. Even with all these brain-hacks, though, I'm surprised that a complete meltdown has not happened. Someone shot at me . . . and I'm not a quivering lump of a woman in need of a tranquilizer. How is that possible?

The sounds of this place might prove my downfall now that the shock is wearing off, however. So many different types of noises are keeping my tension high. I can hear someone shouting from down the hall, and the beeps and rumbles of all sorts of equipment are creating a cacophony of sensory overload. There is an elevator door opening somewhere to my left—are people getting in or out? High heels in the hallway sound like gunshots.

"Do you have any idea who could be behind this?" Sergeant Rawlins asks.

It takes me a few seconds to bring my focus back to this conversation. I shake my head. "I can't think of anyone."

"Did you see anyone while you were waiting for Mr. Hernández to arrive at his office?"

"I saw a lot of people walking or driving by, but no one I recognized or anyone who stood out." Lots of things in my curtained area are blinking and beeping and whooshing. The blood pressure cuff tightens on my arm. I shiver and take a deep breath but can't fill my lungs all the way. I often tune in to my senses to keep me present; I'm not sure how to tune out.

There is something I want to ask the sergeant, but I'm struggling to remember . . . Is it about Sophie?

No.

Mr. Hernández?

No.

Trigonometry?

And then the elevator door shuts, the high heels disappear, the blood pressure cuff deflates, and my mind blessedly clears for a moment!

Trajectory! That's what I wanted to ask him about.

I turn to look at him straight on. "Did you find the bullet?"

He hesitates, and then nods. "It was embedded in the cinder block of the building."

Truth.

I remember landing on my right side. My whole right arm is aching, and a half a dozen other places on my body will likely have a variety of bruising tomorrow. Fortunately, I managed to protect my head. I can't afford another brain injury.

"How high up from the ground did it hit?"

"Pardon?" Sergeant Rawlins asks.

"If it was eight feet high, then they were probably just trying to scare me, right? But if it was less than five feet six inches, then they probably wanted me dead."

Dead.

Paraquat.

I take a deep breath and invite in pink light to keep me focused.

"Um, I'm not sure," Sergeant Rawlins says.

Lie.

"That's a lie," I say before I think better of it.

He startles. "Excuse me?"

I feel my cheeks heat up with a blush. I am too muddled to handle this with my usual awkward grace.

"You know where the bullet hit." The blessed clarity is fading, and my anxieties are rising to the point where I can't afford to wait until I'm alone to tap my meridian lines again. I raise my left hand and begin to tap my index finger against the side of my left eye. I care more about my own mental health than I do about what Sergeant Rawlins thinks; healthy adults manage themselves, and I work very hard to count myself within the category of "healthy adult."

"I deserve to know what I'm up against, Sergeant Rawlins."

Tap, tap, tap.

"I would like to know what you're up against, too, Mrs. Dupree." He's watching me tap, and he's speaking more slowly, as though I seem more ignorant now than I did before. I find that ironic since the tapping improves my overall processing abilities. I don't bother to explain it, though. Something tells me he doesn't put a lot of stock into energetics.

"Ms.," I correct him. *Tap, tap, tap.* "How far up on the wall did the bullet hit?"

"I'll update you as soon as I have more information. In the meantime, is there somewhere you could stay for the next few days while we investigate?"

I shake my head and start tapping underneath my eye to clear the energy from the stomach meridian, specifically the fear and anxiety which so often settles into that part of the body. I can feel the heat in my belly receding, making space for calm. Having space is the first step, only then can I fill it with the energy I want.

"Until we know what we're dealing with, it would be best if you didn't go home," Sergeant Rawlins continues. "We can put you up in a hotel."

"How high up on the wall was the bullet?"

"Let's focus on how we can protect you going forward."

"Sergeant Rawlins," I say, holding his eyes as the world goes silent for a moment. I stop tapping and focus all my energy on him. "You want me to trust you, but you won't tell me what a hotel is going to protect me from. Where did the bullet hit?"

He clenches his jaw, and we stare at one another for the length of time it takes for me to say hippocampus three times. He takes a breath. "The bullet was approximately four feet from the ground."

Truth.

I stare at the ceiling and let the information sink in. "It was a shot meant to kill me, then." I feel validated for having taken the Snapple and the candle as seriously as I did. I was right! But being right means that someone *is* for real trying to kill me, which deflates that validation pretty quickly.

"Now will you agree to police protection?" he asks.

"What kind of gun?" I ask, still looking at the ceiling.

"We won't know until we've finished our forensic investigation."

He's lying again, but a soft lie. An *I'm not certain.* Maybe the type of gun doesn't matter yet.

"Something glinted," I say, though I am pretty sure I'd said that before.

"Scope, probably," he says. "We think the shooter was on top of the shops across the street. We're talking to some people who may have seen something."

On top of the shops, I repeat. Like a sniper. I think about Afghanistan and James Bond movies and the old video game where you shot animated ducks with a plastic gun.

"We can put you up in a hotel for a night or two while we find some answers," he says again.

I shake my head. "I want to go home."

"I understand that, Ms. Dupree—" he begins, but then his phone rings. He pulls it from the heavy-looking belt he wears around his waist, then glances at me. "Sorry, I need to take this."

Truth.

"Of course," I tell him, glad for the break.

He stands up from the stool he's been sitting on and identifies himself into the phone. He pulls back the curtain, then closes it behind him. As his voice fades into the general melee of the ER, I am relieved to have a few minutes of relative aloneness even though the hospital sounds get loud again in my ears.

I start tapping again, this time tapping all the different zones on my body to get the full benefit—eyebrow, outer corner of the eye, under my nose, below my collarbone, and so on. I glance at one of the monitors and see that it's 10:38 a.m.

I only work Monday through Thursday; Fridays are my days off or when I reschedule for clients who couldn't keep their regular appointment during the week. Everyone kept their usual time this week, so I was planning on catching up my laundry, going to the grocery store, and making some Body Toddys; one of the two boutiques I sell my Good LuLu products through is running low on inventory of my signature body scrubbers. Today was supposed to be a normal day for things like that, and a longing for that normality waylays my tapping for a moment.

I close my eyes and let the visualization of what today could have been overtake me. I picture myself folding laundry while I watch a Sandra Bullock movie, making creamed eggs in the air fryer for lunch, and laying out what I need to make the Body Toddys—louffas, coconut sugar, and my Good LuLu Body Washy that becomes an all-in-one body scrub. The visualization calms me and helps me remember that the overwhelming emotions I'm feeling right now won't last forever. One day I will be able to have the day today should have been. It's something to look forward to.

A minute later, the ER nurse comes into my curtained area and does a final set of vital signs before telling me I'm ready to go if I feel up to it. Everything hurts when I stand, but my dress made it through unscathed, which is a little bit of a shiny lining. I shift my weight from one foot to the other, tightening individual muscles one at a time as I get my bearings.

The nurse watches me. "You're okay? Not feeling dizzy?"

"I'm good," I assure her. I mean, I'm still overwhelmed and overloaded and scared and confused, but the tapping and meditation helped. Even the beeping seems softer.

I take a few careful steps, wincing at an ache in my hip and a twinge in my knee, but then force myself to stand up straight and walk normally. "I'm good," I tell the nurse again.

She nods and says she'll be back in a few minutes.

I find Kermit at the foot of my bed and then locate a vending machine down the hall where I buy two bags of fruit snacks. I mean to save one for Mr. Hernández but accidentally eat them both on my way back to the emergency room. I throw away the wrappers so I don't have to admit what I did. When I am back to the curtained areas of the ER, I bend down to look beneath the other curtains to see if I recognize Mr. Hernández's shoes until I realize that he'd probably be lying on a gurney like I had been.

There are only two curtains pulled closed, which means I have a 50 percent chance of finding him on the first try and a 100 percent chance of finding him on the second.

I peek into the first curtained area, and Mr. Hernández looks up at me from where he is sitting on his gurney. He is doing something on his phone one-handed but that's because his other arm is in a sling. He puts his phone down when I enter.

"Your glasses broke." There isn't anywhere for me to sit, so I remain standing even though my hip is throbbing.

"Yeah," he says flatly, lifting his left hand to push the damaged lenses up his nose. The right earpiece is missing, and there is a crack running diagonally through the right lens. "I'm going to take the replacement cost out of your retainer."

I'm not sure his replacement glasses should be my responsibility, but then again, paying for a pair of glasses is a fair exchange for him having saved my life.

I watch as the cuff around Mr. Hernández's sling-free arm inflates to take his blood pressure. The beeping makes me shiver, and I notice the smells that I've managed to ignore thus far. Sterile, medicinal, rubbery smells. My stomach feels icky. His phone chimes with a text message, and then another one almost immediately after the first. He ignores both.

"Are you alright?" I ask.

"Not really, no," he says, lying back against the pillow but continuing to watch me. "I tore my rotator cuff and will probably need surgery. Every other joint in my body hurts."

Truth. Relatable truth.

"I hope saving my life was worth it."

"So do I."

Ouch.

"Did the police talk to you?" he asks.

I nod as my eyes get stuck on the heart monitor. Maybe I should have stayed in my own curtained area after all. I seem to have adapted to those sounds better than I'm adapting to his.

"I think they're taking you seriously now," he says.

I cock my head slightly to the right and pull my eyes from the monitor to look at him. "Are *you* taking me seriously?"

He nods. "Someone is definitely trying to kill you."

Truth. Relief floods my chest, and I let out a breath. *He believes me!*

The blood pressure cuff releases with a hiss, and I rub the gooseflesh on my left arm with my right hand, even though moving my right arm hurts. At least it's not in a sling like Mr. Hernández's.

"The police don't want me to go home," I tell him.

"Well, someone *has* tried to kill you there twice."

"I guess that's true." I stare at the floor, hating the idea of not going home after a day like today. The distraction of my hobbies is centered there. It's my safe place. Or, at least, it used to be. But it is also where someone has tried to kill me two out of the three attempts. It isn't safe, is it?

When I look up from the floor, Mr. Hernández is looking at me. "Are you okay?"

"Um, no," I say with what I mean to be a laugh but ends up sounding like a huff. "But I'm still alive, so there's that. I really want to go home, not to some hotel."

His phone starts to ring. He picks it up with his good hand and silences it before giving me his full attention. "I agree with the police—you shouldn't go home until this is settled."

I look at my toes that I painted bright yellow yesterday. They don't improve my mood as much as I would have liked.

"They are offering you protection, and, as your attorney, I think you should take it."

"The police," I say with irritation. "Sergeant Rawlins wants me to trust that they'll protect me, but they didn't want to help the first time I went to them, and they still aren't telling me everything."

"It's not their job to tell you everything. It's their job to protect you."

"But I deserve to know the truth of what I'm facing, and I don't like Sergeant Rawlins playing games about that." I put my hand on my chest. "He certainly shouldn't lie to me. It's my life on the line, after all."

Mr. Hernández is watching me closely, and I shift beneath his stare. "That's a pretty strong allegation, LuLu. To say he lied."

It's the first time he's actually called me LuLu, and it makes me feel like maybe we're friends. I hope that's true. "He *did* lie. I'm the one who got shot at, and, well, you did too. We both deserve to know more details than the average Moe."

"What did he lie about?"

"He said he didn't know how far off the ground the bullet hit, but he did. It was four feet from the ground. It was meant to kill me."

"So, he *did* tell you."

"Not until I caught him lying."

"You accused him of lying to you?"

I weigh how much I want to say. Mr. Hernández is my attorney, and I need him to trust me. "I can tell when people are lying. How can I trust the police if they won't be honest with me?"

He pauses for a moment as though taking this in. "What do you mean, you can tell when people are lying to you?"

"I *know* when people lie to me." There aren't that many ways to say it. "It sets off an alarm inside me." I glance at him for a reaction before scanning the curtained area for something to focus on that doesn't make me feel dizzy. I really don't want to tap in front of him, but my anxiety is rising. "That's what I mean."

"You feel an alarm?"

I shrug. "I don't know how to explain it better than that. I can just tell when someone tells me the truth and when someone lies to me. I feel a little . . . ping in my chest. I think it's probably an energy they emit, or a pheromone or something. I don't really know how it works, but I'm not making it up and I'm not *guessing* that Sergeant Rawlins lied. I *know* he lied and when I caught him in it, *then* he told me the truth. It doesn't inspire a lot of trust when I have to demand the truth about my own safety."

"So, you have to be with someone in person to feel this . . . ping? Physical proximity?"

I guess we're not done talking about that. Maybe if I answer his questions, we can move on to how much I'd rather go home and make Body Toddys instead of stare at the bland art nailed to the wall of a cheap hotel room.

"I can't spot a lie over a phone call if that's what you mean. And gestures or movements don't trigger the same awareness—I mean, sometimes I can tell by the way someone acts, but I think everyone can do that. The . . . alert I feel is triggered verbally somehow. I know, it's weird."

He watches me for a few seconds. "My favorite color is green."

I look him in the eye again even though I'm ready to move on from this topic. His eyes aren't a bad thing to focus on; however, I've always been preferential to brown eyes. Maybe because mine are so blue. People have called them striking or piercing or intimidating depending on the circumstances of their commentary. Brown eyes seem so much softer. Although his stare isn't soft—it's intense.

"That's true. Green *is* your favorite color, but do you mean a bright Kelly leprechaun green or a woodsy evergreen?"

He thinks a moment. "Evergreen."

I feel the ping. "That's a lie."

He raises his eyebrows. "I like cheese."

"True, but everyone likes cheese except vegans, and you're not friendly enough to be a vegan."

He huffs a laugh. "My mother's name is Esmeralda."

Lie.

This could go on all day. I look at him square in the face.

"Did you get kicked out of the DA's office because you interfered with the investigation of a woman you had a romantic relationship with?"

The story had been all over the news when it happened, though I hadn't been particularly attentive. I hadn't been working for Fiona yet, but she told me about it a couple of months ago when she mentioned that her other nephew was moving to Sedona. The first nephew she told me about was Jordan; he helps her with a lot of things, and I know all about him. I didn't know about the other nephew. I had looked up the details after my first meeting with Mr. Hernández on Tuesday. I don't judge people too hard for who they once were in hopes that such grace earns me the same mercy.

His face flushes, but he doesn't answer the question, which is what I expected. He looks away to fiddle with his watch on the wrist of the arm in the sling. It's a few seconds before he looks up at me again.

"You're a little . . . different, aren't you?" he says.

I hold his eyes and consider, again, how much to tell him.

CHAPTER 4

"If I'm to help, which I hope to be able to do," he says when I don't immediately explain why I'm different, though I sense that's what he wants to hear about, "I need to understand who you are and your history. I want to help, but I need more information than what I currently have if I'm going to be effective."

Truth.

No one aside from my medical team knew me when I moved here, and no one on my medical team ever knew the woman I was before the accident—back when I was Catherine. Talking about the accident isn't my favorite topic, much like my lie detecting. But I have asked for his help. He did push me out of the way of a bullet. I take a breath and imagine white daisies to fortify myself. Visualizing flamingos is for when I need to stop a direction of my thoughts. Pink light for focus. Daisies are for when I need to be brave. Talking about the accident that changed everything requires courage.

"I was in a car accident outside of Tucson just over five years ago," I explain, looking at the track in the ceiling where the little thingies that hold the curtain in place slide back and forth. I pull the curtain one direction a few inches, then back, impressed with how smoothly the thingies move in the track. They sound like the wheels of tiny, well-oiled roller skates. "I suffered a brain injury and was in a coma for a few weeks."

Twenty-four days to be exact, which is why twenty-four is not my lucky number. I still like the number four though. And twenty. "I still deal with some of the effects of the brain trauma, which, I guess, does make me a little different than other people. Information organizes differently in my head, and I sometimes forget details."

"Brain trauma, huh," he says, though there's little inflection in his voice. "What caused the accident?"

"We're not sure," I shake my head and move the curtain again. "It was just me, no other vehicles, and it happened at night. The investigation concluded that a rabbit had jumped in front of me or something. I lost control, flipped the median, and rolled several times. I don't remember it."

"You don't remember anything?"

I shake my head. "In fact, I don't remember much from the weeks of my life before the accident, and only bits and pieces of the first few months of rehab that followed; that's what first introduced me to Sedona—it's where the rehab facility was that I was sent to. Even after all this time, about five months of my life are either gone entirely or very hazy."

I do remember with painful clarity how I tried to go back to being Catherine Wright Dupree in Seattle after I finished nine months of rehabilitation, though. I wasn't Catherine anymore, and once I better realized who she'd been, I didn't want to be her again. Catherine's friends couldn't make the transition. They were ambitious, high-powered grinders without space for the version of Catherine who couldn't work or go out for drinks and didn't always know the right place to laugh in a conversation. When Covid happened, I went to Spokane to stay with my mom and used the time-out to reconsider my future that I had been so certain of before the accident happened.

My family in Spokane adjusted to the new me better than my friends in Seattle had, but Catherine had done a fair amount of damage to those relationships too. My mom is really the only person from my old life who has truly embraced me as LuLu, and we're closer now than we ever were before, probably because I *want* to have a close relationship. Catherine didn't. Mom's the only bridge left, other than Sophie, between my old life and my new one. By the time Covid restrictions had lifted, I was ready to start over completely. And so, I did.

"You really don't remember the accident at all?" Mr. Hernández asks, bringing me back to topic.

"I remember a few details from the days before the accident, but nothing important." I can see my hand turning up the AC in an unfamiliar car—probably the rental car I'd been driving. Two stacks of typed papers held together with black binder clips. A road sign for Picacho Peak exit, which was the next exit I'd have reached if my car had stayed on the road. I might be able to remember more details if I tried, but I prefer to put my energy and focus toward creating a life I am excited to wake up to every day. A life someone doesn't want me to have anymore.

"And I'm doing very well," I say when he doesn't comment further. I continue moving the curtain back and forth, enjoying the swishing sound; it helps drown out the other sounds of the ER that are battering against my eardrums. "Better than anyone thought I would in those early months. I drive and work and cook again. I make chemical-free soaps and hygiene products that I sell in boutiques around town, and I do yoga when I plan ahead well enough to get to the classes." Which is about three times a month.

As for my limitations, I'm not great at social cues, and my time management is pretty bad, which is why I keep a simple schedule and set a lot of reminders on my phone. I have a financial adviser and a bookkeeper to manage my finances, and I have a therapist, Dr. Cindy, who helps me sort things out—like the time a woman confronted me in the park for staring at her, which I hadn't realized I was doing. Or when I didn't understand that when someone doesn't return multiple text messages, it means they don't want to continue contact.

I don't stare at people's clothing anymore, thanks to Dr. Cindy helping me understand why that had made the woman uncomfortable, and I have a strict "three unanswered texts means I should back off" rule, which is why I showed up at Mr. Hernández's office today instead of continuing to text him.

"I've learned a lot of tricks and tools to deal with my quirks, and most of the time, they work pretty well, but I am a little, different, as you said."

"Huh," Mr. Hernández says. "Sounds like you've been through a lot."

I nod and watch the thingies move along the track some more. I *have* been through a lot, but I'm at peace with my new life for the most part. Not everyone can say that.

Catherine couldn't. I'm not sure she knew what peace was.

From what I know about Mr. Hernández, and the tense vibe I get from him even when he's telling me the truth, I'm not sure he can say he's at peace with his life either.

"You're really okay now, though?" Mr. Hernández asks. "I mean, since the accident. You live a normal life?"

"Yeah, mostly. Numbers don't work in my brain anymore, and I couldn't live in Seattle—the weather gave me horrible headaches and I could never get warm." I think about Sophie's upcoming visit again and swallow. I haven't shared any of what's happening here with anyone back home, of course—not even Mom—but if I don't figure things out, Sophie can't come, and the idea of Sophie not coming . . . I cut off that line of thinking by picturing a flamingo in a Hawaiian shirt playing a ukulele.

"Do you miss Seattle?"

I shake my head as the flamingo grapevines off stage. "Just Sophie. And fresh seafood. Oh, and my mom, although she's in Spokane." I force a smile but know it isn't coming off as sincere. My anxiety is rising, so I take a four-count breath—inhale four seconds, hold four seconds, exhale four seconds, hold my lungs empty for four seconds. It helps to reset my parasympathetic nervous system.

"How old is your daughter?"

"Thirteen. Today is her last day of seventh grade."

She came to visit me by herself for spring break in April—the first visit we had where it was just us. We hiked and cooked and painted rocks. She loves Arizona. It went so well that Forrest agreed to let her stay for a full *six* weeks this summer without Mom needing to chaperone, the longest visitation he's allowed yet.

"Why doesn't she live with you?"

I take another four-count breath. "Her dad had primary custody while I was recovering from the accident, and it ended up making the most sense to keep that arrangement. For Sophie's sake."

There have been a lot of bad days since my accident—days of pain and fear and struggle—but the day Forrest told me that he would go back to court and deem me incompetent if I tried to fight for more custody had been the worst of all the bad days. We both knew he would win, and I had already realized I couldn't live in Washington State anymore. It broke my heart.

"Ah," Mr. Hernández says with an uncomfortable yet validating amount of pity. "Sorry about that."

"Me too." I pause for two blips of his heart rate on the screen and move the curtain one more time before letting it go. I turn to face him and push up my smile again. "But I have a job I love in a city that invigorates me and my own little house that I adore. *And*, when Sophie turns fourteen, she can change the current custody arrangement."

He holds my eyes again. "It would probably help if we could find out who's trying to kill you and put a stop to that before Sophie gets here."

I appreciate that he's attempting some levity and smile even though his expression remains stoic. "Yes, I think so too."

He's quiet and pulls his eyebrows together. "If you were from Seattle, why were you in Arizona? When you had the accident, I mean."

I have a tendency to jump from topic to topic so I guess I can't be critical when someone else does the same. "I was dating a guy from Tucson. I mean, we worked for the same company in Seattle, but he grew up in Tucson. We had come here to meet his family I guess."

"You guess?"

I shrug, but it doesn't deflect as much discomfort as I would like it to. "Like I said, I don't remember much about the weeks leading up to the accident. Dane filled in some of the gaps. We'd been dating a few months and had gone to Phoenix for the weekend. We had dinner with his parents that night in Tucson."

"You weren't staying in Tucson?"

I shift awkwardly. It's weird to repeat a story you've been

told about your own life. And I hate how Mr. Hernández is staring at me. "No, we were staying in Phoenix."

Mr. Hernández is still watching me. "Was he in the accident too?"

"No." I shake my head, my tension rising. The only people I ever talk to about the accident are my elderly clients, and they take the facts in stride. They've lived long enough to see my near-fatal, single-car collision as one of those things that happens in life. Most of them have cheated death a time or two themselves. And they don't ask a lot of questions. It's been a long time since I've spoken openly about this. "We drove separately because he planned to stay the night at his folks, and I wanted to go back to the hotel. I had my accident on the way back."

"You drove separately from Phoenix? So, you had two rental cars?"

"It's not as weird as it sounds," I explain even though it suddenly does sound really weird. "Catherine would have wanted her own car. She didn't like being inconvenienced by anyone else's schedule, and she wouldn't have stayed at a person's house. She was a hotel sort of gal."

A hotel two hours away from where Dane's parents lived even though Tucson has an international airport. Even though visiting Dane's parents was the whole point of the trip. I've stumbled into these odd details from time to time over the years, but I don't have anywhere to go with them. I can't ask Dane my questions. We're not in contact anymore. So, I ignore the questions when they come up and keep my focus on the present. I've never had anyone else asking those questions, however, and it feels strange and uncomfortable to not feel certain about my answers.

"You call yourself Catherine?" Mr. Hernández asks, bringing my attention back to him.

I feel my cheeks heat up when I realize what I've said. "Oh, sorry, before the accident I went by Catherine, and that's how I think about the woman I was back then. I know that sounds weird." I shake my head and take a breath, hating that I care what he thinks. "When I moved here, I started going by LuLu, which was a nickname my family used when I was little." I shrug again. "Anyway, the accident happened, I recovered at a rehab here in Sedona, and when I realized that I couldn't live in Seattle anymore, I came back. The vortexes energize me, and I've built a new life." I smile and hope it looks confident.

"And this Dane person?"

An entire chorus line of flamingos starts to dance off stage in hopes of distracting me. I politely thank them and close the curtain. I can do hard things, and Mr. Hernández has to understand my history if he's going to help.

I am LuLu, and LuLu is great.

"We kept in touch for a while, but I think that might have mostly been because he felt . . . obligated, since he'd been here when the accident happened—I don't really know. He had transferred to Yakima by the time I returned to Seattle. According to Facebook, he's married."

I try to swallow the renewed embarrassment about the whole text message thing with Dane almost . . . gosh, two years ago now. I hadn't thought about why he didn't respond to several text messages sent over a period of a few weeks. When he finally replied to tell me that my messages were making his fiancée uncomfortable, I sent multiple texts explaining myself, which led to his threatening a harassment charge. It was after that when Dr. Cindy helped me craft the three-text-maximum rule that has saved me a great deal of embarrassment since then. I see Dane's posts on Facebook from time to time, which is how I know he married the cute redhead and, apparently, found Jesus. Every other post is about salvation and coming into the light. I wish we were still friends, but I'm glad he's happy.

"I really don't want to talk about this anymore. Can we find a new topic, please?"

Mr. Hernández nods, his eyes still boring into me. "Sure. Want to talk about the CIA?"

I sigh. "I already told you that I didn't finish the application."

"But they recruited you?"

"They recruited upcoming graduates of Seattle University, and since I minored in forensic accounting for my undergraduate degree, I was a good fit. I had an interview with a scout and started working on the application, which is an absolute bear, by the way, but then I was offered a job in the private sector that paid about three times as much and things were getting serious with Forrest and so I didn't finish the application. I really don't think that has anything to do with someone trying to kill me now."

"Who's Forrest?"

"Oh, my ex-husband. Sophie's dad."

"Got it," he says with a nod. "And Russia?"

"I did an internship with an international bank the summer before graduate school and lived in Moscow for three months. I didn't meet Putin or anyone from the Federal Security Service as far as I know. Really, I've lived a pretty boring life."

"But someone wants to see you dead badly enough that they shot at you in public in the middle of the day. There must be a reason."

"Yeah." I nod, feeling the weight of the attempts on my life and furrowing my eyebrows to once again think over the people I know. I work so hard not to have contention in my life that's it's difficult to think of any negative relationships, let alone someone who would want me *dead*.

My brain clicks with the realization of one, no, *two* negative relationships, however. I turn to face Mr. Hernández quickly, pulling my shoulders back so I'm standing straighter. "Do you think it could have something to do with the embezzlement charge? People wouldn't *kill* for something like that, would they?"

CHAPTER 5

I start to explain what had happened last spring, but Mr. Hernández tells me to stop talking until we have more privacy. I am paying a lot of money for his advice, so I do as he suggests, even though he says it rather rudely. I stay silent in his cubicle for a few minutes until the sounds of the ER become too much.

"I'm going to wait for you outside," I say.

He nods and watches me leave.

I am on my way toward the exit when my young nurse, flustered and irritated, runs up to me and tells me I didn't have authority to leave my own area.

"You told me I was done."

She scowls, turning her pretty features not so pretty. "Wait here. I need to get a wheelchair and your discharge paperwork."

Five minutes later, she's wheeling me outside in a wheelchair, and I'm looking around in hopes no one sees me. If they are going to insist people must be wheeled out of the hospital, they should let us hold signs that say things like "I'm feeling much better now" or "Don't underestimate me based on these corporate policies."

"Is someone picking you up?" she asks when she brings the wheelchair to a stop at the curb.

"No."

"How are you getting home?"

"I have no idea," I say, kicking up the footrests so I can stand. "I'm waiting for Mr. Hernández and probably Sergeant Rawlins." My car, George Flemming III, is still at Mr. Hernández's office, which makes me frown. The black leather upholstery is going to be flaming hot since the parking spot probably isn't shaded anymore.

The nurse huffs. "If you're just waiting, then come back inside. It's cooler in there."

I move toward a shaded bench instead. She's right about the temperature, even in the shade, but I wouldn't go back inside for all the air conditioning in China. "I would rather wait out here, thank you."

She huffs again and takes the wheelchair inside, leaving me outside alone, which is what I wanted all along. I kick off my flip-flops and stand in the dirt at the base of a bigtooth maple tree. It isn't the grounding I had envisioned in the grass of Posse Grounds, and I can feel the distance from the vortexes since the hospital is in Cottonwood—a larger town twenty miles south of Sedona—but it will do.

The nurse's irritation is bothering me—I don't understand what I did wrong. Mr. Hernández's questions about the accident are bothering me—I hate thinking about it. And being at the hospital is bothering me. Oh, and knowing someone wants me dead, that's bothering me a lot.

I spend five minutes with my eyes closed and my hands pressed together at the level of my heart while picturing swirling white light all around me. My breaths lengthen, and my thoughts stop feeling so chaotic. I hear several people walk by, but I don't let myself think about them or their potential judgments about the weird woman in a foofy dress meditating underneath a tree in the heat of the day. I focus, instead, on forgiving the nurse for being testy and on accepting that Mr. Hernández needs to understand my history if he's going to appropriately advise me. It's a relief to let these things go. I blink my eyes open and sit down on the bench.

I look up some silly memes on my phone about the end of the school year and send them to Sophie. I send a funny reel about bad haircuts to Mom. Then I play the bubble-pop game. There are studies that say screen time is bad for your brain, but games were part of my rehab and serve as a good distraction. I'm also really good at this game, which brings a nice shot of dopamine every time I complete a level.

I've completed six levels of the game and am feeling nicely centered when a slinged Mr. Hernández and uniformed Sergeant Rawlins are suddenly next to my bench, making me jump. I hadn't noticed their approach. The bubble-pop game can be very engrossing.

"Sergeant Rawlins thinks it's a good idea for you to stay at a hotel for a couple of days," Mr. Hernández says as though this is new information and not something we talked about twenty minutes ago. "I agree with him, not only for your own safety, but for neighbors and anyone you might interact with for the next few days."

I look between them like a child with two dads telling her what to do. I am still resistant to the hotel option but haven't thought about the risk other people take on being around me. To consider it now makes my throat go dry as though I just ate toast without butter. What if one of my neighbors got caught in the cross fire of yet another attempt to kill me? The idea of someone else suffering because I selfishly wanted to use my own shower is horrible to consider. A glance at Mr. Hernández's sling further emphasizes what the right decision is here.

"Okay," I say. "And the police will be investigating in the meantime?"

"Of course," Sergeant Rawlins says.

Truth.

"I would plan to stay for the weekend at least," he adds.

The whole weekend? I swallow the rebellion that rises in my throat and take a breath. I can accept this.

It is what it is.

I'm okay.

Everything works out perfectly for me.

"Can I go home long enough to pack a bag?" It was only a few days ago that I thought about the fact that I never go anywhere overnight. I should have thrown a chip over my shoulder while I had the chance.

"Sergeant Rawlins is going to drive us by your place to get your essentials and then back to my office." Mr. Hernández is looking at me in a way that makes me think he's trying to tell me something he isn't saying. I have no idea what the subliminal message is, but I nod as though I do even though that sort of pretending has gotten me in trouble before. I follow both men to Sergeant Rawlins's police car, and he invites me to sit in the front seat. I feel sorry for Mr. Hernández when he has to fold himself into the back seat that smells like sweat and stale cigarettes.

"What will happen next?" I ask Sergeant Rawlins once we are en route.

"We'll continue to investigate," Sergeant Rawlins says simply, which he's already told me. I was looking for *additional* details. Is Mr. Hernández planning to turn over the candle and Snapple bottle to the police? Can the police get test results quicker? I don't dare ask these things, however, since I haven't had time to counsel with my attorney. "We may need you to come in and answer additional questions," he adds.

"Okay."

"Please add to your reports that I am retained representation for Ms. Dupree," Mr. Hernández says from the back seat.

Sergeant Rawlins pauses a few seconds, then nods. "Noted."

"Does that mean you have to be present if I talk to the police?" I ask, looking over my shoulder through a grate that separates the front seat from the back seat. It's weird to look at Mr. Hernández through the little square gaps, and it makes me uncomfortable, like he's a bad guy. I face forward again.

"Yes," both men say with equal gravity at the exact same moment. The synchronicity makes me smile despite how uncomfortable I am.

"You live on Yellow Sky, right?" Sergeant Rawlins asks after a minute.

I look at him in surprise.

He glances back at me with raised eyebrows before going back to his driving.

Oh, right. Police can access all sorts of things about me. This makes me uncomfortable too. I guess I also gave my address when I went to the police on Monday and made my "neighborhood complaint" about someone trying to blow up my house. And as part of intake at the hospital.

"Northeast end. Last house."

"Nice," he says conversationally as he pulls up to a light. "All BLM property behind you, right? Not far from the Kushman's Cone Trail?"

"Yeah," I say. "I really like the area." The Kushman's Cone

has several trails that make for excellent night hiking, and having no houses behind me means the desert is like a backyard I don't have to pay property taxes on. Plus, I'm almost straight west of Boynton Canyon, one of the identified energy vortexes, and like to think that I am living in its energetic shadow.

"My brother-in-law used to live on Moonlight."

Lie.

Probably to try to create a point of connection between us. This sort of lie isn't unexpected, but I still hate being lied to. I am reminded to be on guard.

"He liked it out there," he continues. Another lie, since his brother-in-law didn't live there. "Good affordable housing in that area."

The part about affordable housing is mostly true. Sedona is a small town in regards to census population—ten thousand or so—but it's luxury living. I wanted a home that was small and simple with lots of open space around it and good energy, which is exactly what I found a few miles outside of the city center but within vibrational range.

"*Relatively* affordable," I agree, settling in and deciding to use this conversation for my purposes too. "Are you from Sedona, Sergeant Rawlins?"

He hesitates, and I wonder if he's trying to decide if I have some ulterior motive to my question. Which, of course, I do. "I grew up in Gilbert," he says. "Moved to Chapel some seventeen years ago now."

Truth. Chapel is south of Sedona, about the same distance my house is from the city center to the east. And more affordable than Sedona itself but farther away from the vortexes.

"What brought you here?"

"A job."

Truth.

"With the police department?"

He glances at me with a look I know well. It is an "are you really this dumb?" look. I smile and wait. It helps me determine a person's honesty when I ask very specific questions even if those questions make me look like an idiot. Being underestimated works in my favor quite often too. The questions I'm asking are soft pitches anyway, so there's little reason for him to outright lie about things; the *way* he answers is just as telling.

"Yes," he finally says.

Truth.

"You must like it to have stayed so long."

"It's a great town."

Truth. But Sedona is the greatest of all great towns.

"Do you have a family?"

"Three kids."

Lie. Interesting.

"No wife?"

"Not anymore."

Also true, but I don't know if it's a divorce or a death. I decide not to ask because I can tell he's uncomfortable.

"I'm sorry." This works for either situation.

"How about you?" Sergeant Rawlins asks. "How long have you been in Sedona?"

Mr. Hernández pipes up from the back seat. "I would counsel against answering any personal questions, Ms. Dupree."

That puts a damper on the whole exchange, and I go awkwardly silent. I turn and watch the desert landscape pass outside my window for the next few minutes while we finish the drive.

Being from West Washington, where it rains almost as often as it doesn't and everything is drenched in green, the desert had seemed washed-out to me at first, like a bright curtain sun-bleached from hanging too long in the same window. Over time my eyes and my understanding adjusted, and now I see color everywhere. A thousand shades of green and brown and red. There's so much life and strength in what seemed to be barrenness at first.

Sergeant Rawlins turns onto Red Moon Drive and then makes a quick left onto Sunset Hills, which winds around until it takes us to Yellow Sky. He pulls into my driveway a minute later, shaded by a cottonwood which covers George's usual parking spot. I reach for the passenger door handle.

"Hold on a minute," Sergeant Rawlins says, putting out a hand but not touching me. "Let me check things out before you head inside."

I frown but follow his instructions, though I don't stay in the car. It smells terrible despite the vanilla air freshener hanging from the rearview mirror. I let Mr. Hernández out of the back seat, and we stand against the car even though it's noon and scorching hot. The shade of the tree helps, but not as much as I had hoped.

Sergeant Rawlins walks around the perimeter of my house with his hand on the gun at his hip.

Everything works out perfectly for me, I affirm in my head even though things are feeling very imperfect right now.

I watch Mr. Hernández look at my house and wonder what he thinks about it. It's nothing fancy, which is part of why I absolutely love it. Manny—the handyman who is also the most handsome man I know—says he loves my house, which makes me all jiggly inside to think about. He's been to my house half a dozen times for a variety of minor repairs, and twice he's stopped by to drop off his latest version of his evolving No-Bake Cookie recipe. Other than that, I don't get a lot of visitors.

"It was painted a dull green with gray trim when I bought it," I tell Mr. Hernández, waving toward the house that is now navy blue with white trim and a hot pink door that matches the three pink plastic flamingos stuck into the salmon-colored dirt next to the porch. Sometimes I dress them up with Santa hats at Christmas or hula skirts for Hawaii's Statehood Day in August. They are not dressed up right now, though, and maybe that's for the best. This is not a festive occasion.

Mr. Hernández makes what I think is an approving grunt.

"I call it Casablueka."

"Casablanca?"

"Casa-blue-ka, with a *k* in the last syllable. *Casa* is home in Spanish, blue because it's blue and that's my favorite color, and K-A is *ka*, which is the Egyptian word for the creative life force. Casablueka."

"Right."

He doesn't get it. That's fine. Casablueka is cozy and tidy, and when Sophie is here, my home holds all my most precious things.

"The inside was painted six different colors—all of them dark, very 1990s. I painted everything white so it's bright and open."

"Good call," he says.

When Sophie and Mom came out for a few days last Christmas, we painted one wall of Sophie's room butter-yellow—her favorite color—and bought mismatched colorful bedding from the half a dozen thrift stores in town to create a vintage boho look. Sedona brings out a different side of my daughter; I adore seeing her bloom in the desert.

"You, uh, like butterflies?" Mr. Hernández asks, waving toward the fourteen metal butterflies of all colors, sizes, and designs affixed to the front of my home as though migrating through, which monarch butterflies actually do through Sedona every September. I've found these in secondhand shops over the years, too, and there are so many of them now that the different tones and colors match somehow.

"Butterflies are good luck."

"They are?" he asks, giving them a skeptical glance. "I haven't heard that before."

"Well, you've never asked me before."

Sergeant Rawlins comes around the far side of my house, carefully stepping between some agave plants and a particularly stunning prickly pear cactus I have let grow as wild as they choose.

"So, butterflies are only good luck for you?" Mr. Hernández asks as we both watch the sergeant draw closer.

I shrug. "They might be good luck for other people too. I don't know."

"Do you always leave your back door unlocked?" Sergeant Rawlins asks as he walks toward us.

"Yep," I say as I start toward the porch. "Front door too. I'm terrible at keeping track of keys." Manny installed one of those number-pad locks last fall, but I don't like the beeping it makes when I push the numbers.

Sergeant Rawlins puts his hand out to stop my progress toward the front door. "Hold on."

I stop but also clench my teeth together and take a four-count breath. Mr. Hernández and a cop are with me; I feel pretty safe.

"Let me go in first and make sure everything is clear," Sergeant Rawlins says.

I nod and fall in step behind him because he didn't say I couldn't.

Mr. Hernández brings up the rear. "You should always lock your doors," he says from behind me.

"I lock the doors when I'm inside," I reply over my shoulder. "Most of the time." I don't think I'd locked the doors the night the candle showed up on my stove, but I'm not sure.

I've let the yard remain natural desert so that it's not a draw on resources—either water or my time—but I did move some rocks around to outline the path to the front door. The cottonwood that shades the driveway is established, and the two saguaros in the front yard are equally self-determined. They are both at least forty years old, and the one, which I call Beatrix Potter, has eleven arms—the universal number for good luck—and six buds this year that should bloom a week or so after Sophie gets here. I'm so excited for her to see it!

The smaller saguaro is dying, the base slowly yellowing, and he has no blooms this year. One day he'll dry into one of the saguaro skeletons people pay good money for. I named him King Tut in anticipation of his inevitable mummification. The real estate agent who helped me find this house recommended a company that would remove him. I thanked her politely, but I never even considered it. Several of my neighbors have elaborately desert landscaped yards—quite impressive—but mine is more of a DIY creation that suits me and has more open space that some people might call barren but I call . . . open space.

Mr. Hernández and I wait on the porch while Sergeant Rawlins "clears" the house. I feel the prickle of sweat in my armpits and on my scalp, which makes me think of my hair for the first time. It's probably a complete disaster after the sidewalk impact, ambulance ride, and gurney situation. I can't believe I haven't thought about fixing it until right now and am suddenly eager for a mirror.

"So, how long have you lived in Sedona?" Mr. Hernández

asks. He wipes sweat from his forehead. If his shirt wasn't navy blue, he'd have some pretty good sweat tacos going on under his arms. Also, if he weren't wearing such a dark color maybe he wouldn't be so hot. I never wear dark colors anymore, but I'm also getting sweaty, so I'm not sure where I was going with that particular critique of his clothing choices.

"I've been here three years. I rented an apartment for a year before I bought Casablueka—I'll have been here two years next month." July 13 is my purchase anniversary date. Last year, I celebrated with a cold glass of Diet Peach Snapple, watching *Romancing the Stone*, and browsing Facebook Marketplace for a cat like Kathleen Turner had in the movie, which I did not end up getting once I'd slept on the idea.

This year Sophie will be here. Maybe she'll want to repeat what I did last year. Maybe she'll have a better idea of how to commemorate the anniversary.

"And you live here alone? No boyfriend or roommate?"

"No," I say, making a face at the idea of sharing my home with someone else. Other than Sophie, of course. What if someone wanted to move my measuring cups to a different drawer or preferred warm showers in the summertime?

For the first time, I wonder if Sophie will hate taking cold showers. When she came out with Mom for a week last summer, I turned the pilot light on for them. I haven't thought about that yet for this year, and I make a mental note to talk to Sophie about it. Maybe she'll find cold showers as invigorating as I do?

Sergeant Rawlins comes back to the front door. "All clear. I'll wait out here while you pack—make it snappy."

Mr. Hernández comes in behind me and closes the front door. "I want to make sure that you're clear on our relationship," he says.

My eyebrows shoot up as I turn to face him.

"Attorney–client," he clarifies.

My cheeks heat up, and I quickly face forward and head toward my room in hopes he doesn't notice my misinterpretation. He follows. I haven't really thought about whether I find him attractive, but his inference of a relationship prompts me to evaluate this. He *is* good-looking, but his overall grumpiness is definitely an unattractive feature. And he answers my questions strangely, either with his own or evasively. Probably just a character trait, but it gives me pause now that I'm thinking about it. I'm also not sure how old he is—I'm not very good at guessing that sort of thing—but I think he's a little older than I am. Or a little younger. He definitely isn't twenty-five, and I'm pretty sure he isn't fifty.

Manny is forty-four; three years older than I am, which is about perfect for a secret crush. I raise a hand to touch my hair but stop myself. I'll have the opportunity to fix it soon enough and don't want to draw attention to my vanity.

"If the police contact you for any reason when I'm not with you, you need to let me know," Mr. Hernández says.

"Does that mean you'll answer my calls?" I ask over my shoulder.

"Yes," he confirms as we reach my room. He doesn't hesitate to follow me in, which feels a little strange, but we need this time to talk about some things, and since there's nothing romantic between us, it's probably okay to have a man in my bedroom. "You say absolutely nothing to them unless I'm with you," he says.

I open the closet and pull Lisa from the top shelf. "Nothing at all?" I ask, picturing myself in a room while half a dozen police officers ask me if I'd like a drink, or if I'm too hot, or what my favorite color is while I refuse to answer. "That could be awkward."

He sits on the edge of the blue velvet chair I keep in the corner for meditation mostly; her name is Bunny because she's super soft. "Don't answer any questions about the attempts on your life or about your history. You can explain that your attorney has advised you not to talk and then they can't keep asking you questions. Sergeant Rawlins said that he might have more questions for you. That's expected. Just make sure I'm there when you answer, okay?"

"Alright," I say with a nod as I dump everything already in Lisa onto the bed. That's where my good can opener went! I set it aside to be returned to the kitchen later. I honestly can't remember why or when I put it in there.

"I convinced Sergeant Rawlins to get you a room at the Arroyo. That's where I'm staying."

I look at him as I cross to my dresser to get a few unmentionables. "They put you up, too, then?" I distinctly remember Sergeant Rawlins stating that Mr. Hernández was not at risk.

"No, I've, uh, been living there for the last few months," he says. "I asked Sergeant Rawlins to get you a room there so we would be in close proximity to each other. The Arroyo has surprisingly affordable rates for long-term stays in the offseason."

Lie.

"Oh," I say, trying to hide my curiosity on why he isn't being truthful about that. There are a few different Arroyo hotels in Sedona, all of them nicer than I would expect the police department to pay for or someone to live in long term. "Affordable" isn't part of their marketing. Plus, he knows I can tell he's lying. I don't pursue it, though. I'm not sure his reasons for living in a hotel are applicable to my situation, and I'm glad he and I will be in the same building. He's the only security I have right now, something I would not have expected based on either of our meetings at his office. I've chosen to trust him.

Chosen.

That's an important detail. Trust always comes down to a choice.

I roll up a few pairs of underwear and an additional bra in my pink nightgown so that he won't be able to tell what they are when I cross back to Lisa.

"Now, tell me about this embezzlement charge," he says.

I tuck my underthings into the bag and head toward the closet to pick out a few dresses. "Well, let me say up front that I did *not* embezzle anything. Gloria was an owner on the account and well within her rights to do what she did. And I didn't take any compensation for the advice I gave her. Mrs. Roberts had equal rights to the money from the originating joint account, and there was a comprehensive paper trail outlining every step she took to protect her portion. There was no embezzlement."

"So you helped Mrs. Roberts hide money from her husband."

"No," I say, shaking my head as I turn the stack of folded dresses sideways and put them in the bag. "We didn't hide anything. Gloria had every right to half of the liquidity of their assets under the community property laws of Arizona. The judge agreed that Gloria could keep the money we'd managed to protect, and the criminal charges against me were dropped. Mr. Roberts was a real creep, and she is so much better off without him. You'll have to take my word for that."

"I'd actually prefer to take his word for it."

I pull my eyebrows together, confused. I don't think Mr. Roberts would confirm his own creepiness. Not many people possess that sort of objectivity. The last time I'd seen him he'd been glaring at me from across the corridor of the Magistrate Court, blaming me for foiling his plans.

"How much money are we talking about?" Mr. Hernández asks as I grab an additional pair of flip-flops from the closet, just in case. They teach you in Girl Scouts that you should always pack an extra pair of shoes. That might have only been when you're going camping, but still.

"Eight hundred and seventy-two thousand dollars."

Mr. Hernández leans forward, and his eyes go slightly wide behind the lenses of his glasses. The cracked lens distorts that eye, so I don't look at it for long. "They had that much money in a savings account?"

"No, they had *twice* that amount in a savings account," I say with a nod, heading toward the primary bathroom for my toiletries. Thankfully, Mr. Hernández stays in the bedroom.

I finally have the chance to look at myself in the mirror and stifle a groan. My hair is halfway out of the bun on one side and completely lopsided. It looks like I slept on it this way while having very bad dreams.

I begin to untangle the elastic I'd used this morning from the rat's nest that is my hair and raise my voice so Mr. Hernández can still hear me. "I completely agree with you that it is not best practice to have the money in a regular savings account well above the FDIC insured levels. The fact that Mr. Roberts had always managed the money in their relationship gave him a false sense of security and control that worked to our advantage, however." I wince as I comb through the tangles with my fingers but keep talking. "Once we learned about the affair, we had to get Gloria's share of their joint assets secured before Mr. Roberts left her high and dry."

"Right," Mr. Hernández says from the bedroom while I wind my hair back into a messier version of my original messy bun, but it's not lopsided anymore. In Seattle, Catherine had brown hair she kept highlighted, cut to her shoulders and maintained via salon visits every five weeks. After a year in Sedona, I had become a "natural" blonde thanks to regular exposure to the sun; I would never have guessed that would affect my hair color so much. It also turns out I have a bit of natural curl, which helps keep my bun in place. One of the first Good LuLu products I ever made was my Deeply Conditioning Deep Conditioner—I call it DC/DC—that keeps my hair from feeling like straw.

"Eight hundred thousand dollars sounds like a pretty good motive for attempted murder if you ask me," Mr. Hernández says from the bedroom.

"Really?" I wrinkle my nose as I wind the hair elastic around my pile of hair and fluff it a little bit. Not my best work, but also not my worst. I turn away from the mirror and start filling my makeup bag with everything I'll need overnight. "It wasn't even a million dollars."

"When I was in the DA's office, I prosecuted a case where a man killed his brother over less than $500."

"That's terrible," I say, frowning. Their poor mother. "But killing me now won't change anything, and it's been more than a year since all that stuff happened."

I do a final check of what I've packed: deodorant, a Body Toddy, facial cleanser, toothbrush, toothpaste, dry shampoo, regular shampoo, conditioner, dental floss, lip gloss, nail clippers, and my homemade linen spray. I think that's everything I need from the bathroom and return my attention to the conversation.

"The divorce has been final for several months now, and Gloria moved to Miami in November. She's dating a very nice man—retired dentist. I told her to make sure she gets a prenup, keeps her finances separate, draws up a new revocable trust to ensure legacy, and uses an accountant for organizing her finances and taxes." I come out from the bathroom with my hygiene kit and put it in Lisa, who still has a bit of space I feel obligated to fill. Who knows when she'll have another chance to live up to her potential as an overnight bag.

I add the notebook next to my bed and my packet of colored pens but debate on whether to bring my laptop. I don't use it very often, but I don't love the idea of leaving it behind, so I throw it in. With that, Lisa is completely full, and I smile.

"And Mr. Roberts? Does he still live in Sedona?" Mr. Hernández starts up his interrogation again.

"Yeah—same house and everything. I see the mistress at Safeway sometimes but pretend I don't actually see her because, well, I don't want to talk to her." I grab my fuzzy pink sweater from the closet. Maybe I will get to take a night walk—it will be a nearly full moon tonight. I stuff the sweater into space that isn't really there. Lisa is bursting at the seams.

You're welcome, Lisa. I know how good it feels to be useful.

"As soon as we can shake Sergeant Rawlins, we're going to track down Mr. Roberts," Mr. Hernández says with a sharp nod, finally sitting back in the chair even though I'm done packing and therefore ready to go. "You can use your Spidey senses to see if he's the one who wants you dead."

"Spidey senses?" I repeat because I am super confused. I hate spiders.

"Your lie detecting."

Oh. I see. "Spider-Man has increased sensory abilities—literal amplification of his natural senses. I can just tell if people are lying. It's not the same thing at all."

"Close enough. And on our way to his house, you can tell me all about Mr. Roberts and the girl."

"The girl?" I ask as I lift Lisa to test how heavy she is. Not bad. I mean, I wouldn't take her on a hike, but house to car and car to hotel will be fine.

"The mistress," Mr. Hernández clarifies. "The woman you see at the grocery store who might also have a motive to murder you."

"Oh, well, I can tell you all about her—it's a matter of public record now—but she's hardly a girl. Maryanne turned seventy-six years old while I was working with her, so she must be seventy-seven now."

CHAPTER 6

Sergeant Rawlins drives us back to Mr. Hernández's office and does the same sort of inside-outside check before allowing Mr. Hernández to go inside to get his laptop. I stay outside and use a tissue from Kermit to wipe some bird poop from George's windshield. I look around with pensive tension, but there's nothing that gives any indication of the crime committed here other than the hole in the cinder block. I can't stop staring at it.

Shouldn't there be police tape everywhere and the sidewalk blocked and then when people ask what's happened, the story of how I was shot at on a Friday morning would be shared? It's not that I want the fame or anything, but it just feels like people would like to know, and if they did, maybe somebody would say, "I know someone with a sniper's rifle and a propensity for yucky no-name candles. You should go talk to Small Fry down at the Harvester Bar. He always sits at the third stool in from the door." That's how it would happen on TV. Small Fry from the Harvester Bar. TV makes everything look so easy as opposed to my situation where there aren't any actual leads. At all.

Mr. Hernández thinks Mr. Roberts might be involved, but he had his hand slapped hard by the judge and has pretty much disappeared from Sedona society since then. Everything had been fairly low-key until the newspaper articles—whispers instead of black-and-white print. Most of his friends and family distanced themselves from him after that.

After Mr. Hernández locks up the office, Sergeant Rawlins leaves us standing within a few feet of where I was shot at earlier. If he suspects we have a different agenda than going to the hotel and waiting quietly for him to call us with an update, he doesn't show it.

I look anxiously at the tops of the office buildings on the other side of the street and the cars parked in front, wondering where the shooter had been. I'd seen the glint but can't remember exactly where it was. A woman comes out of one of the offices on the other side of the street and heads toward her car. Does she even know what's happened here?

"I am feeling very vulnerable right now," I say, warding off a chill despite the heat radiating up from the sidewalk and down from the summer sun.

Mr. Hernández pushes his broken glasses up his nose with the hand not in the sling and casts his own look around the block. "Me too. Let's go. Are you good to drive my car?" He lifts his slinged arm with a slight grimace.

"We can take George," I assure him, turning back toward my car.

"Who?"

"My car. George Flemming III." Haven't I told him the name of my car already? Last March, I tore off the undercarriage of my Prius for the third time—I called her Princess

Hufflepuff—and while I was arranging a rental car to drive during the repair, I realized that I needed a car that was higher off the ground and the name *George Flemming III* came to me as though in a vision.

Once Princess Hufflepuff was fixed, I took George's name with me to every used-car dealership within fifty miles of Sedona and knew the instant I saw the putty-colored 2017 Subaru that he was my George. The woman helping me with the sale thought the name was fantastic, which was unnecessary, but still the validation was appreciated. I traded Princess Hufflepuff in and drove George off the lot the same day. George has been an amazing addition to my world. He can drive anywhere, his color matches the desert, he's small enough to fit into compact parking stalls, yet rugged—an all-over stand-up kind of guy. I adore him.

"Your *George* is full of stuff," Mr. Hernández says, looking narrow-eyed into the front seat, which is, in fact, full of stuff. Mail, library books, an Amazon package I keep forgetting to return, rocks I have collected the last few weeks to put around the base of Beatrix Potter, and bottles of Diet Peach Snapple that got warm before I opened them as well as several empty bottles I drank when they were cold. I've got a floral comforter in the back seat that one of my clients gave me last week. It'll be a good extra blanket for Sophie's room once I remember to take it inside.

I unlock George and open the passenger door to start throwing everything from the passenger seat to the back. There's plenty of room back there, even with the comforter taking up most of the space on the seat.

"Let's just take my car," Mr. Hernández says from behind me.

"I'm the one driving, and I prefer to drive my own car."

"I have remote air conditioning and seat coolers. I promise you that my car is a better ride."

This statement does not trigger as a lie or the truth because it is neither. It's ridiculous supposition, is what it is. I throw the last Snapple into the back seat, straighten, and move around to the driver's side.

"You've never driven in George so you can't know that your car is a better ride," I tell Mr. Hernández. "And his AC works really well. We'll be cooled off by the time we reach Main Street. I want to drive my own car."

"And I want you to drive mine."

We stare at each other over the top of the car.

"If not for pushing you out of the way, I would be able to drive," he continues. "Since you're therefore responsible for my injury, I should get to choose."

Truth.

He really believes that? "You're saying it's my fault I was shot at?"

His cheeks darken with realization of what he's said, and he looks away.

"Victim blaming just lost you two points, sir. I drive." I get in on the driver's side and push the start button. George growls to life, and I turn up the AC. I might have been exaggerating that we'd be cooled off by Main Street. It's really hot in here. My Jimmy Buffett playlist starts up, and I turn off the stereo. Though there are few situations that cannot be improved by a Jimmy Buffett song, now *might* be one of them. Plus, I'll be tempted to sing along, and I'm not a very good singer thanks to the intubation tube from the accident that left a fair amount of scar tissue behind. When I go to church, I sometimes just hum the hymns, that's how bad my singing voice is.

Mr. Hernández pauses a moment but then gives up the fight and slides into the passenger seat.

I suppress my victory smile as best I can, but it isn't easy.

My phone alarm cuts off my internal gloating, and I hurry to fish my phone out of Kermit. It's my first reminder to call Sophie this afternoon. She has a last-day-of-school party tonight, which means we'll miss our usual Friday evening call. We agreed to 2:30 instead. I was worried that the change of routine would be hard for me to remember, so I set alarms on my phone to remind me at 12:20, 2:00, 2:15, and then at 2:32 in case I *still* forget.

"Everything okay?" Mr. Hernández asks.

"I need to FaceTime Sophie at 2:30," I tell him as I return my phone to Kermit and roll down the windows a little to help the air circulate quicker. Mr. Hernández pulls his door shut.

What will I tell Sophie when she asks how my day has been? I wonder.

The thought forms a pit in my stomach. I hate being dishonest. But is it better to burden the people I love with the truth?

"Duly noted," Mr. Hernández says as he pulls the seat belt across his chest. He can't quite manage the buckle, so I lean toward him and take the belt from his hand. Our eyes meet. Hold. Then he looks away, and I finish securing the seat belt without saying anything, though I am very aware of him being so close to me right now.

He makes a grunting sound that may or may not be a thank you.

"So," Mr. Hernández says with a changing-the-subject tone as I pull out of the parking spot. "I've been thinking about all three of these attempts that have been made on your life."

Truth.

He continues. "Poisoning a Diet Snapple and lighting a candle are passive aggressions—hands off. But then they use a gun? In broad daylight, no less." He shakes his head. "It's weird."

"And a sign of escalation," I say, remembering that word from a documentary I saw about serial killers. I don't watch things like that after 1:00 p.m. anymore because of the way they stick in my brain. Point of case.

"Yeah," Mr. Hernández says with a nod. "Definitely escalating. The poison might not have been detected at all if it had been successful. A house fire is more overt and would trigger an investigation, which is a risk for whoever is behind this, but a shooting is aggressive and even riskier for the perpetrator."

"Increased acts of desperation," I say, using another term that makes me feel smart. "I still don't understand why anyone would want to kill me, though. I'm . . . nobody."

"Power," Mr. Hernández says.

Truth. As a former prosecutor for the district attorney's office, he has a lot more experience with this sort of thing than I do.

I glance at him, but not for long because I'm driving. "Power? I don't have any power."

Catherine had power. She craved it and sought it and wielded it like a machete in every part of her life—work, relationships, motherhood. I just want peace in every part of my life now. Calm, kindness, and peace.

"Not to take *your* power necessarily," Mr. Hernández explains. "But that's why people kill—to either get or keep power."

"I thought people killed for love or money," I say.

"Which are forms of power."

"So, I am standing in the way of someone's power. How?"

"Well, for example, Mr. Roberts was lying to his wife in order to retain the money he was making from disposing of their assets. That money was a form of power, and he wanted as much of it as he could get. Mrs. Roberts wanted her equal portion of the power they had built together over the course of their marriage."

"And I helped take that power away from Mr. Roberts, which you think could be motive for him putting a deadly herbicide in my Snapple."

"Right."

Lie. So, Mr. Hernández *doesn't* think Mr. Roberts could be behind these attempts on my life? This gift of mine doesn't always help me out very much.

"But why come after me a year later? How does that restore his power?"

"Well, you damaged his reputation by pointing out what he'd done—both morally and financially. He might think that getting rid of you would give him more . . . self-esteem."

I turn right toward Highway 179, which will take us south toward the Roberts' affluent neighborhood. "That's just gross," I say. I change lanes, enjoying the soft click-click cadence of George's blinker.

"Yeah, well, murder is pretty gross."

Truth.

"So, tell me about the Robertses," Mr. Hernández says. "How long did you know them? How was the affair discovered? What was the process used to move the money?"

I answer the questions as succinctly as I can. Each question is followed by another one, several of which I have already answered. By the time we turn up Schnebly Hill Road, he's asking me some of the same things for the third time.

"If you don't believe me, you can check the public record. It's all in the transcripts."

Mr. Hernández glances at me. "You think I don't believe you?"

"You keep making me repeat my answers. That's what cops do when they are trying to catch you in a lie." I've seen that on TV.

"I'm not a cop," Mr. Hernández says, facing forward again as I look both ways before pulling into the street.

"Well, you're sort of like a cop. All official and interrogating."

"I'm nothing like a cop," Mr. Hernández says, sounding irritated. "I'm an attorney. I represent private citizens to make sure they are treated fairly."

"Sort of like a cop does."

He turns to look at me. "I'm not a cop!"

"Okay, you're not a cop," I say, shrugging. I still think he's like a cop, though, just without a uniform. And neutrality. He works for me although he talks to me like it's the other way around.

We are silent for a couple of blocks. My arm aches but complaining about it can't change what's already happened. At least I'm not in a sling like Mr. Hernández. He keeps shifting in his seat as though he can't get comfortable even though George's seats are super comfy.

"How did you know how to protect that money for Mrs. Roberts?" Mr. Hernández asks.

"Arizona is a community property state and—"

"That's not what I'm asking," Mr. Hernández cuts in with that brisk way of his that makes me feel like I've done something wrong. "You advised an elderly woman how to navigate a fairly sophisticated series of financial transactions to secure a significant amount of money under the nose of a man I expect to be pretty savvy, yet you turn off the gas to your house in the summer."

"I'm not sure what one thing has to do with another."

He makes a scoffing sound. "You said that after your, uh, accident, you couldn't do numbers, but you can move hundreds of thousands of dollars through multiple accounts?"

"I have my master's degree in finance. I know money. And *I* didn't move anything; that would have been illegal."

"Right, but you said you can't *do* numbers since the accident," Mr. Hernández says.

"I can't . . . *read* numbers," I clarify. "And I can't factor complex formulas because I can't *translate* the numbers. But I still know how to manage assets." Amid the knowledge I retained is the startling statistic that 90 percent of single women over the age of sixty-five live below the poverty line. It's the reason I make a point to ask my clients early on how they are set up financially. Most of them have no idea. Their generation notoriously left the finances up to their husbands, and often a child took over when they found themselves widows. Most of my clients didn't know where their fixed incomes came from when I asked them. I find this frightening.

I've empowered several of my clients to get curious and even excited about financial strategizing. Since I am not a licensed financial adviser anymore, the only thing I have dared to do is encourage them to switch their savings account to a higher-yield money market account. Those clients who want more advantages, or are working with higher dollar amounts, I refer to my financial adviser in Scottsdale. Patty feels the same passion I do that women should know their financial footprint and become wise stewards of their assets. She changes lives.

Helping my ladies has been a nice way to continue to use

the skills I worked so hard to build but can't use the way I once did. It also feels like atonement for some of the terrible ways Catherine used her abilities. She could have done so much good for people; instead she became the person that cheating husbands or dishonorable business partners came to when they didn't want to deal fairly with whoever they were financially connected to. Catherine helped her clients hide assets, deed property out of reach, launder money, and skim earnings undetected. There was nothing she enjoyed more than being involved in someone's scheme. Understanding the laws only made her better at skirting them to her clients' advantage. I hope that what I do now is helping to balance the universal scale I sometimes imagine hanging over my head.

"You can't *translate* numbers?" Mr. Hernández repeats, bringing me back to the present. "I don't understand what that means."

I make the final left turn toward the house the Robertses built thirty years earlier, before Sedona became such a mecca for both investors and people on their personal path to peace and enlightenment. Mr. Roberts owned a construction company that built up a lot of this area in the '80s then sold the company and a fair amount of the land he'd developed for a premium when he retired.

"Well, when I say two plus two, you probably see the actual numbers in your head with a plus sign between them and an equal sign to one side." I can't even remember what side the equal sign would go on because I can't actually picture the equation I am explaining. I've learned with the help of an occupational therapist how to explain this disconnect to people who *can* picture the equation though.

"Yeah," he says.

"I can't do that."

"See two plus two?"

I shake my head. "It was like that with letters in the beginning, too, when I was first doing my rehabilitation, but I was able to relearn them so that I can read again. Numbers never came back though. I *know* numbers and what values they represent, and I can do some things in my head, but I can't make numbers work outside of my brain. I have an app on my phone I can type numbers into—like in a recipe—and it will give me the word description. I'm better with semantics these days."

I look at a mailbox not far ahead and slow down so that we are facing it. "That's a five at the start of the address on that mailbox," I say, pointing.

He is quiet for a moment. "What's the next number to the right?"

I look at it. Sort of circley on top. "A nine." I've memorized certain features the way someone who learned French in junior high can read the road signs in Paris twenty years later but gets huffy eye rolls when they try to speak to a local. I've spent hundreds of hours trying to memorize the shapes of numbers, but the recognition doesn't stay. My neurologist says it's due to the damage specifically relating to my inferior parietal lobe. I eventually chose to take his word for it and stopped letting my numeric illiteracy affect my self-concept.

I am LuLu, and LuLu is great!

"And the last number?" Mr. Hernández prompts.

Stick shaped. "A one."

"Huh."

I start driving again. "Did I get it right?"

"The first number was a two, not a five, then a nine, and then a one."

"Well, I got two right." I smile at my success even though I know it's more about luck. Deciphering numbers is literally a skill I have not been able to re-create. "But you can see why going back to my job as a financial adviser in Seattle didn't work. I know a lot of the information I knew before, but I can't see numbers right, and I can't process things as quickly as I once did."

"So, with Mrs. Roberts you explained to her what to do, but that's why she had to manage all the transactions."

Haven't I explained this three times already? "Well, I educated her about her options and talked her through the processes to execute the transfers, but I didn't do anything myself. If I had, that would have been a securities violation. I'm not a licensed financial adviser anymore, but I can educate and direct my clients toward licensed professionals who can help them protect their assets and determine the best investment products for their situation. We didn't have time, nor did we need, a licensed professional for what Mrs. Roberts did. It wasn't actually that sophisticated."

"Right. Okay, I think I get it."

I turn onto the Robertses' street, quickly recognizing the dead and dried-out saguaro I use as a landmark to remember which windy driveway is theirs. I slow down and look at the saguaro skeleton as I make the turn. I'd never seen those before coming to Sedona, and I find them fascinating. The cactus, once fleshy and solid, literally dries out once it dies, leaving behind what looks like driftwood . . . from a cactus . . . which isn't wood at all. That's what my saguaro, King Tut, will be one day. I would never want to hasten the demise of any living thing, but I'm also looking forward to having a saguaro skeleton of my own. Sorry, King Tut.

Mr. Hernández doesn't speak as we slow to a stop in front of the creamy brown Mediterranean-style home set into the hillside. It has clay roof tiles that help manage the Arizona heat, and the rock formations of Schnebly Hill frame it from behind. The views are the house's best feature in my opinion.

Mr. Hernández whistles under his breath. "Nice place."

"I guess," I say, shifting into park.

"You guess?" Mr. Hernández says incredulously as he begins to open his door. "It's probably a two-million-dollar house."

"Well, yeah," I agree, trying to look at it more objectively as I lean forward to see the boxy house better through the windshield. "But it's the wrong brown for the desert, and just, I don't know, too big. And everything inside is automated. Mr. Roberts loves that sort of thing." I shudder, remembering all the hums and whooshes I had to try to block out when Mrs. Roberts was my Tuesday and Thursday afternoon appointment. "The location is amazing, though."

"The whole thing is amazing."

I shrug. To each their ownership, I guess.

I had started working with Gloria after she had a stroke, which had weakened her left side. She was one of my first clients when I started doing home care. She regained a lot of function over the year and a half that I worked for her, thanks to her commitment to the therapy regimen recommended by her medical team. The last time I saw her, a few days before she moved to Florida, she barely had a limp and could finally look at the future as an adventure—able to imagine the future at all, really. Her husband's betrayal had been the sort of devastation that makes a person go to sleep at night with the hope that they won't wake up in the morning. There were a lot of days during my own recovery where life felt impossible, and I clearly remember when I began to look forward to the sunrise instead of longing for an infinite night. It is the sort of mighty change a person does not forget, and I am grateful to have been a part of Gloria's journey toward that light.

"For a house built in the middle of the desert, it's rather cold," I say. "Figuratively speaking. No carpet, no . . . softness. Just hard lines and hard floors and way too much operational noise."

Mr. Hernández makes a scoffing sound as he lets himself out and then bends down to look through the car at me. "Are you coming?"

I raise my eyebrows. "You want me to? I thought *you* wanted to talk to Mr. Roberts."

"I'll need to know if he's lying. Come on."

My palms are sweaty before I step out of the car. Then all of me is sweaty because it is so crazy hot. I follow Mr. Hernández to the front door, my anxiety building as we approach. I hadn't done anything wrong when I helped Gloria secure her assets, but having charges pressed against me had been embarrassing. There were articles in a couple of the Arizona papers, and two of my clients said they didn't need me anymore. That was in addition to losing Gloria, who moved to Florida, and Maryanne, the mistress, who I fired as soon as I learned she was the reason all of this happened. Well, Mr. Roberts was the actual reason, but Maryanne played her part.

I stand slightly behind Mr. Hernández as he rings the bell. A few notes of Pachelbel's Canon in D ring inside, and I wrinkle my nose. I played the cello for a couple of years in junior high and Pachelbel's Canon in D was the most boring cello part of any song I was given. I always knocked when I came to work with Gloria to avoid the tinny rendition of a song I do not love. The doorbell isn't a sharp enough sound to scatter my thoughts, just raise my annoyance. My heart rate is increasing in anticipation of seeing Mr. Roberts again too. My stomach feels queasy.

I feel the vibration of footsteps moving toward us as Mr. Hernández adjusts the strap of his sling, making me think that, despite his bravado, he is nervous about this too. I hear the click of the doorknob being turned from the inside, and at the last second, my anxiety spikes. This is going to be an ugly confrontation, and I need another minute to emotionally prepare myself. I step behind Mr. Hernández.

I really did think I would wait in the car while Mr. Hernández verified my story, and I haven't had time to ground myself.

Mr. Hernández tries for a moment to pull me forward with his good arm, but I dodge his attempts and picture pink light for focused thoughts. *I can do this*, I tell myself.

I am LuLu, and LuLu is great.

Everything works out perfectly for me.

Then the door is open, and Mr. Hernández stops trying to grab me behind his back. I hold my breath and imagine myself as Thumbelina all curled up in a walnut shell. In Pittsburgh so that I'm a long ways away from here.

"Hello?" a woman's voice says.

It's Maryanne.

Why hadn't I considered she would be here? I pull my shoulders to my ears to make myself smaller, appreciating the additional girth that Mr. Hernández's bulky sling adds to my hiding place but knowing my full-skirted dress isn't allowing me to truly hide. I clench my eyes closed and wish I were a person who was capable of taking in information, making a decision based on that information, and then moving forward with that decision in smooth and calm ways. I don't really *do* confrontation these days, and the impulse to make a run for it is strong though juvenile.

"Good afternoon," Mr. Hernández says. "Is Mr. Roberts at home, please?"

"I'm sorry to say he isn't," Maryanne says in her very clear voice.

Lie. Unexpected curiosity steps onto the stage of my mind, eclipsing some of my anxiety. Does that mean that Mr. Roberts is here and she's lying about that, or is she not sorry that he *isn't* here?

I stay behind Mr. Hernández a little longer.

"Is there something I can help you with?" she continues.

"Well, do you know when he'll be back? My name is Jaime Hernández. I'm a local attorney here in town, and I had some questions I wanted to ask him."

"Uh, well, I'm afraid he'll never be home," she says in that same sweet tone. "He's recently passed away."

Truth.

CHAPTER 7

I put a hand to my mouth as a rush of emotion explodes in my chest. Mr. Roberts is dead?

Mr. Hernández pauses, then clears his throat. "I'm sorry, did you say that Mr. Roberts has passed away?"

Suddenly Maryanne's face is peering around Mr. Hernández's shoulder. "LuLu?"

I close my eyes again, wrestling with my shock as I stay right where I am and picture bright white light, even brighter than Mr. Hernández's gluey smile in that online headshot. White light invites peace and calm, which I need if I'm going to manage the next few minutes.

"LuLu, is that really you?" Maryanne asks.

I keep my eyes closed. I just need a few more seconds to ground myself in this new reality. White daisies pop like popcorn on the screen of my mind's eye.

"It is you!" Maryanne says with what sounds like delight.

LuLu works out perfectly for me.
I am perfect, and perfect is great.
Or something like that.

I'm out of time and take a fortifying breath before I force my eyes open. I step out from behind Mr. Hernández in time to see Maryanne's penciled eyebrows shoot up her wrinkled forehead. Her lips are fuller than I remember, and she's got fake lashes that are too black for her fair skin. Her hair is that same shade of auburn Gloria had blamed for her husband's straying. "Like Jolene in that Dolly Parton song," Gloria had said after we discovered the mistress's identity. Gloria and Maryanne had known each other for years before Maryanne decided to steal Gloria's husband. The whole thing was just awful.

Maryanne steps forward and throws her arms around my shoulders, which causes me to automatically hug her back despite my shock. Doesn't Maryanne know whose side I'm on? Once in the hug, I don't know how to get out of it without hurting her. Maryanne is a very slight woman, and I imagine her fragile joints popping apart if I were to pull away too quickly.

I meet Mr. Hernández's eyes over Maryanne's fluffy hair. He raises his eyebrows, and I shrug to show that I don't know what's happening either. I would not have imagined in a dozen visualizations that Maryanne would be pleased to see me.

"Oh, my goodness, but it's been an age," Maryanne says as she steps back, her birdlike hands on my shoulders.

I cannot think of what to say.

"Do come in, LuLu, and bring your friend."

Maryanne takes my left hand, pulling me into the house. Her skin feels papery cold and gives me the shivers.

Mr. Hernández follows us through the foyer and into the sunken living room. Gloria's kachina doll collection is no longer on the mantel and there's a new rug, but the rest of the furniture is the same, which feels as wrong as it would if everything were different.

"Sit, sit," Maryanne says—one command for each of us

I assume—while making a pressing motion with her bony hands. "I've got cake. Let me put some on a plate for us. One minute."

Mr. Hernández and I sit side by side on the leather sofa, but I can't feel comfortable when there is no Gloria in Gloria's house. She had been so proud of the details that were her ideas in what she'd called her dream home. That double-tray ceiling in the foyer—Gloria's idea. The spiral staircase that goes up to the attic studio, and the playhouse in the backyard that looks like a miniature of this house—Gloria. Without her here, there is no charm at all for me.

Maryanne sets a glass plate in front of us, along with a stack of napkins. I stare at the slices of bundt cake that I instantly recognize as Gloria's poppyseed cake—soft and buttery with a citrus glaze on top. The cake Gloria brought to every potluck she'd been invited to for probably forty years and a recipe she and I made together several times as part of her occupational therapy to improve her dexterity through practicing familiar, everyday tasks. We printed it out and taped it to the inside of one of her kitchen cupboards, though that was for my sake not hers. She had the recipe memorized years ago.

I feel heat starting to rise in my chest. If Mr. Hernández reaches for a slice of that cake, so help me, I might karate chop his arm!

My eyes move to follow Maryanne as she sits on the edge of one of the Queen Anne chairs Gloria chose for this house, layering her hands on one knee. She has sparkly gold acrylic nails to go with the false eyelashes and puffy lips.

Back when I had helped Maryanne with the housework and cooking at the townhome she rented near the city center, Maryanne's daughter paid my wages because Maryanne's fixed income couldn't afford me. Two of my clients right now have a similar arrangement: Fiona's other nephew, Jordan, pays my wages, and Mrs. Gambretti has a daughter who manages all her finances. The contrast of how much Maryanne's circumstances have improved through her deception really churns my butter.

"Oh, it's lovely to see you, LuLu. I have so missed our visits."

Truth. And . . . a weird thing to say.

Maryanne waves toward the cake and smiles as though if she pretends nothing happened that means nothing happened. "Please, help yourself."

I do not smile back and hold myself tightly. I can't count how many times Gloria and I ate this cake at her kitchen table and talked about whatever seemed important at the time: grandchildren graduating from high school, the javelina that ate all her tulip bulbs, the strange letter she received from the tax division about the sale of a property they owned which Mr. Roberts tried to explain away but Gloria couldn't stop thinking about.

Mr. Hernández clears his throat. "I am, um, sorry to hear about the loss of your . . . uh."

Maryanne watches him expectantly but says nothing. Mr. Hernández is lying about being sorry about the loss, but of course that's only because he's trying to get additional information. I can forgive that sort of lie.

"About Mr. Roberts," Mr. Hernández finally says.

Maryanne cocks her head prettily and gives him a soft and appropriate smile. "Oh, thank you, dear. That's very kind of you. Did you know my husband?"

Husband!

I feel my thoughts spin like a three-legged stool with two legs knocked out even though I shouldn't be surprised. I find myself wondering how Mom's doctor appointment went yesterday and what the expiration date is on the milk in my fridge—all attempts my brain is making to disengage from the present moment.

Please, please, please help me, I beg, picturing a flamingo in a rowboat. *This matters. I need to be here.*

I am LuLu, and LuLu is great.

You've got this!

There is purpose in being here.

I feel my anxiety settle as that inner part of me accepts that I can distract myself later because this moment will never come again. My heart rate slows. I open my eyes when Mr. Hernández speaks.

"No, I didn't. But LuLu has told me about him."

"All good things, I hope," Maryanne says, laughing as she crosses one bony ankle over the other and tucks them both beneath her chair. She has excellent posture and is wearing those expensive ballet-type slippers with the turquoise soles that cost hundreds of dollars. I've heard they aren't that comfortable. Fixed-income-Maryanne could never have afforded shoes like that.

"No, actually," I cut in, officially anchored. "I told Mr. Hernández how Mr. Roberts tried to rip off Gloria after you and he started having an affair."

Maryanne's face shows her shock.

Mr. Hernández shifts on the sofa and clears his throat.

I stare at the older woman without blinking. "I guess you two got married, then?" They hadn't been married during the trial because the divorce hadn't been final yet. In fact, Maryanne had disappeared from Sedona while all that was happening. I learned through the grapevine that she had gone to Lake Tahoe to stay in the Robertses' vacation house that hadn't yet been liquidated. It was later sold as part of the divorce decree, and then Maryanne was in town again, buying name-brand canned vegetables this time. Of course she married him. She wanted what Gloria had, which means legal qualification.

I wonder why Gloria hasn't told me they married. Then I wonder why she hadn't told me about Mr. Roberts's death. We don't talk as much as we used to, but surely these sorts of details would be something she would share. We'd become very close through her rehabilitation after the stroke, our *non-criminal* financial planning, and shared understanding of how quickly one's life could change. Car accidents and men who don't keep their promises could irrevocably shift your entire existence.

There is silence for a few beats. When I hear Mr. Hernández take a breath as though he's about to speak, I turn my head and give him a look that makes him close his mouth. I look back at Maryanne with the unblinking stare of my blue-blue eyes. Seconds audibly tick by on a clock somewhere in the room, with all the hums and whooshes of this annoying house providing backup. It is hardly silent, but I let the not-talking get heavy as I wait for her to answer my question. I am anchored and engaged.

"Um, yes, we were married not long after all that . . . business."

Truth.

"And then he died?" I press. "When?"

"Last month."

Truth.

"I didn't hear about his passing. It wasn't in the paper." I don't actually read the paper, but my ladies follow the obituaries like a financial adviser watches the spread of the stock market, which some of them also follow now that they've improved their investments. Those terrible newspaper articles that had made me look guilty had been big news; Mr. Roberts's death a year later would not have gone unnoticed.

Maryanne shrugs a shoulder. "I'm still working on the obituary and memorial service."

Lie.

"Why haven't I heard about it?"

Maryanne cocks her head. "How would I know that, dear?" She laughs as though we are making small talk.

I hold her eyes and feel the menace behind her innocent expression. "Are you trying to kill me?"

Maryanne's eyes go wide, and Mr. Hernández laughs awkwardly. He scoots forward on the sofa. "Uh, well, thank you for your time, Mrs. Roberts," he says, adjusting the strap of his sling. "I think that maybe we should come back another day."

"Do not call her Mrs. Roberts," I say to Mr. Hernández without looking at him. I put a hand on his knee to keep him from standing. I'm not done. I keep my focus on Maryanne. "Someone is trying to kill me, and Mr. Hernández thought it might have something to do with the embezzlement charge. We came here so that he could talk to Mr. Roberts about it. Since Mr. Roberts is already dead, you're the only one left with motive. Are you trying to kill me, Maryanne?"

Maryanne's expression of shock shifts into something hard, but not frightened or put off. Smug is the best description I can think of, and it gives me the chills.

The silence goes from awkward to heavy again. I keep staring, my hand tightening on Mr. Hernández's knee to keep him in his seat. I'm in the zone now and have the solid focus I had asked God to provide. I won't waste the answer to that prayer.

Finally, Maryanne leans into her high-backed chair and

crosses her arms over her chest, emanating that smugness in waves. "Now, why on earth would I do that, LuLu?"

"I cost you and Mr. Roberts a lot of money," I say, thinking of Mr. Hernández's theory that motive for murder was always a form of power. "It would be understandable if you were angry about that even though you had been breaking the law and all manner of ethics and decency."

Mr. Hernández clears his throat. I grip his knee even harder.

"Angry?" Maryanne repeats. She spreads her arms out wide, showing the pale, saggy skin hanging down from her upper arms. "Gloria got roughly a million dollars, and I got all this, his half of the retirement accounts, *and* his life insurance when he died. Who cost who?"

CHAPTER 8

My face tingles with comprehension of Maryanne's words, and I drop my restraining hand from Mr. Hernández's knee.

After several seconds, Maryanne speaks again. "If anything, I have you to thank for all of that, LuLu. I'd been trying to get Bart to leave Gloria for more than a year, but he had one hang-up after another. When everything blew up, well, the marriage was over, and his kids weren't speaking to him. I was the only person there to offer support and encouragement."

Her tone is sweet again. But a yucky sweet—like when you eat full-sugar ice cream right after drinking a Diet Peach Snapple.

"By the time everything settled, he'd lost every friend in this town and was ready to make an honest woman of me." She smiles, looking to all the world like a sweet grandma just dying to bake you some chocolate chip cookies without any nuts. "We enjoyed a lovely year together, and then everything came to me when he died so unexpectedly."

"You instead of his children?" I say. Everything is pinging as truth in my chest, and it's making me dizzy. "There was a will and a trust."

Maryanne shrugs one thin-as-a-bird shoulder. "Both the trust and the joint will were dissolved during the divorce, and the last thing Bart wanted to do was sit down with another lawyer and draft up new documents. There's some probate to work through because of that, of course, but Arizona has excellent inheritance laws, and we did manage to change it so I was the beneficiary on all his accounts and insurance policies before he died. The children's inheritance will be Gloria's problem, which is only fair since she turned them against poor Bart in the first place."

Truth.

My thoughts are starting to pop like water on a hot skillet. The Robertses' children—all older than I am—and most of the Robertses' friends here in Sedona *did* distance themselves from Mr. Roberts after everything that happened. Are the children *still* so out of contact that they don't know their father is dead?

Mr. Hernández stands quickly, startling me and effectively breaking the stare down Maryanne and I have been in while I processed the implications of what she's said.

"Alright, well, I think we have everything we need," Mr. Hernández says.

"How did he die?" I ask without standing. My focus is fracturing like a windshield crack on a cold Seattle morning, but I'm trying to hold on. Pink light all over the place! No flamingos!

"Heart attack."

Lie.

The absolute awareness after she's downloaded so much truth hits me like a hammer in the center of my chest.

I clamp my teeth together as understanding unfurls. Because of his alienation from friends and family and no public notification of his death, no one even knows. I mean, the coroner and some official people must know, but if the surviving spouse doesn't publish an obituary, inform friends and family, and arrange a funeral—if she makes no mention of it—then no one might notice he's gone because his poor choices had isolated him to this prison on the hill. Maryanne was the only person in his life.

Mr. Hernández grabs my right arm and pulls me up from the sofa.

"Nice meeting you, Mrs. Roberts," he says too loudly.

"*Gloria* is Mrs. Roberts, not this geriatric trollop!"

Maryanne's eyes go wide, and her mouth falls open with a dainty gasp of offense as she puts a hand to her chest.

Mr. Hernández pulls me out of the sunken living room and into the foyer. He drops my arm long enough to open the door but then grabs me again and pulls me onto the porch.

I turn back to look at Maryanne, who has followed us, her face a hard shell of victory as she stands on the threshold. She is staring me down as she begins to close the door.

"Gloria is living her best life with a clear conscience!" I yell before the door closes. "Stop making her cake!" The door shuts, sealing Maryanne in and us out.

Mr. Hernández pulls me toward the car and pushes me into the driver's seat before hurrying around to the passenger side. I automatically lean over to help him with his seat belt when he gets into the car, and he pushes my hand away. "Just go. Get us out of the driveway."

George growls to life, and I back down the driveway. I have

only just turned onto Schnebly Hill Road when Mr. Hernández tells me to pull over. I could use a minute, so I do as he says as soon as there is a wide enough shoulder for me to do so safely.

My brain is on overload as I shift into park and cover my face with my hands. My arm is hurting too—he pulled me around by the one I'd already hurt in the fall—but I can handle physical pain. I'm not crying; I just need to feel like I'm tucked away somewhere for a minute until I can face the reality currently remapping my brain. I focus on my breathing and picture a rainbow over the valley where white daisies spring up in every nook and cranny. This is a new visualization for me, and I go with it. Rainbows represent peace and acceptance and a better day. I want all those things right now!

I hear Mr. Hernández turn toward me as best he can with that bulky sling, but I continue my visualization until I feel capable of looking at him, which is about the same time my visualization turns into a Lucky Charms commercial. I open my eyes, and he stares at me for a few seconds before speaking in a low, controlled voice.

"What. On earth. Was that?"

"What was what?" I ask, looking in the rearview mirror for the topic of his question. Does he mean the saguaro skeleton?

He stares at me, then shakes his head. "That whole interview—what is wrong with you?"

Instant heat spikes in the center of my chest as I whip back to glare at him. "Wrong with *me*?" I retort in a tone bordering on a yell that makes him jump within George's relatively small interior. "You're the one who wanted to go there. You're the one who tried to treat it like a kindly neighbor dropping in to say hello. *I* wanted to stay in the car!"

He blinks at me in surprise.

"There is nothing *wrong* with me," I continue, making a

backhand slapping motion in the air with my left hand to push that thought as far away from me as possible. It's a dangerous one to keep around. "And I didn't do anything *wrong*. Have you any idea what that conversation in there means to me?" I point back toward the house. "Do you have any concept about what that means about what I've *done*?"

He stares back at me for a few seconds, then puts out his uninjured hand, palm facing me in either a show of surrender or the way you might try to calm down a wild peacock. "Okay, sorry." He sounds sincere, which surprises me, quite frankly. "I, uh, meant to say that I did not expect you to be so aggressive in that interview."

Truth. His apology cools some of my fervor. But only some. I sit back against the driver's door. "Well, I didn't expect to have such accusations thrown at me or to uncover such a heinous crime."

Mr. Hernández's eyebrows come together. "Crime?"

"She killed Mr. Roberts."

His eyebrows shoot up his forehead.

"She was lying when she said he died of a heart attack," I continue as I face forward and grip George's steering wheel. I need to feel physically connected to something. I'm so glad we didn't drive Mr. Hernández's car. How would I work through all these thoughts and emotions in a strange car that probably doesn't even have a name? I take a breath and let it out. "And I think she's managed to keep the community and his family from even knowing he's dead."

The alarm on my phone goes off, startling me. I shuffle through Kermit to pull out my phone. It's the second reminder I set about Sophie's call, and I feel a spike of panic about having forgotten about it. "I have my call with Sophie in half an hour."

Mr. Hernández lets out a breath of his own and slumps into the corner made between the passenger seat and the window. He lifts a hand to his face and covers his eyes for a moment before scrubbing his hand down his face to his chin. "Alright then, I, uh, let's go to the hotel and get you checked into your room in time for your call." He faces forward. "I think we could both use some time to process things."

I agree and ease back onto the road, but the beeping of the fasten seat belt alarm makes my head want to explode, so I pull over again and help get Mr. Hernández buckled in. We are content to stay in company with our individual thoughts as I pull back onto the road and drive. His words "What is wrong with you?" echo in my head, though, and my skin remains flush with what those words bring up for me.

I've wrestled with "wrongness" a lot since the accident. Everyone in Seattle had expected me to be *Catherine* by the time I finished my rehabilitation here in Sedona. Watching how I failed those expectations over and over again had been excruciating. People asked what was wrong with me a lot. And I lost my temper about it—like I did with Mr. Hernández—over and over again, or I became awkwardly emotional. Something about the accident changed the way I process information and seemed to have knocked out the pretenses upon which Catherine built her life. I didn't care about winning. I didn't prioritize my hair and clothes and weight like Catherine did. I wasn't *her*.

No one in Catherine's life was willing to let go of their expectations of her, though. They wanted me to be Catherine again. And I wasn't. To them, this made me wrong. Catherine would have lied about making the phone call, she'd have pretended that she liked people she didn't, and she often skirted ethics to help her clients pull a fast one. I know these things about my former self just as I know how to manage assets through a variety of investment products, but they were terrible things to accept about myself.

An important part of my new life is believing that I am not wrong for being different and that LuLu is not a damaged version of Catherine, but an entirely new woman. That's where my affirmation came from: *I am LuLu, and LuLu is great.* I am not Catherine anymore, and that's not a bad thing.

I definitely have some lingering limitations and quirks, but even people without brain injuries have those. Mr. Hernández, for example, is grumpy, moody, and obviously unhappy in his life. Maryanne is a liar, a cheat, and a murderess. Catherine was shallow, arrogant, distrusting, untrustworthy, and a disconnected mother who treated her child like an item on her to-do list. I've done the work to be a different person now. I *am* happy in this life. If anyone was wrong, it was Catherine. Not me.

I am not wrong.

I am not wrong.

I am not wrong.

I am LuLu, and LuLu is great.

The Arroyo Roble is on the same side of Main Street as the Robertses' house, but Oak Creek runs between them, so I have to drive back to Highway 179 to get across. As I wind my way back, I take my four-count breaths and repeat the affirmation *I am not wrong* a few more times before letting it change into the higher vibration of *I am okay.* I let my muscles relax, imagining that they are absorbing the words as I say them. My brain is okay. My body is okay. My quirks are okay.

I am okay.

I am okay.

I am okay.

"Are you okay?"

I startle to hear Mr. Hernández's voice repeat my affirmation as a question. I glance at him. "What?"

"I'm sorry I hurt your feelings."

Truth. And surprising humility.

"Alright." I continue to drive, keeping my eyes locked on the road ahead of us.

"I just did not expect that level of assertiveness from you," he continues. "I thought I was going to lead the discussion."

Truth.

"Okay," I say, still feeling tense but not about to apologize for taking the lead. Under the circumstances, it was absolutely necessary.

"It *was* my idea to go there," he continues. "You didn't even want to go in and then you . . . led out pretty strong. It took me by surprise."

Truth. I take a deep breath and allow my defenses to soften even more.

"It took me by surprise to hear that she'd married him," I say, "though it shouldn't have. I hate that she got exactly what she wanted by hurting so many people. It's not fair." I hate unfairness. I hate good people getting hurt. I hate liars.

"The information *was* unexpected," Mr. Hernández agrees in a careful tone, as though I could blow at any second. I don't mind him feeling that way if it means he'll be a bit more diplomatic. "But we learned what we needed to know. I don't think she's trying to kill you."

"She doesn't *need* to kill me," I say. "Apparently, she benefited from what I did to help Gloria, and now Mr. Roberts is dead." I place my right hand over my stomach, wishing I could draw out the discomfort that has settled there. I wish I didn't have to drive right now. I wish I were in the middle of the desert, lying on the warm sand, watching a hawk circle in the blue-blue sky overhead and thinking about absolutely nothing. I wish I were sipping a nice cold Diet Peach Snapple.

I slow down for the roundabout.

"Are you sure you're okay?" he asks after a few more seconds.

"I am okay," I say, repeating out loud what I've been telling myself.

We're silent for the few seconds it takes to navigate the exit from the roundabout.

"Are you certain she killed Mr. Roberts?" Mr. Hernández asks.

I nod, but then stop and pull my eyebrows together. *Am I sure?* "I guess I'm not completely sure she killed him, but he didn't die of a heart attack, and I don't think she's informed his family. Gloria would have told me. Maryanne said he died last month—that could have been three weeks ago or seven weeks ago if it happened May 1. People would be talking about it if anyone in their circle knew."

Why not inform his children of his death? No matter how estranged they might be. "You saw how cold she was, how . . . greedy and calculated," I continue. "Oh my heck, we need to tell the police!"

I am dismayed that I haven't thought about that before now and pull Kermit into my lap, trying to fish out my phone, which I hadn't put in the phone holder attached to my vent. I shouldn't be doing this while I'm driving, but having not already done it has me feeling panicked. What if I hadn't thought of it at all? What if Maryanne got away with murder?

"We can't tell the police," Mr. Hernández says, pulling my purse off my lap before I've taken hold of my phone.

"We have to!" I say, turning to face him, but only for a moment because I'm still driving.

"We can't . . . yet," he says. "We need to figure out who's trying to kill *you* first. If we go in there to report a totally new crime, we're going to make everything we've already told them seem less believable. We need to help secure their belief that you are in danger, not give them reason to suspend it."

Truth.

"But she lied," I say, glancing at him again. "And I really do think she killed him."

"And if she did, we need to do something about it—I totally agree. Just not yet. Let me pull the death certificate and find out if there was an autopsy. We can check the date, see how his death was processed, and where his body is now. Let's gather the evidence we need to present a solid case without compromising your safety. I don't mean this to sound wrong, but Mr. Roberts is already dead. We can't stop that from having happened, but we can hopefully keep you from joining him by keeping our focus. Can you go along with that? Um, turn right on the second street coming up, yeah, just there."

I settle against my seat and think through what he's saying while following his directions even though I know where the Arroyo is. Not telling the police feels like I'm protecting Maryanne somehow. Yet I can see Mr. Hernández's point. The police are trying to find my killer while Mr. Roberts's killer isn't going anywhere. I want to do *all* the right-best things.

"Can you pull the autopsy tonight?" I ask.

"I can start the process," he says. "It's a bit more involved than going online and downloading the PDF, but I can get it."

Truth.

I tap my thumbs anxiously on the steering wheel. "I need you to promise me we're not going to ignore this."

I imagine myself waking up six months from now and realizing that I never reported Maryanne at all and then the police won't take me seriously because I'd forgotten for six months and—

"We won't ignore it," he says, cutting off my looping thoughts as well as picturing a flamingo would have.

Truth.

I consciously relax my shoulders and nod in agreement. Of course I won't forget. And Mr. Hernández is helping me. *I am okay. Everything works out perfect—*

I can't finish that affirmation. In the middle of such horrible circumstances, it doesn't feel truthful or fair to think that everything is working out perfectly. How can everything be perfect when marriages blow up, children have lost their inheritances to a scheming woman, and someone wants me dead?

"We just need to maintain our focus a little longer, and let the police maintain their focus too. Hopefully we'll have a lot more answers by tomorrow."

Tomorrow. How has so much happened today and it's not even two o'clock in the afternoon?

My room is on the second floor of the Arroyo and, thankfully, available for early check-in. I don't argue when Mr. Hernández goes to the elevator instead of the stairs. Elevators aren't my favorite thing, but if I can handle police interrogations and face off with a homewrecking-hussy-murderer, I can handle the unnatural movement of an elevator with its irritating dings and whooshings.

Mr. Hernández pushes the elevator button then clears his throat. "How about we take the next hour or so to settle in. You can do your call with your daughter, and I can look into some things."

"Like Mr. Roberts's death?"

"Yeah, that too."

I don't get a ping telling me this is a lie, but I have a feeling he'd forgotten all about Mr. Roberts. What other things is he wanting to look into?

The third alarm I set about Sophie's call goes off, and I pull out my phone to silence it. My fear that I might forget to turn Maryanne in mixes with the fear that I might forget to call Sophie even though I still have one more alarm. There is so much stuff in my brain right now.

I start my four-count breathing and then picture a flamingo sliding down a fireman's pole to keep from thinking about Sophie's visit that can't happen if we don't find out who's trying to kill me. I wish I could pull all the thoughts out of my head and sort them into piles like I used to do with M&M's when I was a little girl—arranging them by color and then in order of the most of each color to the least. There is satisfaction in order and routine, and I can't figure out how to institute either of those after everything that's happened.

And yet, I never would have imagined I could navigate all that's happened today without a complete meltdown, but I have. I've stayed present, I've relayed information, I even managed a confrontation. And I haven't needed that many flamingos to keep my mind focused. It's surprising.

I would prefer not to test myself further, however. I hope I can log into my Netflix on the hotel room TV. If so, maybe I can binge-watch *Sabrina the Teenage Witch*. I adore her talking cat.

Mr. Hernández continues. "If you want to come up to my room around three o'clock, we can order lunch and talk about what we need to do next."

"Lunch?" I repeat, looking at him. "In your room?"

"Is that a problem?"

The elevator opens, and we step inside—the only two

people going up at this time of day. It isn't lunch that shifted my attention, and it takes me a few seconds to articulate my thoughts. When the doors close, I turn to look at him. "Why are you doing this, Mr. Hernández?"

"I'm involved." He lifts his shoulders and lets them drop, though he winces slightly with the motion of his hurt shoulder.

Truth. But . . . while he's not lying to me—he *is* involved both as my attorney and as an eyewitness to the shooting—I feel like he's leaving something out.

"Not really," I say. "I mean, yes, you are involved, but you don't have to be. I hired you to test Snapple, not all this." I wave my arm and hope he knows that I'm being a bit more abstract with the gesture than only referencing the inside of the elevator.

He moves his jaw while considering his answer. He thinks before he speaks a lot, giving the impression that everything he does say is important because he's thought it through. But it's only the *impression* of importance; it doesn't mean he's a sage. I need to remember that. The elevator stops, and we step out. The hallway is empty. We don't move down the hall as the elevator closes behind us.

"I want to understand what's happening here," he finally says, turning to face me. "It's not every day something like this lands in your lap."

Truth. But a sad truth if he's just here for the thrill of it. He was once a big-city attorney in the middle of high-drama cases. Is this close to the excitement he used to feel on a regular basis?

"You were already shot at because of me," I remind him. "You're taking additional risks to stay in this."

"*You* were shot at. I was just . . . nearby." He laughs but the joke falls flat.

I don't smile. His smile fades, and we're both looking at each other with serious expressions.

"I'm involved in this, LuLu, and I know a thing or two about criminals. I think I can help."

Truth.

"While I'm relieved the police are now taking this seriously," he continues. "I think you and I can do more than they can. Or at least help them find the answers more quickly. I have a few things I want to look into while you get settled, then we can talk over lunch."

I look at him a few more seconds. His explanation hasn't completely resolved the questions I have, but he's told the truth. I do appreciate that I am not going through this alone, and his involvement *does* feel intentional, not a whim.

"Lunch in your room at three sounds great," I finally say, setting aside my concerns.

For now.

I have a very important phone call to make.

CHAPTER 9

As Mr. Hernández takes the elevator up to his room, I unlock the door to my room and then jump when it slams shut behind me—fireproof doors. I take a breath to calm my racing heart and draw on pink light to unscatter my thoughts broken up by the crash. It takes a few seconds before I'm back on track.

I text Sophie to see if we can do a voice call instead of our usual FaceTime. If she realizes I'm in a hotel room, she'll ask questions that only have scary answers. She's thirteen years old and already lost one version of her mother. The mother she has left is more fun and fairly worships her but lives more than a thousand miles away and sees her a handful of times every year. Sophie had no say in the circumstances of her life, and I don't want to add to the burdens she already carries.

I wonder if I'll tell her when it's all over and decide that I can make that decision later. At 2:19, Sophie calls me instead of replying to my text about not doing FaceTime.

"Hi, Mama," she says cheerily into the phone. "I'm glad you texted. I forgot about our call."

I swallow the hurt and remind myself that I'd have forgotten, too, if not for the alarms I'd set. "No worries. How's my girl?"

"I'm really good. School is out for the whole summer now!" She goes on to tell me about signing yearbooks with the few kids whose parents made them go the last day. "Mom is taking me to Dahlia's Bakery on the way to the party so I can pick out something to bring."

"Mom" is Shanna. She married Forrest a couple of years after the divorce—a few months before the accident. Prior to my fateful weekend trip to Phoenix, Sophie called her Shanna. It wasn't until I returned to Seattle that I realized Sophie had started to call her *Mom*, and then I became Mama at some point. Sometimes the jealousy makes me cry. Sometimes I feel overwhelming gratitude that Sophie has so many people in her life who love her.

"I'm so excited to see you on Wednesday, Mama. Dad's helping me get everything packed, and he bought me some Chaco's. He said that's what locals wear."

"Well, he's right," I say, keeping my tone light. "People love sandals down here. What color are they?"

"Sort of rainbow," she says. I hear the mumble of Shanna's voice in the background. "Pink, yellow, blue. I'll send you a picture. Uh, I've got to go."

"Of course," I say, smiling even though we're not on FaceTime. "We can finalize all the travel plans on Sunday's call, okay?"

"Okay, thanks, Mama. Love you."

"Love you too, sweetie. Have a great time at the party."

My emotions are a tangle when I end the call, and I fall back against the bed, throwing my arms out wide and letting out a breath I feel I've been holding all day despite all the breathing exercises I have employed to keep me present. I want to call my own mom and talk this through with her—she's my best friend.

And she'd jump on the first plane if I told her what's happening here.

She's been so good to help me with Sophie's visits these last few years and super supportive of Sophie coming alone now, though I knew she also worried. We FaceTimed her every day when Sophie was here over spring break, and I think that helped all of us.

Mom will be coming out here for the last week of Sophie's stay this summer, and I'm excited we'll have that time together. I can't burden her with this when there's nothing she can to do make it better. And I just gave myself a deadline: This has to be solved by my phone call with Sophie on Sunday. If it isn't, I'll have to tell Sophie she can't come. I'll have to tell her why.

I close my eyes and resist the urge to cry. Not that I'm against crying, but I want to have enough time to do it properly, and I'm meeting Mr. Hernández in his room for lunch at 3:00. No way can I do a full cry-out in that amount of time.

Instead, I turn off the 2:32 alarm that I set in case I forgot to call Sophie in time, and I take a blessed four minutes to focus on deep breathing and repeating some empowering affirmations before listing all the things I'm grateful for: Sophie, Mom, sunshine, birds, thick hair, Diet Peach Snapple, dresses, comfortable underwear, police protection, salads, air fryers, cell phones, energy vortexes, drawer organizers, chocolate-covered cinnamon bears, cheese, Manny, Sandra Bullock movies, those squishy stuffed animal things, peanut butter, mangoes. It energizes me enough to get me off the bed and reengaged in the day.

I haven't stayed in a hotel room for . . . well, probably since that weekend trip to Phoenix more than five years ago that ended in a helicopter ride to the trauma center in Tucson. I'm not loving that connection to this experience, but I set about getting unpacked and settled. If I'm going to be here all weekend, I had better start homing-it-up.

I unpack the clothes from Lisa into the drawers and closet, put away all the signs about lights and check-out times that scream "This is not a home!" then set out my hygiene items in the bathroom.

I'm spraying Good LuLu linen spray over the soft surfaces to improve the vibrations of this place and thinking about taking a shower even though it's the middle of the day, when my phone rings. I cross the room to pick it up from the desk, hoping maybe it's Sophie remembering something she wanted to tell me, then frown at the name that shows on my screen—Fiona.

My phone had already rung twice before I reached it, and I let it ring twice more so that the call goes to voicemail. Does that make me a bad person? I just . . . Fiona is a difficult woman on a good day. On a day like today, she feels impossible.

I stare at the phone after it goes silent and wrestle with my decision before deciding that I'll call her back after the shower. She's probably following up on my visit to Mr. Hernández's office this morning, but I simply don't want to *Fiona* right now. I head toward the bathroom.

I truly don't mind my cold showers in the summer—they *are* invigorating and, if I'm honest, not all that cold since the ground warms the water some, but the warmer water is so comforting and relaxing today. Because my showers have been cool ones for weeks, they are usually short, but I take a full eight minutes to really enjoy this one.

When I'm out of the shower, dressed, and moisturized, I pick up my phone and am surprised to see that Fiona left a message. Has she ever left me a voicemail before? Has she ever called me, in fact? Despite her age, she prefers short, direct, borderline rude texts to communicate.

I toggle to open the voicemail and listen to her clipped voice. "LuLu, this is Fiona Hernández. I have something for you. Please stop by my house at your earliest convenience. The front door will be unlocked, and you have permission to come in."

I listen to it twice. It's formal, as most older people's messages are, but also . . . strange.

Not only has she never called or left me a voicemail, but she doesn't routinely give me things, either. Well, she gave me a Diet Peach Snapple a few weeks ago and a sweater that she didn't like several months ago. I didn't like it either and gave it to the local thrift store. My clients give me things fairly often. I think they like to feel like they are making my life better with their swan-themed china and too-tight shoes. I've never had any of them want to give me something outside of our regular appointments.

It's tempting to ignore Fiona's call altogether and just deal with it on Monday when I'll be back to clean her bathrooms and scrub her floors, but I'm hyperaware of unexpected things right now.

I decide to see if Mr. Hernández thinks it's safe for us to go to Fiona's before I respond. I don't want to put Fiona in danger.

I head toward Mr. Hernández's room a few minutes before 3:00. My wet hair is in a single braid hanging down my back, and I'm wearing my gray-and-turquoise sundress with the straps that cross in the back. I have nice shoulders, and I like the way this dress shows them off. I usually wear the turquoise pendant I got at the Trading Post my first month in Sedona with this dress, but I didn't think to pack it. Manny once complimented this dress. I've never forgotten.

The first thing I notice when Mr. Hernández opens the door is that he's traded out his broken, clear-frame glasses for a pair of wire-rimmed ones.

"I like your glasses," I comment as he steps back so I can enter his room, which is the exact floor plan of my room two levels down. His space looks a bit more lived-in, however. There are cords plugged in, and the desk has stacks of papers as well as his laptop. A big black thermos with a silver logo I don't recognize sits on the windowsill. He's opened the drapes but left the see-through ones closed—to filter the bright afternoon sun probably.

"My old glasses," he explains as he closes the door behind me. "Are you hungry?"

Am I hungry? I haven't had anything but those two packs of ER fruit snacks since the creamed eggs I ate for breakfast, but it's hard to pick out "hunger" from all the other emotions and sensations I'm feeling. The grounding at the hospital and the meditation and shower here at the hotel helped, but I still feel disconnected from my body.

"I think so," I finally say because I probably should fuel my body even if I'm not feeling the effects of famishment.

"Good. I ordered you a chicken salad."

"You ordered me a salad?" Isn't that what men order for their girlfriends to suggest they need to lose weight? Catherine was obsessively thin and never quite came to terms with the widening of her hips after having Sophie. She'd eat a chicken salad without dressing or cheese whereas butter and heavy cream might be my love language, though I buy the hormone-free, grass-fed versions.

"Yeah," he says without looking at me as he heads over to the small table by the window that's stacked with papers and life debris like fingernail clippers, headphones, and some supplements in white plastic bottles. "I figured since you don't cook much in the summer that's what you would like."

Okay, maybe there's some consideration in there, but why not wait until I got here and let me choose my own food? I don't know if it's misogyny, efficiency, or oblivion but I also don't want to make an issue. And I do like salads. Especially if they have dried cranberries. A salad just isn't the same without dried cranberries. I fish through Kermit and triumphantly find a snack baggie of them at the bottom. I'm not usually prepared for salad emergencies and being on point today seems like a good omen. Maybe the first good omen I've encountered. Other than Mr. Hernández being willing to help me out with all this for reasons I still don't understand.

"I got a call from Fiona," I say. "I didn't answer, and she left a voicemail saying she has something for me and wants me to stop by and pick it up. Do you think it's safe to go over?"

Mr. Hernández pulls his eyebrows together.

I lift Kermit's strap over my head and hang it on the only open hook on a set of five near the door. "And she said 'please,'" I point out.

Though Fiona is the sort of woman to reprimand a stranger's child for displaying poor manners in a grocery store, she herself does not reflect those same niceties on a regular basis.

"Hmm," Mr. Hernández says as he returns to clearing the last few items from the table. "Any idea what it is she wants to give you?"

"No."

"Does she make a habit of giving you things? What I'm asking is whether this is a common thing."

"It's definitely out of character. She once gave me a sweater she didn't like, and a few weeks ago, she had a Diet Peach Snapple for me when I was leaving." The Snapple would have socked the shock off me if I wore socks, and then my gratitude seemed to annoy her and she told me to stop being so dang gracious. She is a tricky one.

Mr. Hernández narrows his eyes at me. "She knows you like Diet Peach Snapple."

"Everyone knows I like Diet Peach Snapple. It's my signature drink."

"And she gave you one a few weeks ago?"

"Yes," I say, recognizing that he's going into interrogation mode. His body tenses, his eyes narrow slightly, and he is almost glaring at me with that unflinching, super-uncomfortable gaze of his. The only mood I *have* liked of his, now that I think of it, is his humble mood, which I've only seen when he apologized for asking what was wrong with me.

"Had she ever given you a Snapple before?"

"No," I say, shaking my head. "Some of my clients stock up on Snapples for me, which is very sweet, but Fiona isn't one of them. I usually bring one with me for our appointments and put it in her fridge so that it's cold by the time I leave. She'd never had one for me before that day, and I saw it as a sign that our relationship was improving." It's one of the only improvements I saw in eleven months of working together. "But she was just as sharp with me in the weeks that followed and never gave me another Snapple."

"What does 'a few weeks ago' mean?" Mr. Hernández asks. "Two weeks ago? Five?"

I think this through so that I make sure to give the right answer. This week's visit had been when Fiona suggested I meet with Mr. Hernández after I told her the police hadn't listened to me. The week before was when I wiped down all the kitchen cabinets while she complained about the quality of workmanship in her house. The week before that was when I went early because her hairdresser could only see her at 11:00 that week, and it was the week before *that* when she gave me the Snapple. I'm sure of it.

"A month ago," I say with the sort of pride a kid shows when he wins an art prize in third grade. Being able to review a timeline and figure out this sort of detail *is* a win for me. "Four appointments." I get my phone out of Kermit still hanging by the door. "May 14."

"A month ago," he says, turning to face me and leaning his hips against the waist-high dresser. "And you drank it?"

I shrug. "Probably."

His eyebrows come together yet again. "You're not sure?"

"Well, I mean, it was really sweet of her to give me the Snapple, but it wasn't cold. I put it on George's passenger seat to put in the fridge later. I only like my Snapples cold, and I'd put one in the fridge when I arrived that morning, so I drank that one on the way to my afternoon appointment."

Mr. Hernández considers this with that disapproving look on his face that once again makes it very hard for me not to think that he's disapproving of *me*. I look away and return my phone to Kermit.

"The Snapple Aunt Fee gave you wasn't cold?" he asks.

"No," I say—again.

"But you think you did drink it eventually?"

He's asking very particular questions, and before I answer this one, I take a few seconds to think about where these questions are headed. Maybe I can save both of us some of this interrogation. I lift my eyebrows when the snap of connection takes place in my mind and look at him sharply. "Are you trying to make a connection between the poisoned Snapple and the one Fiona gave me?"

"I'm trying to be thorough."

Truth. Shocking!

"She's your elderly aunt!"

He looks at me with no shame at all. I feel guilty just realizing *he's* thinking there might be a connection between Fiona and the poisoned Snapple.

"I'm trying to be thorough," he repeats. "You got the poisoned Snapple from the fridge at your house that day last week, right? It was cold? Not a Snapple from the floor of your car."

I nod, but I have an icky feeling in my stomach and take a deep breath before filling in a teeny-tiny detail that he's going to freak out about. "I did get that Snapple out of the fridge that day last week, but when I get too many Snapples rolling around on the floor of my car, I'll take as many as I can carry into the house and put them in the fridge."

He stares at me. "You have multiple Snapple bottles in your car at any given time?"

I am starting to feel judged, but I hold his eyes and don't shrink away. I haven't done anything wrong, and if he'd been paying attention when I cleared out the front seat of George prior to our drive to the Robertses' house, he'd have seen that this behavior has precedence. I think I have five Snapples on the floor of the back seat waiting for me to remember to return them to the fridge.

"I only like them cold," I repeat.

"You've gathered car Snapples since Aunt Fee gave you that bottle? You've transferred them from your car to your fridge within the last month?"

I nod slowly. We both stare at each other.

He curses and takes a few steps toward the window, running his hand through his hair but stopping when his hand is on top of his head, which then looks like he's holding his whole body down. He has big hands. Michael Jackson had big hands. So does Anthony Robbins.

I don't say anything but that sick feeling in my stomach gets worse as I consider the implications of this conversation. I can't hold on to the idea that Fiona would have given me a poisoned Snapple. It feels like a really scary possibility to accept.

He turns toward me sharply, his hand still on his head. "Did Aunt Fee know you were coming to see me this morning?"

"Yes," I say. "I called her yesterday to see if she had any other number for you since you weren't calling me back. She said she didn't and suggested I go by your office this morning."

"*She* suggested it," he says.

I nod slowly. "I was already considering that option if she didn't have a secondary number, but I acted as though I hadn't thought about it because that seemed the gracious thing to do. I thanked her for the idea and said I would go first thing."

He takes a deep breath and then lets it out slowly. "Does she know you turn off the gas to your house in the summer?"

"I don't think so . . . Wait, yes, I told her on Monday, when I was upset that the police hadn't taken me seriously. That's when she referred me to you."

"Monday," he repeats. "*After* you found the candle."

I nod.

"You're sure you hadn't told her before the candle incident?" His voice is sharp.

I shake my head. "I talked to Carla about it—Carla is my Monday afternoon appointment—because she complained about increasing utility costs, and I suggested turning off her pilot lights for the summer, and she told me that sounded like crazy talk." I shrug. "And Manny knows because he's the one who showed me how to turn on and off the gas and relight the pilot lights, but I don't think I have ever told anyone else until I told the police, then Fiona, and then you."

"Manny?" Mr. Hernández says in that same sharp tone. "Who is Manny?"

I feel my cheeks get warm, so I look away from him. "Manny is a handyman in town—Handy Manny. He's done work for me and several of my clients too." I leave out how good his No-Bake Cookies are because it doesn't seem pertinent to this discussion.

"And you *think* he and Carla are the only people who knew you turned off your pilot lights prior to the candle incident?"

I nod.

"Which means anyone else would expect that the gas would be turned on and a lit candle would blow up your house."

We are staring at each other across the room when there's a knock at the door that startles both of us. A voice calls, "Room service."

Mr. Hernández opens the door and takes the tray from the room service attendant before turning back to the table. I look between him and the server, then go to my purse and pull out some cash, since Mr. Hernández doesn't seem like he's going to. We sit down at the table a minute later, our respective meals in front of us—chicken salad for me and fish tacos with beans and rice for him, which looks way better than my salad, but whatever. I'm grateful for the meal.

"Are we going to Fiona's after this?" I ask him as I start cutting up my salad—most restaurants keep the leaves so big it's awkward to eat. Especially in front of other people. Mr. Hernández is silent and seems thoughtful.

"Yeah."

That's all we say before we start eating, both of us thoughtful now. I eat so fast that once we're heading back to the parking lot, I can't tell which has made me more uncomfortable—the salad I ate too quickly or the increasing anxiety about this possible connection between Fiona and the poisoned Snapple. It feels absolutely mad to consider Fiona could have anything to do with this. Taking action feels better than waiting for something else to happen, however.

I ignore Mr. Hernández's slight scowl when we reach George in the parking lot, but he doesn't put words to his dislike, and I pretend I don't notice. I put my phone in the holder attached to the vent this time and buckle my seat belt.

"Is that your daughter?" he asks.

I glance at the dance recital photo currently showing on my screen—I have a few dozen photos that rotate through as my wallpaper—and feel my chest soften. Sophie's hair is pulled up into a puffball on top of her head, and she's wearing a pink leotard with a full tulle skirt. She has her hands held to her head like moose antlers.

"That's my Sophie," I say with a smile as I start the car and pull out of the parking spot.

"She's beautiful," he says.

"And crazy smart," I add. She *is* beautiful, but I don't want her to stand out only because of that.

I barely remember the recital when this photo was taken. Catherine had sat as far back in the auditorium as she could and spent most of the performance texting with her assistant, who was working on a report Catherine had to have first thing in the morning. She had promised Sophie they would go to their favorite ramen restaurant for dinner afterward, but they ended up getting drive-through sandwiches because Catherine had to get back on her computer. She promised Sophie a sit-down dinner at a restaurant of her choice another time to make up for it, but I don't think she ever followed through on that. By the time this photo had been taken, Sophie probably no longer counted on her mother following through on her promises.

The recital had been just a few weeks before my accident. It's the last Sophie "event" I had attended as Catherine.

"Her dad is . . . African American?" Mr. Hernández asks.

"Yes," I say while I slow down for a stop sign. "Forrest and Sophie prefer being referred to as Black, though."

He looks at the photo another moment. "She has your eyes."

I glance at him, pleasantly surprised.

Sophie's eyes are dark brown like Forrest's, but the *shape* of her eyes—large, almond, and deep set—is mine. Not many people notice that detail because Sophie looks so much like her dad. I love it when someone sees that she and I belong together too.

"So, you're related to Fiona through Johnny, right?" I ask after a couple of blocks. He's asked a lot of questions about my life and the accident that changed everything. It's only fair I get some information too.

"Yeah," Mr. Hernández says. "Uncle Juan, though he preferred Johnny, is my dad's brother."

"She talks about Johnny a lot," I explain. "There are photos of the two of them all over the house. It seems like they were really happy together."

"They were," Mr. Hernández says with a touch of nostalgia in his voice that makes me glance at him. I hide my surprise at hearing that sort of softness. "They never had children of their own, so they doted on their nieces and nephews when we were little. I grew up just a few blocks from them. Their house was on my way home from school if I skipped the shortcut through the park. I would stop if I saw Fiona's car in the driveway because she kept popsicles in the freezer for just such an occasion. She was a journalist back then and worked from home before that was really a thing."

I try to imagine this version of Fiona—well, both of them really. The smiling Fiona I have seen in the photographs around her house handing a young Mr. Hernández an orange popsicle on the front porch of her post–World War II brick bungalow with flowerpots and a porch swing. I can see the young and carefree Mr. Hernández taking the popsicle and telling her about his day as he licks the drips before they stain his hand. Both images are so different from who those two people are now. I wonder if they miss themselves. Sometimes I miss parts of Catherine—her confidence, her intellect, the way she knew how to talk to nearly anyone she met. But I wouldn't go back to being her. Not for anything. I wonder if Fiona and Mr. Hernández would go back to their past versions of themselves, though.

"It seems like things changed a lot for Fiona when Johnny died," I say as that image of a carefree aunt and nephew fade from my mind.

"Well, first Johnny got sick," Mr. Hernández says. "That's when things started to change."

"Wasn't it cancer?"

"Yeah, first one type and then another. He'd worked in factories as a kid, like, I mean, a *kid*. I think he was nine years old when he first started working at a tile manufacturing plant in California."

"Nine?" I repeat in shock.

"Undocumented worker," Mr. Hernández says, that edge back in his voice. Edge brought on by the unfairness of child labor. Edge brought on by my lack of realization that things like this happen too, I think. "Paid under the table so there's no paper trail showing how the employers are violating the labor laws. They'd hire Latin American kids without papers to do cleanup mostly. My dad and Johnny both worked there. My dad eventually found other work that allowed him to go to school consistently. Johnny never liked school. I think he stopped attending in sixth grade and went to work full-time at the factory and then, later, at a lumber mill."

"Still under the table?"

"Oh yeah," Mr. Hernández says, nodding as I turn left toward Fiona's house. "When he got sick, they tracked it back to the asbestos he worked with at that tile company. There had been a class action against the company, but Johnny couldn't be a part of it because there was no record of his employment. There are tens of thousands of people just like him." He shakes his head. "Fiona had to get full-time work in order to have benefits, which meant giving up her freelance journalism, and then her income only just covered his expenses. She sort of . . . faded along with his increasing health issues over the next decade. Depression, I'm sure, but also a lot of anger. Johnny's exposure was likely why they never had kids. Most of their family had moved away from Mesa by then, and I think they were really isolated and lonely. Johnny died from Covid early during the shutdown—he was doing chemo and vulnerable to the virus. Fiona wasn't even able to be with him during that final hospital stay after having taken care of him for so many years. She was so upset about that. And then his life insurance wouldn't pay out because of some loophole. I stepped in to help, but we ended up getting less than 20 percent of the amount. It was a scam policy and barely enough for Fiona to get out of the debt they'd racked up those last few years. She was pretty bitter by the time she sold the house and moved to

Sedona. She wanted to be closer to her sister, who then passed away a couple years ago. Fiona is a very different woman than she was when I was young."

"That's so sad," I say, seeing the movie of his story play out in my head as he tells it. "On so many levels."

"Yeah," he says, then lets out a breath as I pull up to the curb in front of Fiona's house.

I wish the drive had taken longer. I want to ask about how many good years Fiona and Johnny had had. What her laugh had sounded like. If she ever baked—I'm pretty sure baking is a hallmark of living a happy life.

When had Jordan, the other nephew, stepped in to help her out?

Was she happier after she came to Sedona? Even a little bit?

But Mr. Hernández's good hand is on the handle of his door and Fiona's car is in the driveway. My stomach fills with butterflies as I catch back up to the unexpectedness of her earlier call and this visit. I cannot believe all that's happened today. Yet I am here, rooted in this moment and moving toward the next.

Everything is going to be okay, I tell myself and then try super hard to believe it.

CHAPTER 10

"Fiona said she'd leave the front door unlocked," I remember to tell Mr. Hernández when we start up the porch steps.

"She never leaves her front door unlocked," he says in a way that makes me think I should have shared that information earlier. I'm embarrassed that I didn't.

I quickly remind myself, however, that I am doing the best I can; I am 100 percent sure of that.

Mr. Hernández doesn't bother knocking, and the knob turns easily in his hand. "Wait here," he says as he steps over the threshold.

"I'm the one she invited to come over," I remind him.

"Just wait on the porch," he says in a tone that implies I am going to do what he says, like he has some authority. That's sort of adorable, like he's taking on the role of protector. Except it's also ridiculous and pompous because I don't need his protection. I mean, yes, he saved my life this morning, but that doesn't mean he's my security detail. And he's already admitted his continued involvement is based on curiosity.

Mr. Hernández seems surprised when he takes a few steps into the living room and I'm right behind him instead of obediently waiting for his permission to leave the porch. Our eyes hold a moment, and then I step past him toward the kitchen and let him close the front door. Fiona has accused me more than once of trying to cool the whole neighborhood when I haven't closed the door quickly enough. I wait for her to reprimand us now, but the house is silent.

It smells like onions, as usual. Fiona likes to cook and adds onions to almost everything. Even tuna salad, which I do not understand. The TV is on in the family room, where she spends most of her time in Johnny's old recliner. Other than those immediate assertations, the house feels very still.

"Fiona?" I call out. "It's LuLu. I got your message and came as quickly as I could."

There is no answer. No movement or sound of any kind other than our own footsteps as we ease further into her home. She told me in her message to let myself in, but I fully expect her to get mad at me for it. Like the time she asked me to clean out the fridge, then got mad, claiming that I wasn't supposed to do it unless I had time after I did the floors. That was the day she fired me for the first time. I cried on the way home. I hate contention and unfairness, and that day was a solid reminder why.

Fiona texted later that day and apologized before rescinding her termination and asking me to come back the next week. It took me a few hours and two donuts before I could agree to try again.

The fact that she wanted me back made me feel that even though she was obviously troubled and unhappy, she needed me, wanted me. Things didn't necessarily improve between us after that—she fired me again a few months later for no reason at all—but I got better at not taking her moods so personally.

And I do think she needs me. Not for the basic housekeeping—which is far below my skill level. Or for financial advice—I tried twice to have that conversation with her, and she shut it down both times. But she needs someone in her life. Even if it's just someone to complain about and order around. She doesn't have any friends that I'm aware of despite having lived here for several years. She moved into this house about a year and a half ago and hasn't connected with her neighbors or attended any events at the senior center. Other than her hairdresser, her nephews, and me, she doesn't have anyone in her life now that her sister has passed away.

"Aunt Fee?" Mr. Hernández calls out from behind me.

Nothing.

We share a look. Should I have called to tell her we were coming? I hadn't even considered calling her back. Neither had Mr. Hernández, apparently.

We continue through the living room toward the kitchen. The air is so heavy with tension I'm sure that if I flicked out my tongue, I could taste it like a snake. I could probably taste the onions too.

Why hasn't she answered us?

Why hasn't she asked if we took off our shoes, which we didn't.

Mr. Hernández and I are side by side as we step through the arched doorway into the kitchen. Some primitive need for reassurance makes me grab his hand. He clasps my hand back without hesitation, sparing me the embarrassment of having instigated unwanted contact. Gosh, it's nice to have a hand to hold right now.

"Aunty Fee," Mr. Hernández says, his voice ringing through the house that feels so empty.

The kitchen bar blocks some of the family room on the other side, but I have a good view of Johnny's chair and Fiona is not in it. I can also see the dining room table holding an empty plate with a wadded-up napkin on top. I've never seen dishes in the sink at Fiona's house, let alone still on the table. She's incredibly tidy and usually washes her dishes as soon as she's finished eating. And she never uses paper plates or plastic cups. No, sir.

If we hadn't seen her car in the driveway, I'd assume she'd left to run a quick errand, though she doesn't leave the house for many reasons. Could she have left the TV on and lain down for a nap?

The kitchen is pristine, as usual. No dishes in sight other than a pan on the stove.

Mr. Hernández continues toward the family room and clears his throat before he speaks to the house at large again. "LuLu and I also want to ask you about . . ."

His voice trails off, and I follow his eyes to the toe of a shoe that extends past the counter. Mr. Hernández releases my hand as he crosses through the rest of the kitchen and onto the carpeted floor of the family room in three long strides. He freezes in the archway between the rooms as he stares at something blocked from my view—blocked except for that shoe.

I am beside him a moment later and cover my mouth with one hand as I look down on Fiona Hernández, who is lying on the floor, dead eyes staring at the ceiling.

A commercial for Disneyland plays on the TV, proclaiming it to be the trip of a lifetime.

CHAPTER 11

Mr. Hernández curses under his breath as he stares at Fiona's body, then turns away with his eyes closed and a hand over his mouth.

I move forward, the skirt of my sundress billowing as I fall to my knees beside her on the floor. "Fiona," I say, patting her hand, which is limp but still warm. "Oh, Fiona. Oh no."

My mind tries to spin my thoughts backward as though to change this course. If ever there was a time my thoughts would want to skitter away, it would be now. I can't let that happen. I take a deep breath, then let it out slowly through my mouth to keep me right here. I give her hand a squeeze with both of my own and take another breath. How is it possible that her hand is still warm?

"LuLu," Mr. Hernández says as he grabs my shoulder. "Get up."

He somehow lifts me to my feet and turns me into his chest for a hug, but I push away from him.

"I'm okay," I say as I look at Fiona's body again. Her face doesn't look peaceful, which makes me even more sad. I stare down at her for a few more seconds before kneeling beside her again and using my hand to close her eyes.

I'm not afraid of death like some people are. Though I don't remember my accident, I know that something happened there that taught me about souls and life after this one. I don't remember the experience, but I feel peace about death being part of the contract, and that it isn't the end, just a transition to a different part of living. The soul part of Fiona is probably happier than she's been for a long time if Johnny was there to welcome her, and I like thinking about the sweetness of that reunion.

Even with all that perspective, however, Fiona shouldn't be dead, and it's shocking to see her this way.

Then I think: *What does her death mean in the larger context of the attempts on my life?* My anxiety starts to rise now that the shock is wearing off. We need to tell Sergeant Rawlins.

I pull my phone from Kermit strapped over my chest and hold it up for Face ID, but Mr. Hernández grabs my wrist.

"Hold on," he says, looking around the room.

"I'm calling the police," I tell him.

"I'm not sure that's the best course," he says, looking pale but otherwise all-business. "Once the police get here, we lose any chance we have of finding anything that might make sense of this. What did she plan to give you?"

My eyes go wide. "You're suggesting we *don't* call the police. Again?" First, we literally let Maryanne get away with murder, and now he doesn't want to report his own aunt's death?

"Yet," he says, keeping hold of my wrist and turning me toward the kitchen. "Let's take a few minutes to see what we can find. Where's her phone?"

"This is a crime scene!"

"She's the link, LuLu." He's still holding my wrist, but I could pull out of his grip if I wanted to. "We can call the police—we *will* call the police—but let's take a minute to look around in case we can figure out how she was involved in the attempts to kill you, and why she wanted you to come over here today. When, exactly, did she call?"

He has a point. "A little after 2:30. Sophie called early, and Fiona called five minutes or so after that call ended," I say, still trying to make sense of his perspective. He released my hand, and I toggle through my phone to see the exact minute. "Yes, 2:32. An hour and four minutes ago."

One hour. How could she be dead in an hour? Would things have been different if I'd answered her call? The thought makes me put a hand to my stomach as a sharp pain springs from my solar chakra at the base of my rib cage.

"It feels wrong not to call," I say as I lower my phone to my side.

"Everything about this is wrong," Mr. Hernández says, looking at his aunt's body and shaking his head. He blinks quickly behind his wire-framed glasses. "Do you think the police would have figured out Fiona's link quicker than we did?"

"We didn't figure out the link until we found her dead in her house!" I return with a sharp voice. "We have information they need, and she should be taken care of."

But as Mr. Hernández and I stare at Fiona, I begin to question myself. I know the difference between right and wrong. Calling the police is the right thing to do, I am certain of that, but . . . someone is still trying to kill me. The police wouldn't have thought to look at Fiona. How could they have made that connection?

I have to face that word Mr. Hernández brought into this—*link*. Fiona may have had something to do with the poisoning. She didn't know that a candle wouldn't burn my house down, and she is the *only* person who knew I was going to

Mr. Hernández's office this morning. If Mr. Hernández hadn't pushed me out of the way, that gunshot would have killed me. A ball of pure sorrow rises in my chest as I accept that Fiona *is* the link between all three attempts on my life.

I immediately argue with myself. Fiona would never . . . She couldn't possibly . . . She likes me. I mean, she's never *said* that she likes me, and she's fired me twice, but she rehired me each time, and I've seen her nearly every week for months. We have a connection. We matter to each other.

Or, rather, she mattered to me.

"How could she be involved?" I say, still looking down at her while Mr. Hernández goes back into the kitchen. I try to swallow that ball of sorrow, but it won't go down. My body shudders with an unexpected chill, and I cross my arms over my chest and rub my upper arms to try to warm myself up. My right arm hurts when I rub it, reminding me to be careful of it. "She wouldn't want to hurt me," I say almost to myself, but of course to Mr. Hernández too.

Mr. Hernández pauses on the other side of the kitchen bar and pushes his glasses up higher on the bridge of his nose. "She might have given you a poisoned Snapple, LuLu. It seems a stretch that she would sneak into your house and light a candle, and there's no way she fired the gun this morning. But obviously, she knows something—*knew* something. Maybe she knew too much, and she was . . . silenced."

Does that make her death my fault? Oh gosh.

Like Mr. Roberts's death?

If one of the attempts to kill me had been successful, would Fiona still be alive?

I close my eyes against the thoughts and picture a bright white light surrounding all of us. I search my mind for an appropriate affirmation that might bring some peace to this particular situation, and it comes to me with another chill: "The solution is already in the room."

"What?"

I look up at Mr. Hernández, not realizing I'd said the words out loud. I'm usually by myself when I draw an affirmation from my mind. If you talk to yourself only when you're alone no one thinks you're crazy. When you accidentally talk to yourself when other people are around, well, that's a house of a different color.

"The solution is already in the room," I repeat.

Mr. Hernández shakes his head and doesn't say whatever he is thinking as he pulls open a drawer in the kitchen. Saying out-of-context things makes me look like the weirdo I would prefer he not think I am. But maybe I am that weirdo. Maybe I can accept his impression of me and move on.

I interpret the affirmation "The solution is already in the room" as a sort of acknowledgment that God knows what's happened here. That finding the truth is possible if I stay open to all options. I use it often.

I look at Fiona again.

The chunky black sweater she wears every day despite keeping her house at 78 degrees year-round is off one shoulder. Her housedress has come up on the right side to reveal the scar from the knee-replacement surgery she'd had just before I started working with her—that's why I was hired in the first place. A lot of my clients hired me for multiple visits a week due to an acute need, but then settled to one appointment a week when they no longer needed that much care.

I want to cover her up with the crocheted blanket that's on the back of her sofa, but I also know not to interfere with the crime scene.

As I walk back toward the kitchen, my eyes move past the

fingers of Fiona's left hand and cross the carpeted floor before landing on a familiar bottle lying on its side. No lid, a darker area of carpet radiating out from it. Diet Peach Snapple. I would recognize those bottle contours anywhere.

"Mr. Hernández," I say as I change my course to get closer to the bottle.

"What?" Mr. Hernández says, looking at me across the kitchen bar that separates us while closing another drawer.

"She drank it," I say, pointing at the bottle though he can't see it from where he is.

Mr. Hernández comes around the counter and moves toward the bottle, then goes down on his knees and leans close to the carpet, inhaling deeply before looking up at me. "Paraquat," he says as he struggles to his feet, the sling making standing more difficult than it would otherwise be. "It has the same smell your bottle had."

"Which means . . ."

What does it mean?

Did Fiona try to kill me and then . . . kill herself? Or did someone force this on her?

"We need to find her phone," Mr. Hernández says. "We need to know who she's been in contact with."

I nod and start in the family room; he goes back to the kitchen. I imagine finding the phone and discovering the whole terrible plot against me via text message threads. Would I find that she looked up legal lethal poisons? I don't imagine she does much internet surfing on her phone, however.

Her house is so clean and clutter-free that there's not a lot to sort through. The phone isn't in the crumb-free cushions of her recliner or the couch. It's not in her yarn basket or under any of the furniture.

When I stand up from looking under the couch, I notice

the empty dishes on the table again. There's a plate, fork, knife, and spoon set on a place mat, but no glass to complete the setting. I close my eyes and imagine her sitting at the table, eating her lunch—her last meal—with the Diet Peach Snapple set in place of a glass. She cuts each bite meticulously, waiting to drink anything until she's finished, and then crumples the napkin she had in her lap and puts it on the empty plate.

Or she finishes her last meal with someone standing over her, who then holds out the poison she has no choice but to swallow.

When I open my eyes, Mr. Hernández is watching me closely. We hold each other's worried looks a moment.

"Why don't you check the bedroom?" he says. I nod, grateful for a chance to get out of this room for a moment—the scene of the crime.

The bedroom is as clean as the rest of the house, bed made and blinds open. The normalcy hurts my heart.

If I had come straight over after her call, could I have stopped her? If I'd called her back, would she have told me what she was planning to do?

On the nightstand next to her bed is a notebook I'd bought her for Christmas. I gave one to each of my ladies last year. I open the front cover to see my own handwritten note:

Dear Fiona,

I have found journaling to be such a healing process, and it's my hope that this notebook can be a step toward your own healing. You deserve joy!

Merry Christmas,

LuLu

Fiona had seemed put out by the gift. She hates clutter and made a point to remind me of that as she'd set it aside. I haven't seen it since the day I gave it to her, tied with a gold ribbon. But here it is. Navy blue cloth cover with colorful butterflies scattered across the bottom half, thick gold spirals, and the matching gold pen clipped to the cover. Butterflies are good luck to me; when I see one, it always reminds me of God's hand in my life. Looking at this notebook doesn't make me feel that. It just makes me sad, butterflies or not. I hesitate to turn additional pages out of respect for her privacy but then remember Mr. Hernández's voice saying, "She's the link."

I pull back the inscription page in hopes she'd left some insight behind. How was she the link?

Why?

Did she give me the poisoned Snapple four weeks ago?

Did she buy a candle from Walmart with the intention to burn down my house with me in it?

The first page behind the inscription page is blank. I quickly thumb through the other pages, all of them as blank as the first. The disappointment is sharp as I close the cover and turn my back on it.

I don't look at Fiona's body when I come back into the living room. Mr. Hernández is shuffling through the cabinet above the sink. I know what's in there: cookbooks and user manuals for her kitchen appliances.

"Did you find anything?" he asks me.

"No," I say, shaking my head and pointing toward the phone cord plugged in above the kitchen counter. "I wouldn't say she always had it on her, but her phone was never very far away either. Have you checked . . . her?"

He pauses, looks at Fiona's body again, and then says, "Yes."

Truth. I'm glad he did so that I don't have to.

"We need to go," I say as he closes the cabinet. "We need to call the police so that she can be taken care of." I nearly gag on the ugliness of the words.

"I did find this." He points to the fridge, and I turn to see a poor-quality picture of her and Johnny from decades ago held to the fridge with a Cabo San Lucas magnet. Will she get to return to being the happy woman in that photo? Or will she stay the woman she'd become for all of eternity? Hard. Unhappy. Evil?

She's not evil.

She might not have been nice, but she isn't evil, and, in that moment, I am able to forgive everything, even the things I don't know about yet. Hurt people hurt people, and she was hurting. I don't need to punish her for that, nor do I need to hold onto the betrayal. I hope my forgiveness can speed up whatever she needs to do to make things right on the side of life she's on now.

But the photo isn't what Mr. Hernández is pointing to. Next to the photo is a paper I instantly recognize as one of Handy Manny's handwritten receipts from the tablets you can buy at office supply stores. Being reminded of him makes me stand a little bit straighter.

"You didn't tell me that Handy Manny does work for Aunt Fee."

"I told you he works with several of my clients. Most of them are single women and need help with home repairs now and again. He's done work for Fiona a few times, I think. She told me once that he reminded her of a young Johnny." This memory invites a bit more softness, and I soak it in.

"Look at the date," Mr. Hernández says.

I look closer at the receipt and see the date—June 14—written in Manny's scrawling hand. "He was here *today*?" I ask, blinking and reading the date again.

"I'll take a picture," he says, glancing at the clock on the microwave as he pulls his phone from his pocket. It's 3:49. We've been here for twenty minutes. "Is there anywhere else you can think to look for the phone?"

I scan the portion of the house I can see while Mr. Hernández snaps a photo of Manny's invoice. A place for everything and everything in its place, except Fiona's body sprawled across the floor and the empty bottle of poison a few feet away. I shake my head.

"Can we please call the police now?" I ask, another round of chills creeping up my spine.

"We'll call from the car."

I look at Fiona once last time, wishing I had more answers to the tangle of questions in my mind. "I love you, Fiona," I say, then turn and leave the house.

We get in George, who is boiling hot again. I turn on the engine so we can start the air conditioner, and then I pull my phone out of Kermit.

Mr. Hernández grabs my wrist. *Again.*

I nearly scream at him to let me go, but instead I take a breath and clench my teeth while I wait for him to explain himself.

"Don't call yet," he says.

"No," I say, looking at him strongly and pulling my wrist out of his grasp. "I agreed to wait on reporting Mr. Roberts's murder because it wasn't time-sensitive, but this is. We *have* to call the police about this one. We cannot leave her on the floor a second longer."

"If you call them, we lose our edge."

"Our *edge*?" I repeat, meeting his eyes and gripping my phone harder. Again, he's not holding my wrist so tightly that I couldn't pull away. "What edge? We've got nothing."

"We have proof that Aunt Fee is somehow a part of this, and that Handy Manny was here. Maybe he saw something or heard something—maybe he's involved. Let's talk to him before the police do; that's all I'm asking."

This suggestion makes me too defensive too quickly. I clench my jaw and rein in my emotions. I also drop my phone back into Kermit and pull my wrist free from Mr. Hernández's grip. He lets go. "Manny has nothing to do with this."

He doesn't beat a skip. "Before this morning, you'd have said the same about Aunt Fee. If we call the police right now, we're going to be giving statements for hours. Is that what you want? Or is it worth having one more conversation that might get us closer to saving your life?"

I clench my eyes shut against the truth of what he's saying.

I don't want to do this anymore.

I want to give everything to the police and go home . . . except I can't go home, and the motivation to return to my hotel room is thin.

I am in the middle of this. The *very* middle. It's about *me*. I feel like I'm trapped in a ring of mirrors from which there is no exit. What is happening? Why and how was Fiona involved? What if we don't figure this out and I have to tell Sophie she can't come? Or, worse, what if the next attempt to kill me works? What if I never see my daughter again?

I have to fill my lungs with white light and picture an entire football field of white daisies to keep my brain from derailing. I'm not built for this. I don't know how to manage all this stress and fear.

I need perspective. I need to stay present and not spin out into the past or the future. *Right now, in this moment, I am okay.*

Think, LuLu, I tell myself. *Focus.*

We haven't heard from Sergeant Rawlins since he dropped us off at Mr. Hernández's office, a few hours ago.

Sophie is supposed to arrive in five days.

Fiona is dead.

Am I willing to put my life entirely in the police's hands when there is a possibility of bringing all this to an end with one more conversation?

The solution is already in the room.

I open my eyes and let out the breath I hadn't realized I was holding.

"I'll go with you to talk to Manny, but we're *also* calling the police. We can't ignore Fiona's death, and it will be worse for us the longer we wait to report it. It's the best I can do, Mr. Hernández. Yes, we'll end up giving statements, but we'll be able to talk to Manny first and we'll know that Fiona is taken care of." I can live with Manny being the last person I see before I spend the next eighteen hours in a police station.

Mr. Hernández grunts and pulls his phone from inside his sling—he's adapted pretty quickly. He waves for me to start driving as he puts the phone on his thigh and dials 911 with his good hand before lifting his phone to his ear. I'm not sure where I'm supposed to go, but I follow his gestured instructions out of Fiona's neighborhood. A few seconds later, he identifies himself on the phone and requests a wellness check on his aunt. He pauses, then says he hasn't been able to get ahold of her and would like someone to check on her.

Lie.

And even though I know he's lying, and I know why, I don't like how easily he says it. He gives Fiona's name and address, which I'm impressed he knows since according to Fiona he'd only ever visited her one time in the three months since he moved here. When he hangs up, we're both silent for a block or two.

"Where does Manny live?" he asks me, back to business.

"I have no idea," I say. I might have fantasized about him inviting me over to watch him make those delicious No-Bake Cookies, but I don't know where he lives. He might not be wearing a shirt in these fantasies, and the kitchen in this fantasy is rather generic . . . Well, it looks a lot like my kitchen.

"You have his number?" Mr. Hernández asks.

"Yes."

"Call and see if we can stop by."

"I usually text him."

"Then text him," Mr. Hernández snaps.

"Don't talk to me like that," I say as I pull over into a spot of shade and get my phone out of Kermit. "It's so rude."

Mr. Hernández is quiet while I type out the text, push send, and then place the phone in its car holder.

"Sorry," he says.

We sit in silence, waiting for Manny to reply. I can see the rock formation of Coffee Pot from here and wish I was walking that hiking trail right now.

"Okay," I say as an acceptance of his apology. I'm not in the mood to lecture him on good manners.

Three blinking dots show up on my phone screen, indicating that Manny is typing, but then they disappear. We sit for several more seconds that feel way longer than they probably are.

"Why do you go by LuLu?" Mr. Hernández asks, maybe trying to lighten the mood. "If Catherine is your legal name, where did LuLu come from?"

I am grateful for the change in topic and for the distraction. "When I was little, my Grandma Ruth read me a book with a character named LuLu, and I asked her to call me that. Apparently, I thought it was a very pretty and grown-up name. It stuck, and for years that's what my family called me."

That memory is a good one so long as I don't let it expand in my mind too much. I liked being LuLu and Little LuLu to the people who loved me best. Then I got older and the nickname seemed childish. I left it behind along with some other parts of who I was that I wish I'd kept.

My relationship with Grandma Ruth changed after I told her I'd asked Forrest for a divorce. When I—well, Catherine—explained that there wasn't any big drama, I simply wanted an independent life, she had been completely shocked. She asked if marriage meant anything to me, and I admitted that no, it didn't, not really. Not anymore. Our relationship was different after that, and Catherine didn't even care. She got the independence she wanted and only had to be a mom every other week after the divorce. She felt as though she'd beat the system. I think I only saw Grandma Ruth one more time before she died. Catherine was too busy with work to attend her funeral.

I picture a flamingo floating away in a hot air balloon filled with those thoughts to keep myself from going down that particular bunny hole. It's a dark one.

"After the accident, I was a very different person than I had been," I explain to Mr. Hernández. "I started going by LuLu when I came to Sedona. It's felt a lot more . . . me. The me I am now."

The three blinking dots return to the screen, and a moment later, Manny's reply appears.

Manny: I'm home if you want to stop by. Is everything okay?

CHAPTER 12

Manny texts me his address—which isn't far—and we head that direction. I have crisscrossed Sedona today, and though I don't mind driving, the stress of the day has me feeling irritable. But, then, we're going to see Manny and that smooths some of my edges.

The carport along the north side of Manny's house is full—his truck, a car on blocks, and a variety of tools seem to live there—so I park George on the curb, in the sun.

I drop the driver's side visor and use the mirror to apply the blushing pink lip gloss I keep in Kermit for just such occasions. I wish my hair was down, but at least it's not in a crazy bun coming undone like it had been this morning. I don't think Manny has ever seen my hair in a single braid—maybe he'll like it. It's a lucky accident I'm wearing this particular dress which Manny had complimented once. I smooth my hair back; it's starting to frizz as it dries.

"What are you doing?" Mr. Hernández asks, his good hand on the door handle ready to let himself out as he watches me.

"My lips are dry," I explain, smoothing out the gloss.

Mr. Hernández looks through the windshield as Manny steps onto the porch. Mr. Hernández pauses, then narrows his eyes at me.

I pinch my lips together one more time to smooth the gloss and then flip the visor back up before getting out of the car. This isn't a social visit but looking my best when Manny's around seems the least I can do when he is always looking so incredibly gorgeous.

Manny is waiting for us at the edge of the porch, and I'm relieved that there is some shade on the sidewalk where we can stand and talk. Manny is dressed in khaki shorts, flip-flops, and a dark gray T-shirt that clings to the hard muscle beneath the fabric. He's wearing a baseball cap, but I know that his head is as smooth as a stone beneath it because sometimes when he's working, he takes off his hat and wipes his forehead with the edge of his T-shirt. That's also how I know he has a beautiful, brown, flat stomach.

"Good morning, Luh-loo," he says as we approach, his words lilting in that way I adore. He jogs down the steps and meets us at the shaded sidewalk. "I'm afraid I have no cookies for you today."

I smile. "Well, you didn't know I was coming over until five minutes ago."

"That's true," he says, smiling back at me, which feels like that moment in the morning when the first ray of color hits the horizon.

He doesn't put his hand out to shake mine, we've never done that, but he does extend it to Mr. Hernández, who is staring at him like he's a specimen in a jar.

I shift my weight uncomfortably as they shake hands and then get right to business. "Sorry to interrupt your afternoon,

Manny. Thank you for being willing to talk to us. This is Mr. Hernández. He's an attorney helping me figure some things out and, um, he's also Fiona Hernández's nephew."

The image of Fiona's body sprawled on the floor flashes in my mind, swiftly followed by a rush of guilt over not telling him about her death. It's not a lie, but it's not the whole truth, and it feels wrong to withhold it. I try to swallow my discomfort, but some emotions are meant to be felt and I think this might be one of them.

"Oh, yes," Manny says to Mr. Hernández, still smiling. "Mrs. Fiona has told me about you."

Mr. Hernández stiffens slightly. He knows that Fiona had told me he was washed-up and lazy. I can't imagine she'd have shared anything different with Manny.

"We're looking for some information and thought maybe you could help us," I say.

"If I can, I will," he says with no change to his friendly tone.

"Were you at my aunt's house today?" Mr. Hernández asks, staring at Manny with that unblinking look of his. The look that makes you feel like you've done something wrong even when you haven't.

"Yes," he says easily, nodding. "I finished repairing her dishwasher."

"Finished?" I ask.

Manny nods and looks toward me. I stand a little straighter beneath his gaze. "Her dishwasher was leaking a few weeks ago. I replaced the broken coupler, but the new part cracked when I installed it. I wrapped the coupler as best I could and ordered a replacement. I installed the new part this morning."

"What time were you there?" Mr. Hernández asks.

Manny squints one eye and looks up into the tree. "Oh,

um, I think I arrived around noon." He nods and looks back at Mr. Hernández.

"And she was alright when you arrived?" Mr. Hernández continued.

Manny nods and shrugs in a way that is super sexy, never mind the circumstances of this meeting. He has these broad shoulders that taper down to narrow hips. Seriously. This man.

"As much as she is ever alright, yes." He pulls his eyebrows together. "Is everything okay?"

No! I want to yell. And then I want tell him what's happened and let him tell me it's all going to be okay and do I want a cookie? The fantasy is completely ridiculous. He can't reassure me that everything is going to be okay, but I wish he could.

I can feel sweat trickling down my back despite the shade. "Um," I say, trying to choose my words.

"How long were you at her house?" Mr. Hernández asks.

Manny holds my gaze another moment with those liquid brown eyes of his as though trying to decipher what it is I'm not telling him. He slides his attention back to Mr. Hernández. "I was there until almost one o'clock. I had to pull the dishwasher completely out and then make sure the new coupler held up while running the first portion of a cycle. She invited me to stay for lunch, but I had another appointment."

"Another appointment?" Mr. Hernández repeats.

"It's Friday—that's my day for repair work because I'm not on crew. I had two appointments after Mrs. Fiona. I had only been home twenty minutes or so when I received Luh-loo's text."

"On crew?" Mr. Hernández says, sounding irritated. "What does that mean?"

Manny's expression begins to harden.

"He manages a framing crew a few days a week," I explain, trying to soften the edges creeping into this conversation. "And does handyman work on the other days, including Fridays as he said."

"What appointment did you have after Fiona's?" Mr. Hernández asks.

Manny stares back at him. "I don't think that is any of your business, Mr. Hernández. What is the problem?"

He and Mr. Hernández hold each other's eyes for a long, uncomfortable second. Though they are both Latino with similarities that are easy to see, they are very different men. Manny has an accent, his skin is a shade darker, and his manner is more laid back and open. Mr. Hernández, in contrast, is stiff in his body and appears cold and tense and hardened.

"Does my aunt invite you to have lunch with her often?"

"Often?" Manny repeats, raising his eyebrows. "No, sir. I have worked for your aunt, perhaps three times. Once she invited me to stay for dinner when I was there late in the day, and today, she invited me to stay for lunch. I have never accepted her invitations, though I have thanked her for them."

"Why would she invite you to stay for a meal?"

I knew why. Staring across the table at Manny would be like staring into the eyes of Christmas. Manny regards Mr. Hernández with a long look and crosses his arms over his chest, which makes his biceps look even bigger. I swallow the sudden dryness in my throat.

"I suppose you should ask her that question, Mr. Hernández. My guess is that she is lonely and would like someone to share a meal with."

"I *can't* ask her because she's dead, Mr. Handy Manny," Mr. Hernández says in a disparaging tone. "And it's very likely you were the last person to have seen her alive."

CHAPTER 13

Manny's eyes go impossibly wide, and he says something in Spanish. The only part I recognize is *muerta*. "Mrs. Fiona is . . . dead?" he says in English as he drops his arms to his sides.

Manny looks at me, and I frown and nod simultaneously to confirm that what Mr. Hernández said is true. A bead of sweat starts to drip down the left side of my face. Isn't Mr. Hernández's admission incriminating for both of us since we haven't told the police yet? Shouldn't he know better? But, then again, I never expected *not* to own up to us finding her. I only thought I would be admitting it to the police before I told anyone else.

I wipe at the dripping sweat with the back of my hand and clear my throat. "We found her at her house about half an hour ago," I say.

"*You* were the last one to see her alive," Mr. Hernández says, still staring Manny down.

"We don't know that," I say, giving Mr. Hernández a reprimanding look. I look back at Manny and soften my tone.

"We think she died between 2:30 and 3:30. You said you left around one o'clock? Did she seem to be sitting down to eat at that time?"

His expression is drawn and shocked, but he looks at the ground and puts both hands on his head. He mutters something under his breath in Spanish again. I'm guessing it's either a prayer or a curse—both feel entirely appropriate.

"I am trying to think," he says, his accent stronger with his distress. "She started cooking lunch while I was working. Fajitas, she said. They smelled very good. I don't know if she finished cooking before I left."

"Did she invite you to stay when you got there, or did she invite you later during your visit?" I ask. Would things have turned out differently if he had accepted her invitation? It's a version of the question I've been asking myself about how things might have been different if I'd answered her phone call.

"She invited me when I first arrived, but, as I said, I had another appointment. I told her that I would stay for a meal next time."

I share a look with Mr. Hernández whose pinched expression reminds me that this is his aunt. Maybe I can give him a bit more grace on how he is handling things. But also, would it be that hard for him to be a bit more kind?

"And did she say anything in response to that?" I ask, turning my attention back to Manny.

"Um, she said, 'If there is a next time.'"

We lock eyes, and I expect he's feeling the same threat of those words as I am. Yet it is just the sort of defeatist thing Fiona would say, even if she didn't know that would be their last conversation. She said things like "I just want to be with Johnny" and "I don't understand why life has to be so long" on a regular basis. She was so depressed.

I feel a lump in my throat as I imagine her saying this to Manny if she knew that there wouldn't be a next time. If, in fact, she drank that Snapple on purpose.

Will we ever know?

"Had she said anything like that before?" Mr. Hernández asks.

"She always said things like that," I say as Manny nods in agreement.

Manny continues, "Sometimes she would talk about Johnny and say she wished she was with him; life has been hard for her since he died. She said things like that each time I did work for her."

"She talked to you about her dead husband?" Mr. Hernández says, and I bristle again at his tone. Suspicious. No compassion.

"Yes, sir," Manny says crisply, apparently reading Mr. Hernández's tone like I am. "She loves Johnny very much and misses him. She spoke of him a great deal. She, uh, said that I reminded her of him when he was younger."

"She told me that too," I say to validate the information. I hate that I sound like I'm defending everything Manny says, but I feel defensive. He hasn't done anything wrong and doesn't deserve to be talked to like this. Especially since he's being very forthcoming and helpful.

"What else did she say?"

"Nothing," Manny says as he shrugs. "Nothing that I remember."

"Did you see anything unusual while you were there?" I ask, hoping to soften things any degree that I can.

"No," Manny said. "Nothing. But your questions are making questions of my own. How did she die?" He looks back and forth between us.

"Poisoned, we think," Mr. Hernández says, and I am, again, shocked that he is giving so much information. My ex—well, Catherine's ex, really—Dane, was an attorney and any time we watched a cop show, he would yell at the screen for people to stop talking and call a lawyer. Now, here's Mr. Hernández, who is not only a lawyer but a *criminal* lawyer, spilling all this information to a man he met five minutes ago and has treated like a criminal himself.

"Did you see a bottle of Diet Peach Snapple while you were there?" Mr. Hernández continues.

Manny's eyebrows jump up his forehead, and he nods vigorously. "Yes, I saw it on the counter, and I asked her if that was for Luh-loo."

Truth.

They talked about me? I feel oddly comforted by this.

Manny continues. "But she said the drink wasn't for you, Luh-loo. She said—" He pauses and puts his hands on his hips, glancing at the ground. "She said that she was going to treat herself instead, and then she tapped the letter." He shakes his head. "It was confusing."

Mr. Hernández and I speak in unison. "What letter?"

He looks between us. "Uh, the letter. It was on the middle counter, the island. It said your name on the front." He waves toward me.

Mr. Hernández and I look at each other. Then back at Manny. "There was no letter," I say. "What did it look like?"

"It looked like . . . a letter," Manny says slowly, then uses both pointer fingers to draw the shape of a rectangle in the air. "A white envelope like you use to pay a bill."

"It was sealed?" Mr. Hernández asks.

Manny shrugged. "I assume so. It was on the counter beside

the drink and had Luh-loo's name on it. You see her on Mondays, yes?"

"Yes," I say. "But she called me around 2:30 today and asked me to stop by. She said she had something for me."

Manny nods. "The letter I would think. Except you say there was no letter."

"And you didn't find it strange that she told you all of this?" Mr. Hernández asks Manny.

Manny pulls himself up even straighter, which I swear makes his shoulders look broader, his chest look stronger. I can see darker patches of gray on the front of his shirt where sweat has started to soak through.

His expression tightens as he lifts his chin. "Do you have trouble with me, Mr. Hernández? I fixed your aunt's dishwasher, she invited me for lunch and talked about a drink and a letter, both of which were on the counter. Then she paid me, and I left. I have done nothing to deserve your manner of speaking to me, and I will ask you to show me greater respect than this."

Oh. My. Goodness. Could this man be any sexier? It's all I can do to pull my eyes away from him.

Mr. Hernández is both glowering and looking reprimanded at the same time.

I clear my throat, and both men look in my direction, but I focus my attention on Manny, wishing I'd taken the lead on this conversation from the start. "So, the drink was on the counter," I repeat. "And she said she was going to treat herself?"

Manny nods, his expression soft now that he's looking at me. "That is what she said."

"She paid you?" Mr. Hernández says, drawing Manny's

beautiful eyes away from me. "Is that standard practice, for her to pay you at the end of an appointment?"

"No, actually," Manny says, shaking his head. "Her nephew usually pays me—the other nephew, Jordan. He pays me on Venmo after I send him a request on the app. Today, she paid me in cash from her wallet."

Truth. Also, this is the first time I've really thought about Jordan in regards to Fiona's death, and I feel the blood drain from my face. He doesn't even know.

"It's not marked on the receipt," Mr. Hernández says as he pulls his phone from his pocket and brings up the photo he'd taken. He zooms in and turns the phone to face Manny.

Manny leans forward to look at the image, and then his cheeks darken. "That is my mistake. I had already put the invoice on the fridge and did not think to update it since I always request payment from Jordan. Mrs. Fiona paid me as I was leaving."

"Really," Mr. Hernández says, looking at Manny with a sort of knowing, sort of judging look as he returns the phone to his pocket.

"Jordan pays my wages too," I say, nodding fast as though it will distract Mr. Hernández from whatever suspicion is growing in him. We should call Jordan before the police do. He's taken such good care of Fiona since she moved here. Oh, goodness, how will he react to all this?

Mr. Hernández is staring at me. "Jordan pays you?"

I nod. "He's the one who hired me after Fiona's knee replacement."

I've met Jordan in person twice. Once, a few weeks into my working for Fiona. The second meeting happened a couple of months ago when I arrived while he was fixing Fiona's sprinklers. We chatted for a minute, which annoyed Fiona because it made me two minutes late. I'd spoken to Jordan on the phone before he hired me, and we've exchanged texts here and there. I'm pretty sure he's the one who convinced Fiona to hire me back both times she fired me. He's been amazing to her, and I'm sick about how he's going to take the news of her death.

"Did she say anything else while you were there?" Mr. Hernández asks Manny.

"I do not believe so."

"But you're not sure."

Manny's jaw tightens again, and he does that stand-up-straight posture thing again. Mr. Hernández is a few inches taller, but you wouldn't even notice right now. "Do not treat me like a criminal, Mr. Hernández. I have done nothing wrong and am telling you all I remember. I did not expect I would be interrogated about the appointment, so my thoughts are not planned out, but I do not believe Mrs. Fiona and I spoke about anything else."

Truth.

"Did she seem like her normal self to you, then?" I ask, trying to keep these men from coming to blows. Mr. Hernández would certainly be the worst for it, but I don't think Manny would hit a man with an arm in a sling. "You said she seemed as alright as she ever did, but did anything else stand out in her behavior?"

"No," Manny says, shaking his head and putting his hands in his front pockets. "She seemed sad, as she is usually. Sad and lonely." He pauses and takes a breath. He looks at the ground again. "I wish now that I had stayed for lunch."

We are all silent, then. If wishes were fishes, we'd all swim with them like dolphins. I would do anything to go back in time and change what's happened. I imagine myself bursting into Fiona's house while Manny is fixing the dishwasher and asking her about the letter and the Snapple and this morning's shooting. The sense that things did not have to go this way is so strong, but things *did* happen this way. This horrible, terrible way.

After a few seconds, Manny looks up at me. "When I was leaving, she called me Johnny. She said, 'Goodbye, Johnny. See you soon.' I thought she was making a joke or maybe did not notice the wrong name."

I'm thinking something different, though. I'm thinking she called him Johnny because he was the person she was hoping to see next. Was she . . . excited to be done with this life? I blink back tears. Manny may have been the last person to see her alive, but I think I was the last person she reached out to. When did she plan all of this? Before Manny came, certainly, hence the letter and telling him that the Snapple was her treat. But how much of today had she spent making a plan? What did she know about the shooting this morning?

I think about the notebook full of blank pages next to her bed. Is that where she'd written her letter that I am assuming was a suicide note? Or maybe a confession detailing her part in all this?

Written on the paper I had given her in hopes it would help her find some healing?

Was *this* what she saw as healing?

I put a hand on my stomach to quell the ache I'm feeling. My mind begins to skitter to different thoughts: my saguaros, the low supply of Body Toddys I need to remedy, and whether or not I paid the power bill last week. All in an attempt to run away from this, mentally at least. But I can't run. I won't run.

"Thank you for these details, Manny," I say, attempting a smile as I blink quickly at the tears forming.

"I am sorry I do not have more, Luh-loo," he says, then he turns to Mr. Hernández and puts his hand out again. "*Lo siento por su pérdida.* If I can help in another way, please do not hesitate."

CHAPTER 14

We get in the car that is now baking in the afternoon heat, and I watch Manny close the front door after he returns inside.

"I don't trust him," Mr. Hernández says as I pull away from the curb.

I am not surprised but keep my tone and my expression neutral. "Why not?"

"Because I don't know him, LuLu," he snaps. "And I don't trust people I don't know, okay. I don't trust a lot of people I *do* know, point of fact."

I slow down for the stop sign at the end of Manny's block and remind myself that Mr. Hernández's irritation is not because of me. It would be nice if *he* would recognize that and therefore not direct his irritation *toward* me, but . . . everything feels so heavy. It's hard to feel too angry toward him. Neither of us know how to handle this.

"I thought he was very forthcoming," I say in my carefullest of tones.

He grunts and says nothing.

"Why did you tell him Fiona was dead? I didn't see that coming." I am taken back to the conversation we had after leaving the Robertses' house—about him being surprised I led out so strongly. I guess I better understand how he feels now.

He groans and shakes his head. "I don't know. I shouldn't have, but I just . . . He was being so glib."

"He was?"

"Yes, all smiley and 'Isn't it a nice day' and 'Let's make cookies.'" He growls again.

I face forward and wonder if we were part of two different conversations. "He's just a nice guy," I explain. "I didn't see anything I would categorize as *glib*."

"Super convenient that he didn't mark paid on the invoice, too, don't you think? He's usually paid by Jordan, but if she pays him in cash first and he doesn't mark the invoice, he gets paid twice."

"That's not what he was doing," I say, tightening with the defensiveness I've been holding back. I still don't want to come across as too defensive, but I also don't want to play into this weird perspective he's fueling. "He explained that he was leaving when she decided to pay him. The invoice was already on the fridge, and he didn't think to go back in and update it."

"Yep," Mr. Hernández says with false positivity. "I bet a lot of the old people he works for forget they've paid, check the invoice, and pay him again. Not a bad hustle."

"That is not fair," I say, shaking my head. I realize I don't know where we're going, so I just keep driving toward driving toward the Arroyo.

"It's not *not-fair* either," he says, turning his head to look at me. "But I'm not the least bit surprised that you're so determined to give him the benefit of the doubt." He laughs without humor. "And they say men are the ones who objectify the opposite sex."

Okay, I think to myself as I let out a slow breath. *We're doing this.* I pull into a mostly empty parking lot and park under some shade and turn to look at him full-on. He meets my gaze and raises his chin. "What is your deal? You treated him like a suspect from the second we got there, determined to catch him in something. That's not normal behavior, and you know it."

"I think he *is* a suspect," Mr. Hernández says.

I lift my eyebrows. "On what grounds? Because he's the last person we know of who saw her alive? That doesn't make him a suspect." I don't think so anyway. "Maybe a person of interest, but not a suspect."

"I hardly expect you to be objective," he says with a scoff, facing forward again and doing his best to cross his arms, which doesn't really work because of the sling. He winces at his own attempt.

"Meaning . . ." I trail off.

"Meaning that if I'd had a napkin, I'd have handed it to you to control the drooling. That man is pure eye candy."

I feel my cheeks heat up, but although the drooling part is an exaggeration he's using to make his point, he's not wrong that Manny takes my breath away. And I likely have objectified him, a little. And maybe that influences my objectivity, but not to the point that I would make I would make excuses for him if I thought there was any possibility he was involved in Fiona's death.

"I was there to get answers regarding the death of your Aunt Fiona—answers which he was very helpful in providing," I say in my own defense, and quite calmly I am proud to say. "That he's as nice to look at as he is to talk to is just a happy accident."

Mr. Hernández narrows his eyes. "So, you admit you're attracted to him?"

"Absolutely," I say without hesitation. "But that's not why we went to see him, and it has no bearing on the facts of the situation."

Mr. Hernández works his jaw. Maybe he hadn't expected me to admit that Handy Manny makes me weak in the knees. But there's nothing sinister in my attraction no matter how much Mr. Hernández tries to make it seem that way.

"He didn't lie about anything he said today," I tell him. "Not a single detail."

Mr. Hernández huffs. "That you know of."

I almost ask what he means, but I stop myself because I suddenly know what he means. My lie detecting, or whatever it is, works best with direct information, such as "I forgot to mark the invoice paid" and "She invited me to stay for lunch." It doesn't work as well when the person shares their impression of something or answers a question with another question because there's no direct lie in an opinion or a question. Things like "I'm not sure" can be the truth, but a deflecting one—a soft lie like I caught Sergeant Rawlins in at the hospital when I asked what kind of gun was used.

As I become more comfortable with a person and trust them, I don't tune into it the way I otherwise might. For example, I haven't tuned into my detecting with Mr. Hernández for a while because we're working together, and we've felt like a team. In light of his odd behavior regarding Manny, however, I realize that maybe I should be a bit more cautious of him.

"I don't understand why you're doubling down on Manny," I say in an even tone just in case he's trying to bait me into an argument. "He said literally nothing that indicates he had anything to do with Fiona's death. I think you're projecting the emotion of this day on to him, maybe because you feel as desperate for answers as I do. Regardless of how we feel, however, he did not say or do anything that is reason to suspect him of having anything to do with Fiona's death."

Mr. Hernández looks away, but he doesn't counter, which makes me think he might be realizing that I'm right. He *is* projecting. Because he's scared. Because his aunt is dead. Because Manny is an unconnected entity for him and a safe place to direct his anger. Or so a magazine article I read at my doctor's appointment had explained.

I attempt to bring us back on topic, wanting to understand this man as best I can. "Why did you dig into the payment thing? Why was that important?"

Mr. Hernández faces forward and takes a breath. "It doesn't matter."

Lie.

"It does matter. You made a big deal about it."

Mr. Hernández looks out the side window for almost a full minute, then turns toward me again. "What do you know about Jordan?"

I wasn't expecting this question, but I'm eager for the topic as Jordan has been in and out of my thoughts since our conversation with Manny. "He's fantastic," I summarize. "He's done so much to take care of Fiona."

"Like what?" Mr. Hernández asks.

"Well, he hired me, and he stops by and fixes stuff at her house all the time. I think they talk every week or so. She brings him up a lot, though she's not very gracious about his help."

"Does he help her out financially?"

"Uh, I don't know, but he pays me. And I guess he usually pays Manny. He could be paying us from her accounts and just doing the management—I'm not sure. Fiona would not talk about money in any form with me, but I had the impression she was on a very tight budget. I assumed Jordan helped her out a little bit. She said he was quite well off."

"That's all you know about him?"

"Are you quizzing me?" I straighten in my seat and hope I look studious. I wish I'd brought my reading glasses to further exaggerate my performance. "Okay, um, what else do I know about Jordan? He's Caucasian, about five foot ten. Owns a cement company, I think, and lives in . . . Flagstaff?"

For some reason, Mr. Hernández softens. Man, he's confusing. "Yeah, that's all correct. Do you know anything about his family?"

"Divorced. Two kids, I think? Fiona told me about the divorce when I asked about a photo I saw on the fridge with him and his kids."

"Yeah. The divorce was only finalized a few months ago. It was an ugly one."

"Were you his attorney?"

"No. I don't do family law. He moved to Flagstaff after the divorce was over and has been building out that location for his company—yes, he does cement. Let's head toward the hotel if that's okay."

"Right," I say both as agreement on Jordan's cement business and that we should drive. I pull out of the parking lot. The police will likely be calling Mr. Hernández any minute about the wellness check on Fiona, and it makes my stomach hurt to think about. It would be good for him to not be driving around. Plus, we're out of leads to track down on our own.

"What does Jordan have to do with Manny's invoice? Other than he would have paid if Fiona hadn't," I say.

"I'm not sure, exactly, but I've wondered to what extent he

helps her financially. She never said anything about him paying for other things?"

I shake my head. "What does Jordan's financial help toward Fiona have to do with the way you treated Manny?"

Mr. Hernández pauses. "I'm not so sure Manny isn't guilty of something. I investigated a lot of scams when I worked for the DA's office, and the elderly are particularly vulnerable."

Truth.

"So, you interrupted the investigation of your aunt's murder to make sure she wasn't also the victim of handyman fraud?" Now who's being a jerk? I put up my hand to stop both of us from continuing down this road and take a breath. "Why does it matter what Jordan pays for?"

Mr. Hernández is quiet for a few seconds, staring out the front windshield. "I don't understand why Jordan helps Fiona out the way he does. It's nice of him, sure, but Jordan grew up in Tucson, not Mesa where Fiona and Johnny lived. He didn't seem particularly close to Uncle Johnny and Aunt Fee, and I never sensed a special connection between them."

Tucson is where I was taken after my accident. It always stands out to me when people mention it.

"Well, Fiona and Johnny had no children of their own. Maybe he just feels some family responsibility to her, and since he lives close by and has the resources, he does what he can to help. It's very kind of him."

"Yeah, I used to assume that too." He turns to look out his side window.

Truth.

"But you don't anymore?"

"Jordan talked me into coming to Sedona," Mr. Hernández admits, shifting in his seat enough to betray his discomfort with telling me this, though I can't see why he would be uncomfortable. "Everything had gone bad in Phoenix. I had a license but no clients, living off savings and freelance stuff. And then he reaches out to me on Facebook and asks if I want to come to Sedona for a while. He had some contracts he needed updated and wanted my help to expand into the Sedona and Cottonwood market now that he was in Flagstaff: meeting with the city on his behalf, submitting plans and getting permits—stuff like that. Jordan worked out some sort of work-trade thing with the Arroyo and rented that office on a month-to-month basis to have a home base for what I was doing for him." He shakes his head. "Anyway, I'm not sure why Jordan went to all the trouble for me, and that's making me wonder why he went to all the trouble for Aunt Fee."

Truth. All of it. And he's far humbler now than he was when he deemed Manny to be eye candy. Handy Manny Candy. I am careful not to smile at this poetry. Or trust Mr. Hernández's openness too much. His mood swings are unsettling.

I wait for him to continue, but he doesn't, and so I decide to play a little devil's advocacy. "Sounds like a nice guy wanting to help out both his aunt and his cousin who'd fallen on hard times."

"I'm not his cousin," he says, looking at me again. "Jordan's mom is Fiona's sister. I'm related through Johnny. We're both nephews but from opposite branches of the family tree. We knew each other because of a handful of times that Fiona and Johnny involved both sides of the family in a holiday celebration or something. We barely knew each other. We're just connected through them."

"So, then, he's just a nice guy helping a distant relation who fell on hard times."

"Right," Mr. Hernández says with a hint of sarcasm, then takes a breath. "I've been working with him for months and still don't know much more than what you just told me about him. He went to a lot of trouble to get me here, but he could have hired half a dozen other people to do what I do. He probably has foremen and whatnot on the payroll who do exactly what I'm doing, other than the legal contracts. It doesn't make sense."

I sit with this information as I pull into the parking lot of the Arroyo that is fuller than it was when we left. It's regular check-in time, I guess.

I park George, but we don't get out of the car just yet.

"Have you told Jordan about Fiona yet?"

"I want to be thorough," Mr. Hernández says, which isn't an answer.

"Right, but I'm trying to follow your line of thinking here. Are you suspicious of Jordan? Do you think he had something to do with the attempts on my life and Fiona's death?" It feels completely mad to say this out loud. I've met Jordan only twice.

Mr. Hernández shakes his head but says nothing. He knows I can't tell if he's lying unless he speaks.

"What aren't you telling me?" I ask, direct and to the point.

He looks at me. "I need to look into a few things. I don't want to jump the gun."

Evasive answer. Not a lie. Not the truth. "Like you did with Manny? You had no problem jumping that gun."

"That's different. Jordan is family . . . and my boss. I want to be thorough without causing damage to him or our relationship if I can help it."

Truth. But I think there's more to it.

"Let's take an hour then meet up in my room again," he says, reaching for the door handle. "I'll share whatever I've found out by then."

"Can you give me a little more than that? Should I be looking into something?"

"Look into whatever you want," he says as he stands up. "We'll put our heads together in an hour."

All right, then.

We walk into the hotel for the second time today, but I head for the stairs this time. Quadriceps are the most important muscles to keep strong as a person ages. I remind my clients of this all the time, and I hate missing a chance to work them. Plus, I hate the confined space of elevators.

"I'd rather take the elevator," he says.

"Then by all means, take it," I say, waving toward the elevator doors. "I would like to take the stairs."

He grumbles as he follows me into the stairwell like he's my babysitter. I'm ready to have some time apart from him. Time to think over all that's happened in the last hour. Time to try to make sense of it all on my own. Maybe I'll take another shower. When we reach my floor, we walk down the hall to my room in silence.

"Come to my room in an hour and, um, stay here until then, okay? Don't leave without me."

That seems like a weird thing to say, but I nod. "I don't have anywhere to go."

"Right." He turns and heads toward the elevators.

I walk into my room and jump at the crash-close of the heavy door behind me. I'll need to be more attentive to that. I use some pink light to draw my thoughts back together, then take a deep breath before looking around the room. I've been hoping it might feel a little homier now that my things have had time to energetically connect with the room, but it still feels like a generic, though nice, hotel room, and I still don't want to stay here.

I employ another round of my Good LuLu linen spray and think over the day: the shooting, Maryanne's confession, finding Fiona, Manny looking handsome, Mr. Hernández's suspicion of both him and Jordan.

Tucson.

I look at my phone. Will the police call *me* about Fiona? Will they arrest me for not telling them we'd found her?

I take a breath and think back to Mr. Hernández's concern about Jordan. He obviously feels some loyalty to Jordan, but also doubt.

Could Jordan be part of the plot to see me dead?

Why?

Why would Fiona be part of a plan to kill me?

What happened to the letter Manny had seen on the counter?

I'm spraying the linen spray throughout the room and trying to match up details that just don't match when my phone chimes with a text message.

I keep spraying as I cross the room, imagining the golden light of gratitude in every tiny droplet of the spray cleansing every surface it touches. Cleansing me. I think about the affirmation that had come to my mind at Fiona's house: *The solution is already in the room*, reminding me that the answers to all these questions exist. We just need to find them.

I pull my phone from Kermit who I'd hung just inside the door and stare at the notification.

New message from . . . Dane Bohannan?

CHAPTER 15

A tingling rush of energy moves through me as I stare at a text from the man who two years ago threatened to file harassment charges against me if I didn't stop texting him. Aside from the random Facebook post that shows up on my feed—he didn't block me—I haven't heard anything from or about him since.

> **Dane:** Hey there, I'm in town this weekend and thought I'd check in. Give me a call so we can catch up.

Hey there?

As though we're old friends who talked a couple of weeks ago instead of a couple of years.

My brain stutters, and I drop the phone on the bed as I walk to the window and stare out at the desert.

Dane. The person I was visiting Arizona with when I had my accident five years ago.

Texting me. Even though he threatened to have me arrested for harassment.

Texting me today of all days.

It can't be a coincidence, and yet I really, really, really want to believe it is.

But I don't believe that Fiona coincidentally died today of all days. I wasn't coincidentally shot at. I know there is something going on beneath the layers of my understanding and awareness, and Dane reaching out today has to mean something.

Accepting this feels like I'm on one of those amusement park rides that drop you fast. All the blood rushes to my head.

Dane is part of my past, and he's suddenly here in the present. Why?

I told Mr. Hernández about my accident and was uncomfortable about the gaps of information I usually ignore because there's not much choice *but* to ignore them. Gaps I thought just this morning could be filled by Dane if we were still in contact. Connecting those gaps to the current threat I'm under feels ridiculous and obvious at the same time. I'm not sure how to settle that dissonance.

I inhale a deep breath of pure white light and let it settle into my belly as I wrap my arms around my waist and continue to stare into the desert landscaping that surrounds the hotel. The land is full of sharp points that hide a dozen different creatures that are equally sharp. The desert is beautiful and fascinating, but always on the defensive. I'm feeling defensive too. But about what?

I want to sort this out under the covers of my own bed while breathing the oxygen generated by my own plants in my own cute house. But I can't. So, then, what is my next best option?

At first, I don't feel an answer, which makes me realize I

haven't been tapping into my inner wisdom much today. Everything has moved so fast.

Talk to him. The voice of inner wisdom brings calm with it. I am relieved that when I finally reached for it, it was there for me. Then it adds, *Be careful.*

I decide to trust it—myself. I consider talking to Mr. Hernández first but decide against it. There are things he's not telling me, and while I have no expectation of holding this back from him indefinitely, I want to take my own action and fuel my own energy into what's happening around me. Happening *to* me. I heard once that God loves action. And I know that God loves me and wants what's best for me. And so I will act, and I will listen to this inner wisdom, and I will see where it takes me.

I pick up my phone, close my eyes long enough to visualize a field of bright-white daisies to summon courage, and call Dane before I can talk myself out of it.

He answers on the second ring. "Catherine!" he says, then laughs. He's the sort of guy who laughs a lot, even when the conversation is serious. "I mean, LuLu of course."

"Hi, Dane," I say, but then I don't know what to say next. *Why are you calling me?* sounds aggressive. *How are you?* sounds trite. I decide that since he's the one who reached out first, I can let him state his reasons.

It takes a few more seconds for him to take the responsibility I've left dangling for him. "Um, anyway, like I said in my text, I'm in town and wanted to see how you are doing."

"You're in Sedona?"

"I can be."

I pull my eyebrows together. "What does that mean?"

He laughs, but it's awkward. This whole call is awkward, but instead of feeling like I need to fix that awkwardness, as I often do, I let it be what it is. As I already determined—he's the one who reached out.

"I came in to see my family for the weekend and just wanted to catch up. How are things?"

"You told me not to contact you anymore," I remind him. "You said I was harassing you."

"Right," he says, a little less laugh in his voice now but still trying to keep things light. "That was . . . Well, I'm sorry about that. Tiera was upset, but she understands now."

What is it she understands? I wonder. And why *now*? I wish I could tell if he were lying, but it doesn't work with phone calls.

"Is she with you?" I ask.

"No, not this time."

"Does she know you're calling me?"

"Of course," he says, a laugh in his voice again. "Seriously, LuLu, I want to apologize for that last exchange and try to make it up to you. Tiera is totally good with me being here. In fact, it was sort of her idea—I can explain that in a bit. Could we meet for dinner or something? Are you free tonight?"

I sit with this for a few seconds. "Aren't you in Tucson?" I ask, trying to figure this out. His family is in Tucson, which is a four-hour drive from Sedona.

Tucson.

Mr. Hernández had said Jordan was from Tucson. I feel a little tingle at that connection.

"Phoenix. Just landed a little bit ago," Dane says. "I could be to Sedona by . . . uh, seven o'clock."

"So, you flew to Phoenix instead of Tucson on a Friday afternoon to see your family, but you haven't actually seen your family and instead you're going to drive two hours in the wrong direction to have dinner with me?" Maybe I should have thought these words instead of saying them out loud. Then again, maybe saying them out loud is exactly what I should be doing.

He pauses. I let my questions hang in the air between us like a hammock full of rocks. "I've been thinking about you the last little while," Dane finally says, not laughing anymore. "I want to make sure you're okay."

A chill moves through me. "Why wouldn't I be okay?"

He's quiet. I'm quiet. Should I tell him someone is trying to kill me? *No*, my inner wisdom says, and I agree. He's done nothing to earn my trust, and this whole call is bizarre.

"Why wouldn't I be okay, Dane?" I ask again.

"Could we talk over dinner or something?" he asks. "There are things to say."

"Say them now."

"Um, I could do that, but I'd really like to see you. I think it would be better for all of us to explain things in person."

"All of us? Dane, what's going on?"

We go silent again.

He clears his throat. "I want you to know that what I'm telling you is true when I tell it." I didn't think he knew I could spot a lie, let alone that I can only do it in person, but it sounds like he does. How would he know that?

I bite my lip and turn to look at the clock radio next to the king-sized bed. It's 4:27. The idea of sitting down for a meal with him makes me anxious, but despite all the effort Mr. Hernández and I have put into this day, we haven't uncovered many answers.

Talk to him, my inner wisdom repeats inside my head. *But be careful.*

Okay, I answer back.

"There's a Thai place here—Thai Spices," I say. "I can meet you there at seven."

"Great," he says with relief in his voice. "I'll see you then."

I end the call and drop the phone onto the bed before closing my eyes and taking several four-count breaths to stop the roiling in my stomach. Two years of nothing, and now he wants to talk to me.

In person.

Today.

He said there are things to say.

I start tapping, just my collarbone at first, and begin pacing the room while picking thoughts out of the swirling ball that is spiraling in my head. I continue to tap—my crown, my eyebrow, my chin, my collarbone. While I tap, I line up facts, looking for where things intersect.

Dane is connected to Catherine.

Dane is connected to LuLu.

Dane is connected to Seattle.

Dane is connected to Arizona.

Dane is connected to Tucson.

Dane is connected to the accident.

Dane has walked through the door of my life on the same day someone tried to end it.

Dane was there the last time my life nearly ended.

I take a breath, let it out slowly, and expand on these facts.

Dane grew up in Tucson, and because of his connection there, Catherine had come with him to Arizona for a weekend getaway and to meet his parents. They'd flown into Phoenix and stayed at the Kimpton Hotel. On the evening of March 19, they drove separately to a restaurant in Tucson to have dinner with his parents. He stayed in Tucson that night, but Catherine drove back to Phoenix, which is why she was on the I-10 at 10:42 p.m. where she braked for a rabbit in the road or fell asleep or something, which led to a single-vehicle crash. That accident led to a life flight to the Banner University Level 1 trauma center in Tucson and, eventually, Castle Creek Rehabilitation Center in Sedona, a few miles from where I now live. These are the details I know.

The details I've been *told*.

Since that night, Catherine has only existed in the memories of other people; the damage to my brain changed my personality and my ambitions. I had to learn to walk and talk and read all over again. I also learned how to consider other people's feelings and opinions, decided I wanted a closer connection with people, and chose to pursue a simpler life that I could manage with as little stress as possible. Sedona supported my goals.

For the gap between my existence as Catherine and then LuLu, I have had no choice but to rely on what other people tell me happened. I know that my heart stopped twice in the helicopter ride to the trauma center, I spent twenty-four days in a coma, and I cried a lot after regaining consciousness. I *know* these things because my mom and my medical team told me that's what happened. I know that I was in Phoenix with Dane, driving my own rental car to Tucson to meet his parents because he told me that's what happened. He's the one who packed my suitcase at the hotel we'd been staying at and brought it to the hospital after he checked out. Mom told me he was upset about having to leave Arizona, but he had to get back to his work after having stayed close by for those first few days. He confirmed this when we started talking on the phone while I was in rehab. He's one of very few people from Catherine's life who kept in contact. He's the only person who knew what happened in Arizona in the days leading up to the accident.

The *only* one.

And I have trusted everything he told me because . . . why not?

But.

Someone is trying to kill me.

Dane has reached out unexpectedly.

I answered some questions for Mr. Hernández at the hospital today that reminded me of the uncomfortable gaps not only in my memory but also in my understanding.

I start to pace and imagine that I'm drawing energy up through the bottoms of my feet. It's a sort of grounding without actual ground. I kick off my flip-flops to accelerate the process of connecting with all that is. With truth. With as much understanding as I can possibly find. I start asking questions I haven't allowed myself to ask.

Why was I meeting Dane's parents?

I remember the first two months of our relationship and have no memory of feelings other than attraction and . . . passion, I guess. The relationship was casual; Dane was going to be heading up the new Yakima office that summer, and we both knew our relationship would come to an end once he left Seattle. Dane had told me that our relationship had shifted in the weeks before our trip—the weeks I can't remember. I had no reason to doubt him, so I didn't.

Why did we stay in Phoenix and not Tucson?

Tucson has an international airport, and if the point was to meet his parents, why not stay closer to them? Catherine would never have stayed in their home, but I would bet there are hotels in Tucson just as nice as the Kimpton. Because they were staying in Phoenix, and Catherine didn't want to overnight in Tucson, they rented two rental cars and drove separately. That's weird.

I explained away the oddness of having two rental cars to Mr. Hernández this morning because Catherine absolutely would have chosen to drive separately to a dinner two hours away so that she could have returned to the hotel alone instead of staying with Dane at his parents' house in Tucson that night. But would she have driven four hours round trip to meet the parents of a man she didn't really care about that much and had only been dating for a few months? Dane and Catherine hadn't even been exclusive, though I'm not certain Dane was aware that she had been seeing other people.

I feel my cheeks heat up with embarrassment. So much of my life before the accident has taken on a translucent quality that I haven't looked at it too hard. What has mattered to me is the now and here, not ruminating on what feels like a distant and uncomfortable past.

But Catherine *had* been seeing other people. That is a fact even if I'm the only person who knows it.

So, Catherine went to Phoenix and rented her own car so that she could drive two hours separately to a dinner with the parents of a man she was not committed to and still sleep in the hotel they'd booked in another city.

I stretch my arms out wide and turn my face to the sky—er, ceiling—and open my heart to the question: Would Catherine have done that? The answer that fills my head is a swift and short and solid *No*.

I inhale, face the window, and bring my arms up to meet above my head, then drop my pressed palms to heart center.

Four hours of driving round trip with an awkward dinner in between with people she had no future with because she had no future—*wanted* no future—with their son? No way.

This realization fills me with an odd flush of emotion: Anxiety about having discovered something that doesn't fit the narrative I have believed up to this point. Embarrassment to admit to myself that Catherine had been cheating. And relief to know Catherine well enough to know this truth.

My chest is fluttering like a monarch migration as I pull my notebook out of Lisa and put it on the hotel desk. I have the blinds wide open and squint at how the light reflects off the white paper. I grab a pen from the zippered pouch I brought. The pen I grab happens to be turquoise and matches my dress, which I take as a good sign. I flip to a blank page and start making a list of details I can feel a connection between. Maybe seeing the words written will help piece things together.

Dane is from Arizona.

Dane is in Arizona right now.

My killer is in Arizona.

Fiona is dead.

I tap my pen on the paper, making asymmetrical dots in the process. I'm missing key points of information, but if nothing is a coincidence then all this information matters. I add a few more notes to the paper.

My death improves someone else's situation.

Most people are killed by someone they know.

Most of the people I know are in Arizona.

Dane was not Catherine's future.

Catherine would not have wanted to meet his parents.

Catherine would not have gone to the trouble of meeting his parents.

Dane is the only person who knows what happened in the days leading up to the accident.

There's something niggling at me. Something I know but don't know. Something . . .

I write the first thing I wrote again.

Dane is from Arizona.

Then add something else.

Dane is from Tucson.

Jordan is from Tucson.

I tap my pen on the paper some more, kicking myself for not investigating my own accident before now. It had never seemed important, but now it feels very important, and I don't have time to look up police reports, double check reservations, verify the details I have not questioned. I never even thought to call Dane's parents to ask about the dinner. And apparently the police didn't either.

In two hours, I'll be sitting across a plate of yellow curry from the man who has the answers. And I'll know if he's lying to me.

I need to learn as much as I can before then to maximize that opportunity.

I get my laptop—who I call Kumquat because it's a cool word—out of Lisa and set it on the desk. I glance at the time and see that I have only about twenty minutes until Mr. Hernández is expecting me in his room. I feel an anxious tremor in my chest at the prospect of sharing what I've learned when I see him. Will he see connections I don't see more easily than I will? Or am I making this into something it isn't?

I don't do Facebook much these days, but since Dane and I are still "friends" on there, it's easy to get to his page. I scroll through multiple posts covering the last several months that show him with a cute redhead who must be Tiera. They were married last February, I find out, and he looks really happy in the photos.

He also has plenty of quotes about Jesus. I scroll back to what seems to be his first evangelizing post almost four years ago about his new church and his new faith. He talks about regret over the man he was and the hurt his actions caused but rejoices in the gift of repentance. It's touching and seems heartfelt; I'm glad for him.

I take a few seconds to remember Jordan's last name—Pender! I check for Jordan Pender in Dane's friend list, but he isn't there. I look up Jordan on Facebook overall, but while there are several matches for the name, none of them are who I'm looking for.

I return to Dane's page and scroll some more. I stop around the time that Dane and Catherine had started dating. There's one picture of them with a group of other people from work. I'm not tagged, though a few other people are. Natalie, Raul, Tyson. I stare at Catherine's face. I don't look like myself in this photo, but I'm smiling. I seem . . . happy. And I guess I was. I had everything I wanted. Is that what creates happiness, though? Having everything you want?

There's no mention of the trip to Phoenix in March of that year on his page. No mention of the dinner with his parents or the accident or anything else for nearly six months. Then a photo of his parents, who had celebrated their fortieth wedding anniversary in November—I would still have been in the rehab center here in Sedona. I don't think I'd ever seen a photo of them when we were dating. Catherine didn't have any interest in his family, yet she supposedly went to dinner with them. I wonder if I should call them and ask if we met for dinner that night. I make a note to think about that.

I scroll backward, to before our relationship, and see the post where he had gotten his "dream job" at the firm where we met. There's another photo of me at the work Christmas party of that year. I remember that night. I'd met with a high-profile client that afternoon who wanted to leave his wife for his younger girlfriend but didn't want to lose 50 percent of his assets to community property laws. We had outlined a two-year plan that involved moving assets into a holding company and liquidating a few others as quietly as possible. The plan was for him to get out of the marriage with 80 percent of what they had acquired without his wife having any idea she was entitled to more. Catherine had been invigorated by the challenge. I'm so embarrassed for her now and wonder where that man's wife is now. A Gloria who I helped to defraud.

And then I find a photo with a familiar face that makes me inhale deep and slow.

Jordan Pender. The other nephew. In a photo with Dane Bohannon.

Jordan isn't tagged in the photo, though the other three men in the photo are. The fact that his whole name is spelled out like the other men, who are tagged, makes me wonder if he had been tagged once upon a time too.

I read the post to get context. The photo was taken at their ten-year high school reunion.

Jordan and Dane went to high school together.

With hot energy churning in my chest, I turn the page of notes I'd written to get to a blank page. I'm so worried that I'll forget this information. There's a franticness in my chest that does no favors for my handwriting, which gets sloppier the farther down the page my list goes.

Jordan and Dane went to high school together.
Jordan moved Fiona to Sedona.
Fiona is dead.
This last line bears repeating, and I write it five times.
Dane reached out after two years.
Dane knows I can spot a lie in person.
Dane knows Jordan.

Jordan is Fiona's nephew.
Jordan hired me to care for Fiona almost a year ago.
Jordan pays my wages.
Fiona is dead.

I run out of lines and turn the page. The afternoon sun coming through the windows shows the indentations of the notes I just took on the page above. I sit up straighter as my inner wisdom repeats a thought from earlier in the day that I had interpreted as an affirmation: *The solution is already in the room.*

CHAPTER 16

Mr. Hernández opens the door of his room when I knock, then heads back to his computer with an intent that signals I've interrupted him. My body is still tingling, but I am working hard not to show it as I line up exactly what to say and how to say it. I want to be ready to answer whatever questions Mr. Hernández throws back at me. Because he *will* interrogate me. It's who he is.

"What did you figure out about Jordan?" I come into the room and shut the heavy door slowly so it doesn't slam behind me. I can't risk scattering my thoughts when I'm so wound up. After confirming the connection between Dane and Jordan, I had done another ten minutes of online sleuthing, confirming that Jordan owns a bigger cement company than I thought. He has locations in Tucson, Mesa, and Flagstaff with a "coming soon" page about his Sedona location opening at the start of next year. The property for his new site is located on the edge of town, near the sewer treatment plant but closer to the foothills since it's set back from the highway.

"Not a lot," Mr. Hernández says, seemingly irritated. "But I have some questions for you about him. How many times have you met Jordan?"

I'm not surprised that he's got questions. I am ready for them. "Twice," I say, even though I've told him this already. "At Fiona's. The first time was because he wanted to meet me in person. I'd done two appointments with Fiona at the time, I think. The second time was a couple of months ago. He was working on a sprinkler, and we chatted from the sidewalk."

"Was he nice?" Mr. Hernández asks me. "Personable?"

"The first time he was nice enough, seemed to be in a hurry though. The second time he was a little more flustered."

"About talking to you?" He fixes that direct stare of his on me.

"I hadn't thought so at the time, but now I'm wondering about that. I had assumed at the time that his attitude was because he's sort of awkward and was not thrilled to be working on Fiona's sprinklers on a workday."

He narrows his eyes but says nothing. I decide to share what I've learned. "I found a connection between Jordan and Dane."

"Dane?"

I see his expression change with realization right before I remind him who Dane is. "Dane was the guy Catherine . . . um, I was dating at the time of my accident. He and I came to Arizona together that weekend."

"That's right. He's from here," Mr. Hernández recalls, eyes narrowing. "You met his parents."

"That's what I always believed," I say.

He holds my eyes. "You don't anymore?"

"I'm not sure what to think anymore." I walk toward him while pulling my phone from Kermit so I can show him the photos on Facebook I saved. One of the photos is that first one I found, the one from their ten-year reunion. But I also found a photo from high school. "He and Jordan went to high school together. They were on the golf team."

When I saw that photo, I remembered a conversation Dane and Catherine had about high school sports before they were officially dating. Dane had played on the golf team and received a scholarship to Arizona State. Catherine's three years on the high-school softball team had earned her a scholarship to a small junior college in Oklahoma that she turned down. She hadn't seen softball as her future and wanted to go to school in Seattle. Dane and Catherine had discussed these things over martinis at a bar they'd gone to with some other work colleagues. It was a surprising memory because I could remember the attraction Catherine had felt that night. I can remember how she'd considered that maybe, since Dane was going to Yakima in six months, she would go out with him when he asked—and she'd known he would ask. It wouldn't be anything serious. Just safe fun since his time in Seattle would have a deadline attached to it. She didn't want anything long-term.

I let the memory slip through my mind as I hold my phone out to Mr. Hernández. He pushes the wire-framed glasses farther up his nose and squints at the photos.

"I think Jordan used to have a Facebook that Dane had tagged," I say, "but it's been deleted. His name still shows up in the posts though. I Googled his company. He seems to do very well for himself."

"And what does all that mean to you?" Mr. Hernández asks. I realize that he probably uses this look in the courtrooms to pin down people on the stand. I put my phone back into Kermit, still slung over my chest, and take a few steps toward the window as though looking at the view instead of needing more distance between Mr. Hernández and me. I haven't forgotten my realizations that he might not be as trustworthy as I thought, even though I can't prove he isn't and the idea of not having him in this with me feels impossible. But I promised myself I would be more cautious.

"I don't know." I shake my head and watch a little red car back out of a parking space below us. "The connection between Dane and Jordan can't be nothing. My accident happened on my way back from Tucson, which is where they are both from." Saying it out loud deepens my discomfort. Jordan and Dane and Tucson and the accident. The accident that *was* an accident. Had to be an accident? Right?

"Dane's never mentioned Jordan to you?" Mr. Hernández asks.

"No, but I'm going to ask him about it at dinner."

"Dinner?" The sharpness of Mr. Hernández's tone startles me. I turn to look at him, hating the way my heart speeds up at the reprimand I don't think I deserve until I review what I've told him . . . and haven't told him.

I relax my shoulders and smile apologetically. "Oh, sorry, I guess I left that part out. Dane texted me. He's coming to Sedona to meet me for dinner at Thai Spices. He says there are things to talk about."

"You left it *out*?" Mr. Hernández says in clipped tones as he closes his eyes and pushes a hand through his hair in apparent exasperation. "How could you leave out the fact that your ex, who is connected to Jordan, is in town today of all days? How long have you known about this?"

"Don't talk to me like that." I pull myself up to my full height, rolling my shoulders behind me like I'd seen Manny do. "There's a lot happening, and I forgot to mention it. Don't be mean. He texted me after I was in my room—like, forty-five minutes ago."

His eyes narrow as he takes in a long breath through his nose, but he must accept that my reprimand is valid because he doesn't press his point. "Are you planning to go?"

"Yes. I want to know why he's come all the way from Washington to say whatever it is he wants to tell me. We need all the information we can get."

"Then you should have asked him to tell you on the phone. We don't have time for this."

"When did we decide on a deadline for my life?"

He shakes his head but allows a few thoughtful seconds before he speaks again. "I can't believe you agreed to that without even talking to me about it." He takes another deep breath.

"Well, I did." I throw my arms up, which I hope shows exasperation and not surrender. He is so moody. "What did *you* find out?"

He moves his jaw back and forth as he seems to wrestle with my determination not to argue about my decision to meet Dane. It takes a few seconds, but he finally gives in.

"I called my mom."

This is not what I expected.

"She talks to Aunt Fee as much as anyone, so I asked her about Jordan's connection. Mom said that they didn't seem to have much of a connection until a couple of years ago, when Jordan decided to open a location here in Sedona. Fiona had moved here after Johnny died but was in a two-level condo. Jordan helped her get this new place, which is single-level living, and then helped her with the knee surgery somehow. Mom knew he'd hired a caretaker for her; I guess that was you."

"None of this sounds very . . . suspect," I say.

"Except Mom doesn't think Aunt Fee could have afforded

the house," Mr. Hernández says with a nod. "Aunt Fee was excited about the move at first and grateful for Jordan's help, but then got more negative about both."

"Negative about Jordan?" This is surprising after all he'd done for her, except Fiona didn't seem to like anyone.

"Mom didn't know why, exactly, but Aunt Fee had made a comment about Jordan being a busybody. Do you remember how Aunt Fee found your name when she moved here?"

It takes me a breath to go from absorbing information to giving it out. "Jordan's the one who called me. I don't think I asked how he found my name, but I have posters on different community boards around town."

"But Jordan is the one who reached out to you," Mr. Hernández repeated.

I nod. "It's not unusual. Family members contact me first in a lot of cases. They often see the need before my clients do." But none of those other family members had a connection to an ex-boyfriend who is also connected to my accident.

"When was that first call?" Mr. Hernández says in that snappy tone of his.

"Um, about a year ago." I am thinking fast, sorting through my banks of memory. "Yeah, it was just before the Fourth of July. I started working for Fiona the first week of August."

"You're sure?"

I nod. "I had three open spots because of the exodus after everything that had happened with Gloria. I was grateful to fill one of those spots before the holiday weekend. Sophie came for a week with Mom starting July 6. I remember telling her and Mom about my new client. Fiona was the first new client I'd had since the articles had been published."

We're both silent for a few seconds, then he turns back to his computer.

"Did you tell your mom about Fiona?" I ask.

He shakes his head, his expression tight. "I will, of course, but . . . not yet."

This is so yucky. What will Mr. Hernández's mom think when she finds out he already knew Fiona was dead when he called to talk to her? "And the police haven't called you back? It's been hours."

"I haven't heard anything."

Truth. But . . . not enough. I feel that prickle of insecurity again.

"Have you told Jordan?"

He looks up at me, blinking and opening his mouth but then he closes it again. We stare at each other for several seconds while I wait for him to respond. Finally, he shakes his head as he turns away from me. I can't tell if he's lying unless he says the words. He knows this. I had asked before if Jordan knew, and he deflected that time too.

What has he told me and what hasn't he shared? There's no way for me to know for sure. I take a breath and let it settle in my chest.

I think he *has* told Jordan, but he doesn't want me to know that. Why?

"Have you told Jordan that we found Fiona?" I ask again.

He clears his throat while I'm still speaking and blatantly ignores my question. When he speaks, his tone is lighter. "So, if Dane is connected to Jordan and Dane's here in town, he must be a part of this too. I'm not sure it's safe for you to meet with him, but I agree he might have important information. Maybe I can already be at the restaurant, a couple of tables away, just in case."

I wish I hadn't told him where I was meeting Dane. Did I tell him what time? I can't remember.

Mr. Hernández focuses on his computer. "I did find this one thing that's interesting. You said your accident was five years ago, in March, right?"

I could ask about Jordan a third time, but I don't. Deflection. Indirect answers.

I imagine a blue wall around myself, protecting me from this man I *chose* to trust. I was so grateful not to be doing this on my own, but if I look at things from a slightly different perspective, that's different too. I found a lot of information on my own, and it's *my* life hanging in the balance. I need to make the smartest decisions I can for myself. If Mr. Hernández has a different agenda, he's not safe for me. I can't trust him more than I trust myself. That's a choice too.

Also, it would be completely reasonable for Mr. Hernández to tell Jordan that their mutual aunt is dead. If he said he had, I would not be surprised or upset about it. The only reason I can think of for him *not* to tell me is because I might ask additional questions he's not prepared to answer. Honestly, at least. Yet he knows he can't answer them dishonestly either. He's trying to control the direction of our conversation—possibly to avoid me finding out something else. Something bigger than Jordan knowing Fiona is dead.

The blue wall of protection helps me keep my emotional distance, and I decide to continue forward, but carefully. It feels like trying to keep your shoes dry while crossing a stream—trying to choose the rocks that won't roll out from underneath your foot.

"My accident was just over five years ago," I say. "On March 19."

"Jordan started the concrete company about a year before that," Mr. Hernández says. "He bought two brand-new cement trucks. Sticker price of almost $300,000 each. Plus, four regular trucks and a piece of land outside Tucson where he set up his cement yard. Looks at face value to have been a million dollars that I can't find lending on. Maybe he had an investor, but he's the only person on the articles of incorporation for the entity. I want to do a little more digging."

Truth. All of it. But it's mostly facts.

I have some facts at my disposal too. "Before he did the cement company," I say, "he owned another business."

Mr. Hernández turns to meet my eyes, and I can see that he knows what I'm about to say. "Desert Designs, landscaping."

"That's right," he says as though he is just now remembering this detail.

"Landscaping," I say. "Paraquat."

Mr. Hernández frowns and nods at the same time. "Would he still have the licensing to buy paraquat if he hasn't owned the landscaping business for so many years?"

"I don't know," I say. The business license wasn't renewed after he started the cement company. "But it's the closest connection we've found to paraquat so far. Do you think he is trying to kill me?"

"I don't know," he says almost offhand as he turns back to his computer.

Lie. I feel it shiver all the way through me. He knows something he's definitely not telling me.

I want to put him on the spot and ask, again, if he has told Jordan about Fiona's death, but I don't.

Someone removed a letter from Fiona's house before we got there. Could Mr. Hernández have done it without me noticing? He did enter the kitchen first . . . but surely, I would have seen him take something from the counter, and he'd seemed genuinely surprised when we learned about the letter from

Manny. Could *Jordan* have been at the house before us and taken the letter? Had Jordan made Fiona drink the Snapple?

"We need to tell the police to talk to Jordan," I say.

"Not yet," Mr. Hernández says quickly. He's focused on his computer again. "We need to know as much as we can before we confront him."

"I don't think it's in our best interest to do the confronting. We're in over our heads here. We need to go to the police."

And yet, I don't want to go to the police yet either. I'm meeting Dane in less than two hours. In my mind, I see a piñata version of Dane that is going to burst open and rain down information. Not that I want to hit him with a bat or anything . . . maybe that wasn't the best imagery. I can't talk to Dane if I'm giving a statement to the police, but the last thing I want to do is confront Jordan on my own.

I shift my weight from one foot to the other while Mr. Hernández continues to type into his computer, and I try to decide what to do. I can't depend on Mr. Hernández, and the thought makes me sad. And I can't just stand here doing nothing when there is so much to do. So much left for me to learn. Seconds turn to a full minute as I wrestle with what needs to be done. One minute turns to two. Mr. Hernández is still tapping away on his computer. Does he even remember I'm here?

Finally, I make a decision and clear my throat to get Mr. Hernández's attention. I want to separate my agenda—saving my life—from his, which I don't really know. It's time to go my own way on this. I know it, even if it scares the Bee Gees out of me. "I'm going to go to Fiona's while you finish your research."

Mr. Hernández's head snaps up so fast I startle mid-turn toward the door. He pops up from his chair to face me. "What? Why?"

"Th-there was a notebook in her bedroom. I gave it to her

for Christmas, but that doesn't really matter." I pause, feeling off-center. "Well, maybe it does matter." Maybe everything matters. "Anyway, I think it might be important, and I want to check it out." I think the notebook might be the very "solution" my inner wisdom was affirming to me when it told me the solution was already in the room. I just hadn't fully understood what it meant. And it's a good excuse for me to leave Mr. Hernández to whatever it is he's doing while I find my own course through this.

"We are not going back to Fiona's for that notebook," he says with the finality of a father refusing to let his teenager go to a late-night party. It's the wrong stance for him to take as it summons my stubbornness and inner rebel . . . or maybe it is the perfect stance for him to take because it puts us on different sides of a line he's just drawn.

I stand up straighter. "I think she might have written the missing letter in the notebook I found in her bedroom," I explain, watching him closely as I realize how much he's giving away with his reactions. Maybe he's figured out how to circumvent my lie detecting, but that isn't my only option in reading him. He's being a bully.

"The letter isn't in the notebook." He's still talking to me like I'm a child rather than an adult woman who has higher stakes in this situation than he does. He's not lying to me, but he isn't being truthful.

I am not good at strategizing what I say and don't say like he is. So, I will be as open and honest as I feel I can be. "I want to see if there are indentations from what she wrote." I look toward the hotel room door and let out a breath. "I should have brought my notebook up to show you what I mean." I face him again. "You know how sometimes when you write on one page, there are—"

"If you have a notebook, then you don't need Fiona's." He gives a scoffing laugh, and I clamp my teeth together. There is no point in trying to explain anything to him. I watch him cross to the windowsill and, with his back to me, take a long drink from his thermos. He puts it down and looks out the window.

"Why are you acting like this?" I ask him in a calm voice. "I have an idea, and I want to pursue it."

"But it's a dumb idea," Mr. Hernández says, turning around while throwing his left arm up as though I've asked him to build a bridge out of pine cones while wearing boxing gloves.

It's not a dumb idea, and we don't have a lot of other ideas. "You can keep doing what you're doing. I'll see if I can get the notebook, though maybe the police are still there, and I won't be able to. Then I'm going to meet up with Dane." I tune in hard to my lie detecting, even though I think he's been working around that. Then again, if he has been working around that by saying what isn't necessarily truth but isn't necessarily untruth, maybe he'll trip himself up. False senses of security can go both ways.

"You can't go to Fiona's," Mr. Hernández says, folding his arms over his chest. "It's a crime scene, LuLu." Silly-kid tone again. Also, *truth*.

"You didn't care that it was a crime scene when we searched through it for Fiona's phone."

"This is different. The police are probably still there."

Lie.

He continues, "You can't just waltz in and take something."

"It's been hours since you called the police," I remind him. "The scene has likely been processed already. If the police are still there, then maybe I'll wait. I feel like this is something I should do, and we have very little to work with right now."

I stare at him for a few seconds. He holds my gaze without blinking, though his jaw is working and his eyes show his . . . nervousness?

"Did you call the police about Fiona?" I ask him.

He rolls his eyes, and I wonder if it's as much a gesture of impatience as it is a chance to look away from me. He's managing me. Or thinks he is. "You saw me."

Truth, but not an actual answer to what I asked. I saw him dial a three-digit number while I was driving away from Fiona's house. I listened to him request a wellness check. But did he actually call anyone? I'm trying to formulate a question that will force him to lie when his phone rings. He quickly turns to pick it up from the dresser, but not before I see the relief in his expression.

"I need to take this," he says.

Truth.

"I'll come to your room when I finish," he continues. "Don't go anywhere until we've talked this through, okay?"

I don't move, and he looks at me. "It's a client," he says, holding up his phone as though to demonstrate, but the screen is facing away from me.

Truth. I'm listening to more than my truth-about-lying now, though. Jordan is technically his client, right?

I turn to leave. He answers the phone at the same time I pull the door open.

"Yes, hi. Go ahead."

A step forward will take me into the hall. A step to my left will take me into the dark bathroom. He would never expect me to stay behind to listen in on his call—the benefits of being underestimated. I glance over my shoulder to see Mr. Hernández's back to me, then I throw the door open at the same time I step into the dark bathroom. The door to his room hisses closed on its commercial hinges and does that solid slam I had avoided when I came in. I close my eyes and send pink light to my brain to pull my thoughts back together as the crash sends them skittering. It takes only a second to get myself back together, and I move as close to the threshold of the bathroom as I can without revealing myself, pulling the fabric of my dress back tight against my shins to prevent it from betraying me. This might be another situation where pants would be preferable.

"Okay . . . Yes . . . She's gone, but she's putting things together without any help from me and pushing hard to go to the police."

I can't breathe for a moment, but then force myself to do so as quietly as I can.

"What's going on with Dane? No, he's here . . . in Sedona, or he will be. She's planning to meet him for dinner. What's he going to tell her, Jordan?"

I raise a hand to my mouth to keep from inadvertently gasping and put every bit of energy I have into listening even though my brain is begging to be allowed to shoot off to some different thoughts. *Please, please, please.* I bite my lip enough for it to hurt so I can stay present.

Mr. Hernández shares what I just told him about Dane and Jordan's connection in high school and the missing Facebook account, he repeats the part about me planning to meet Dane for dinner, and then he starts yelling about Jordan having gotten him into this disaster. He goes on for several seconds, an absolute rant that leaves me confused. He knows *some* things—certainly more than he's told me—but not everything. He doesn't know why everything that's happened has happened. He doesn't seem to know anything about Jordan's connection to Dane.

"This is maddening." He curses several times. "Well, maybe I could barter with LuLu or the cops for some details you're choosing to leave out . . . Don't give me that—the only person you're protecting is yourself!"

More swears.

Then he's quiet. Listening to Jordan's side of things, maybe?

"Yeah, okay. But we've got to move fast. The handyman knows about Fiona now, and I'm not sure LuLu believes I called the police . . . Oh yeah? I'd like to see you deal with her any better than I am! If it wasn't my neck on the line, I would have turned this over to the police hours ago."

I take a deep breath and accept that I am on my own. But I'm with myself. I funnel all the trust I have been giving to Mr. Hernández inside myself now and take a deep breath. I have done so much more today than I would ever have imagined possible. I can do more. I can do it alone if I choose to trust myself to be more than I have been.

I take another long slow breath, then exhale as though I'm blowing through a straw. I try to gauge where Mr. Hernández is in the room by his voice. I think he's near the window, which is good. It's as far away from my position as possible. I look at the door that leads to the hall and visualize myself pulling it open like I did a few minutes ago. But this time I'll go through it.

He'll hear me, but I'll have a head start. I have the key to George in my purse, and the driver's door unlocks automatically when I'm close enough. Mr. Hernández will be slowed down by his shoulder sling and maybe his unfamiliarity with the stairs.

I'm finding it harder and harder to control my breathing as anticipation starts spreading through my chest and arms with a tingle that borders on numbness. I try to shake it out by wiggling my fingers and moving my arms as much as I dare. I take deep belly breaths, imagining the oxygen fortifying the cells of my body like pumping up billions of tiny bike tires all at once.

His voice sounds louder for a moment. Maybe because he's facing the bathroom? I can no longer understand what he's saying because my focus is so centered on making my escape. I hold my breath and wait one second . . . two . . . three . . . four . . .

When his voice gets the slightest bit muffled again, I lunge forward, pull the door open, and make a run for it.

CHAPTER 17

I am several steps down the hall before I hear Mr. Hernández behind me.

"LuLu!" he calls out. "Stop!"

I do not stop.

I try to focus on only one thought—get out of here. There are a million "shoulds" running through my head: I should have called the police myself after we found Fiona, I should have paid more attention, I should have . . .

There's no time nor is there any benefit to those lines of thought. I didn't do some things I could have done. I did do some things right. Getting the heck away from Mr. Hernández is one of those right-best decisions.

He's getting closer. I can feel it in the vibrations of the floor.

"LuLu!"

To my right, there's a sideboard-style table against the wall with a flower arrangement. I veer that direction and grab the vase without slowing down, go into a spin, and fling it in his direction like a shot-putter. It doesn't hit him, but he's forced to jump out of the way, and he falls into one of the recessed doorways.

The door to the stairs is next to the elevator, and I push through into the vestibule between the door from the hall and the door that leads to the stairway. I have maybe eight seconds before Mr. Hernández comes through the first door. I want to leap down the four floors I need to clear before I reach the lobby level, but of course that only works in the movies. There will be people on the lobby level to help me when I reach it, but I'm wearing a dress with flip-flops, and he has longer legs than I do. I need more advantage than my head start.

I push through the second door, the one that leads into the actual stairwell, but instead of hurtling down the stairs, I crouch so he can't see me through the little window at the top of the door. I sit on the concrete landing and brace myself against the center post of the stairs—going up on the left and down on the right.

I get to the count of three before the door bursts open. I'm ready for it and kick both feet against the door as hard as I can. The force of the double-kick sends the door back into him with an astounding amount of power—quadriceps! I hear an oof and a grunt and the slam of his body to the floor between the two doors.

I jump up, kick off my flip-flops, and hold Kermit against my chest as I run down the stairs as fast as I can.

"LuLu!"

My name echoes off the stairwell when I'm two flights down, the skirt of my sundress billowing out behind me. I hear him on the stairs above, but I have a significant lead now.

He starts jumping multiple stairs at a time. Gracious! Why didn't I think of that? I start taking two stairs at a time; it's all I dare. I've only got one more floor to go when the creak of a hinge indicates that someone has opened one of the doors below me. Probably a hotel guest trying to burn some extra calories and about to be scared out of their wits when they see me rushing toward them. But when I come around the landing for that last set of stairs, I see that it isn't a hotel guest.

Jordan Pender is waiting for me in front of the exit to the lobby.

I try to stop myself, but my momentum propels me forward, and my bare feet slide off the cement stairs. I grab the railing with all my strength, linking my arm around the metal to keep from barreling into him. I look up just as Mr. Hernández reaches the landing above me. He has blood dripping from his nose and covering his chin, which makes my stomach turn. His chest is heaving, and he leans against the wall, holding his slinged arm with his other hand.

Jordan is on the landing below me. Not bleeding, but not pleased. He's wearing a baseball hat with his company logo embroidered on the front. His shirt is bright blue—royal blue. Way too cheery for the hard-faced man who wears it.

"LuLu," Mr. Hernández says in a gasping breath. "You should have stopped, LuLu. You should have talked to me."

"You're a liar," I yell back at him. "You've had all day to tell me your part of this!" I take a staggered breath of my own.

"I didn't . . ." Mr. Hernández starts, but he has to stop for breath and bend forward before he can finish. Blood drips from his face to the concrete landing. I don't look at him.

Jordan walks to the base of the stairs, planting himself there. He's an aging version of the stocky teenager in those Facebook photos, with heavy shoulders and a solid body. Not fat, but thick enough that there's no way around him. Mr. Hernández is blocking any possible escape up the stairs, though I couldn't move faster than Jordan if I tried to go that way. Will he kill me now? Right here in the Arroyo stairwell? Will I die without even knowing why?

The solution is already in the room.

I take a deep breath and remind myself that I am not as fragile as I thought. I am not as limited as I have believed. And I am not out of ideas. I start listing the resources at my disposal in this very small yet incredibly important moment in time.

I make an exaggerated show of standing up straight and untangling my skirts, while unobtrusively reaching into Kermit, which I'm still holding against my chest. My right hand wraps around the rose agate—the solution.

"Look," Jordan says, putting up his hands as though to show me he's not a threat. "We need to talk."

Truth. But I have no trust left for either of these men.

"You're trying to kill me!" I shout back, adjusting my grip on the stone, my other hand covering my purse so he can't see what I'm doing. I likely look like an old woman clutching her pearls. I'm okay with that.

He steps onto the first stair, and every muscle in my body goes tense.

"Jordan," Mr. Hernández says in a warning tone that I do not trust either. I dropped my guard with him so easily, and even after I had my first doubts about him, I kept including him on what I learned.

Now is not the time for self-flagellation, however.

I am LuLu, and LuLu is great.

"I just want to explain," Jordan says, his hands out again.

Lie.

"If you had wanted to explain, you'd have done it before you tried to kill me!"

He's three stairs away from me now. With a good lunge,

he could grab my skirts, pull me down, and then . . . what? Bash my head against the concrete floor? Pull a knife from his pocket and slit my throat? There are no passive options left to him.

He glances past me to Mr. Hernández, and I use his momentary distraction to take the deepest breath I can.

I scream at the top of my lungs while I pull the stone from my purse and draw back my arm. The scream startles Jordan just enough, and I throw the rose agate overhand as hard as I can, hitting him right in the nose and spinning him backward off the bottom step. Thank you, high school softball.

He falls against the wall of the stairwell, almost tumbling down the final flight of stairs that must go to the basement. He grabs for the railing, his legs splayed, trying to maintain some balance.

I leap past him toward the door that leads to the lobby. I reach out for the door handle that is inches away, but he grabs my skirt, yanking me backward as he loses his balance and falls down the first few steps, dragging me with him. I clutch the railing to prevent him pulling me down, but his grip on the fabric is fierce. If only I were a cartoon character with giant scissors I could pull from my purse!

"Let go!" I scream at him as loud as I can, kicking at his hands that are clenched tightly around the fabric of my dress. I am pulling myself up by the railing as hard as I can, trying to counter the downward pull, when Mr. Hernández suddenly hurls past me, tackling Jordan.

I yank hard and pull my skirt from Jordan's grip. I don't look back as I spin away from the two men now tumbling down the stairs together. I recognize the sound of fist on flesh. Once, twice, three times before the door out of the stairwell closes behind me.

There are half a dozen people staring at me when I stumble into the lobby, which startles me until I remember I screamed a few seconds ago for the very purpose of drawing attention.

"In the stairwell," I say, then run for the hotel entrance. A woman ahead of me looks at something over my shoulder, and I watch her eyes go wide. I don't slow down and am halfway to the door when Mr. Hernández grabs my elbow and pushes me forward. It takes all I have to keep up with his momentum. His face is still dripping with blood.

We plow through the front doors, people jumping out of the way as we blink into the brightness of the day. I try to pull away from Mr. Hernández's grip, but he tightens his hold on my elbow and keeps going, somehow both pushing me and dragging me at the same time. I'm barefoot, and the tiny rocks of the hot asphalt cut into my feet as we cross the parking lot. The stabs of pain with each step keep me from wondering where he's taking me until we reach George.

He pushes me toward my car and falls forward, his good hand on his knee, though he looks wobbly as he sucks in a breath. "Go," he gasps. "Get out of here."

I pull on the handle of the driver's door, which unlocks as soon as I touch it. Mr. Hernández is still bent over, trying to catch his breath. Blood is dripping from his face and onto the pavement. If I were a bit more vengeful, I could kick him over right now. Maybe keep kicking him for as long as I want. He's bleeding and broken and . . . telling me to get in my car and leave him here. Jordan probably isn't far behind us. I look toward the hotel entrance, but I can't see it from here.

Mr. Hernández is working with him. *For* him?

Why am I hesitating?

Take him with you.

"No!" I say out loud. To him. To my inner wisdom that does not seem very wise right now. To myself.

I pull the driver's side door all the way open and when I turn to drop into the leather bucket seat, the angle forces me to look at him again. He staggers back a step and reaches out for a parked car to steady himself, still trying to breathe. He exhales through the blood, sending droplets out like a spray bottle. My stomach turns. His face is pulled tight in a grimace of pain as he attempts to roll his bad shoulder. Had that tumble down the stairs added to his injury?

I don't wait for my inner wisdom to repeat herself as I reach forward, take hold of his good hand, and pull him around the front of the car.

His eyes go wide as he looks at me. "Wh-what—"

"Get in," I say, throwing him toward the passenger door. I hear commotion from the front of the hotel. Jordan must be outside. "Get in!" I shout again.

He gets in. Seconds later, George, Mr. Hernández, and I are squealing out of the parking lot.

CHAPTER 18

My heart is beating like the blades of a helicopter in my chest as I pull onto Main Street. The adrenaline coursing through my veins makes me want to fly down this road, weaving in and out of traffic, speeding around corners. Instead, I slow down to the rate of traffic and force myself to breathe as I pull in behind a gold Ford Taurus with a white-haired woman in the driver's seat. I know it will take about three minutes for the rush of chemicals to dissipate, so I focus on the smooth leather of the steering wheel and the hum of the road beneath the tires. I take a four-count breath and blink back tears brought on by so many intense emotions. My whole body is buzzing. But I survived. Again!

"I think you broke my nose," Mr. Hernández says, his voice muffled. Probably from the swelling of his sinus cavity.

"Good."

I'm not sure where to go. Nowhere feels safe. The obvious answer is going to the police, and part of me craves being able to run inside with my hands up and collapse in a cell, if that's where they put me. They can take care of this, and I would be safe. But Dane has things to tell me, and Mr. Hernández has said so many times that going to the police will get in the way of things that I can't seem to un-believe it now. What I need is for my mind and my body to catch up to one another. I grip the steering wheel tighter and take as deep a breath as I can manage, but my belly is too tight to inhale fully. My heart is still racing.

Mr. Hernández groans from the passenger seat. Why did I bring him? My inner wisdom said to do it and that was enough reason at that moment, but now I'm stuck in a car with my enemy who is bleeding all over poor George.

"You're working with him," I finally say as I reach over and pop open the jockey box, stuffed full of miscellaneous napkins from a dozen different fast-food places. "You're part of this."

I hit the roundabout and circle it twice before deciding to take Highway 89. Toward the police station. Toward home.

"Not like you think." He grabs a wad of napkins.

I glance at him and then look quickly forward again. I've seen pictures of myself after the accident and seeing him now reminds me of that—bloodied and swollen. He flips down the passenger visor and startles at his own reflection. He takes a bottle of water out of the side door and pours some on the napkin. I decide to go to the Posse Grounds. I will be able to ground myself there and make clearer decisions. There are a couple of hiking trails that in fifty yards take you from the parking lot to the wilderness. If I need to leave, or leave him there, it's also not far from town.

"Explain it with direct details," I tell him. "None of the tricks you've been using."

"Okay," he says in a surrendering tone. "I'll tell you." He pauses for a breath.

I look straight ahead and brace myself. I'm going to feel

like an idiot for not knowing what was happening right next to me. I can handle that, though. Right now, despite the shaking of my hands and slight popping sensation in my brain, I feel like I can do anything.

"I told you I came to Sedona to work for Jordan—contracts, business stuff. We've talked about this."

"That's why you said you had a phone call with a client," I say, remembering how those words had pinged like truth when he said them; Jordan *is* a client. True but deceptive. I grip the steering wheel again, feeling as though I could twist it apart like taffy if I tried.

"Yes," he says.

"You didn't tell me you knew Jordan wanted me dead."

"I didn't know at first."

Truth? I'm not sure I trust my interpretations of this man, however.

He continues. "About fifteen minutes before our first appointment, I got a call from Jordan saying that he wanted me to tell him everything you and I talked about after the appointment was over." A pile of bloody napkins is growing at his feet when I turn east onto Soldier's Pass Road. "It's a violation of my license to share client information, and he knows it."

"Never mind that it's also a violation of basic ethics," I remind him, but ethics seem to be something Mr. Hernández is rather fluid with.

"Yes, and I told him that, at which point he reminded me that he had given me a job and a purpose and that I owed him."

Truth.

"So you told him what we'd talked about, just like that."

"I did," he says, sounding regretful. Maybe.

The pause lasts for the full block and into the parking lot of Posse Grounds. I park and get out of the car, then take a deep breath as I look at the line of red rock laid out to the east. Sugarloaf, Coffee Pot, and Soldier's Pass, where the soldiers crossed through to Fort Verde two hundred years ago.

Posse Grounds isn't a vortex, or at least not officially, but it's easy to access, and I feel good here. I start toward the trail that will soon make it seem like I'm miles from the world at large. I lost my flip-flops in the stairwell, but the trail is soft dirt, and though the afternoon is still hot, I don't care. I *want* to feel things, even if it's uncomfortable. I want to know things with the same acceptance.

I hear Mr. Hernández close his door and follow me. I glance over my shoulder to see that he's limping, and I take some unholy pride in that. I review everything that's happened today, and although my thoughts are still messy and strewn about, I can manage them. Being barefoot immediately grounds me, and I imagine the energy of Mother Earth moving up through my feet, absorbing into my bones and muscles and skin and brain.

I reach a clearing between a smattering of creosote bushes and juniper trees, wriggle my feet into the dirt, and inhale the scent of the mesquite catkins and cedars. The sense of smell is triggered by actual particles of whatever it is a person smells; I read that in *Psychology Today*. This isn't very comforting in a public restroom or landfill, but I love knowing that I am literally breathing in pieces of the plants right now. The earth. The red rock that surrounds me. I hold the breath in my lungs for the count of four and then slowly let it out as I accept the facts of my situation. I bring my hands to heart center again and breathe deep as I find my energetic equilibrium.

What's happening is what's happening.
Things are what they are.
There is no sense hiding from it.

This is reality.
Fiona is dead.
She may have been involved in the attempts on my life.
Jordan is behind all of this.
Mr. Hernández is involved too.
I trusted him.

I feel so stupid but know I can't dwell on that. It will lower my vibrations, and I need to be at a high frequency right now.
I am not dead.
I am LuLu, and LuLu is great.
I am so much more capable than I thought I could be.

I hear footsteps behind me and open my eyes as I turn in his direction and lower my arms to my sides. Apparently enough trust remains for me to have kept my back to him.

We stare at one another across the clearing. He's a mess. His very nice hair is rumpled, the sling he's worn for less than ten hours has a tear at the elbow, his navy-blue shirt is spotted and smeared with dark splotches of his own blood. His nose is swollen, though cleaner now after he used the napkins and water bottle in the car. He's obviously in pain and exhausted and holds his slinged arm with his other hand. It feels dangerous to empathize with him too much.

It's good for me to be outside right now. My thoughts are settling. The mesa stretched out behind me settles me even further. There is space in my head again, and I decide to trust the intuition that got me out of the stairwell, into the car, and ultimately here with him.

I review what Mr. Hernández revealed to me on the drive over and begin lining up my questions.

"What did you know about me before I showed up at your office that first time?"

"Not much," he says.

Truth. But vague.

"What *exactly* did you know?"

He takes a breath, and I see a shift from his previous demeanor. Surrender? Maybe even relief. I take it with a salty rain but don't dismiss the possibility. "I knew that you worked with Fiona and that she'd referred you to me. Just before you arrived for our first meeting, I learned that Jordan wanted me to tell him everything I learned. I thought he was . . . interested in you. That he was using me to do a background check or something. That sounds really stupid now."

Interested in me? I brush that aside. The important part is that he did not know Jordan's motives and was, instead, guessing. I'm glad I'm not the only one feeling dumb right now. "How did you know about the lie detecting? Jordan told you?"

"Yes."

Truth.

"How did he know?"

"I have no idea. He was very cryptic."

Truth. But Dane knows about my lie detecting, and Dane and Jordan are connected somehow. I still don't know how Dane knows.

Mr. Hernández is not what I would call a passive man. The idea that he would take orders from anyone does not fit his character, yet he's telling me the truth.

"But you went along with it. Even though you should have kept our conversation confidential and had no idea what Jordan's motives were."

He nods slowly. "Jordan is the only person who offered me an opportunity after everything that happened in Phoenix. He gave me work. He found me a place to live. He encouraged me to see this as a new start, and although I was uncomfortable with his request to divulge our conversation, I did owe him, and I had no idea what the stakes were. Like I said, I thought he had romantic interest and wanted to know more about you."

Truth.

I think back to our first meeting in Mr. Hernández's office and how difficult he was to read because he mostly asked questions. All those long pauses I thought were proof of his engagement and well-thought-out responses were really time to make sure he didn't trip himself up. I hadn't cared too much about his honesty; I'd gone to him for help with something I could not do myself. I'd never considered that he would be working against me from that very first meeting.

"And then after the meeting, what, you thought there had to be a different reason because I was so weird?"

He blinks at me, which is answer enough. I do not care.

"You took $10,000 from me and then shared everything I told you with Jordan."

He swallows, looking properly penitent, and nods.

"Use your words," I tell him sharply.

"Yes," he says. "I took your money and told him everything."

Truth.

"I also asked him some questions about the Snapple and candle. He told me it was paraquat in the bottle to keep me from getting it tested."

Truth.

I raise my eyebrows and feel a shiver. Mr. Hernández knew that three days ago?

He continues, "And then he told me that you were a threat to everything he'd done and would send him to prison."

"How was I a threat? How could I send him to prison?"

"He wouldn't tell me. He was all over the place in the conversation we had after the first meeting. I got as much information as I could, but it wasn't a lot. He kept saying that the less I knew the better."

Truth.

"But you knew I was in danger for three days and that Jordan was involved, yet you did not do anything to prevent it or warn me. You didn't even return my calls."

He stares at me and swallows. "I told him that I didn't think you were a threat to anything, but that I needed time to do some research. I assured him that I could keep him out of prison if he did things my way but that he was being reckless and was going to make things worse for himself. He agreed to back off while I learned what I could about you. I thought you were safe."

"You thought I was *safe*!" I repeat. "You knew he'd tried to kill me *twice*, and you did nothing to protect me. What gives you the right to play with my life like that?" I put a hand to my chest.

"You're right," he says, putting his hands out in a way that feels patronizing. "It doesn't make sense now, but it seemed like the best option at the time. He said he was on a big job in Gallup for the next week, and I told him to focus on that and I would find a way to resolve things with you. I wanted to figure out what you knew and why you were such a threat to him, so I started researching everything I could find about you. And then you showed up at my office this morning before I was ready."

Truth. And gross. He played a game with my life as the ante. When he'd told me in the elevator that he was remaining involved because he wanted to understand what was happening, he *was* telling me the truth. Curiosity, and maybe protecting Jordan from prison, was his motivation. Disgusting.

"You told him I was at your office this morning?" I ask,

imagining him sending a text from under his desk while we were talking.

"No," he says. "I truly believed he was in Gallup until that shot was fired. At that point, I realized he had to be the shooter. I texted him from the hospital and told him to get out of Sedona before the cops found him, that he was being an absolute idiot. He said he would go back to Flagstaff and lie low."

Truth.

"So, even after knowing that he was still trying to kill me, you told him to get out of town for his own protection."

"And yours," Mr. Hernández defends. "If he was gone, you would be safe."

"Unless he, I don't know, *lied* to you about where he was going and stayed here in town looking for another opportunity."

Mr. Hernández pauses. "Right." He shakes his head. "Fiona must have told him you were coming to my office today. She's the only person who knew you were coming, right?"

I nod, but it's a little convenient that the only person who can confirm that is already dead. Mr. Hernández could still be leaving things out.

"I followed you outside this morning because you'd just dropped that cryptic information about the CIA and living in Russia. My research hadn't uncovered anything about those things—only that you were top of your game before the accident and very different afterward. That the accident had happened in Tucson was a connection to Jordan I wanted to figure out. I wanted us to keep talking so I could learn as much as possible. I saw the glint off his scope just like you did and acted on instinct."

"Well, I suppose I should be grateful that you didn't have more time to think it through."

He looks away from me and rolls his good shoulder, grunting with the effort and holding his breath for a few seconds. He's really hurting.

"I know what I did was awful. I *know*, LuLu. I'm sorry. I just . . . It didn't seem real." He meets my eyes again and pleading enters his tone. "Poisoning a Diet Peach Snapple? Trying to blow up a house with a candle? Those aren't exactly mainstream assassination techniques, and while I'm not here to defend Jordan—whose obsession obviously runs deeper and darker than I'd have ever guessed before this week—he'd been good to me. He'd been good to Fiona. I thought you were safe while I tried to figure out what Jordan was afraid of and find a different way to relieve his fear about it. After the shooting, I realized this was much bigger than I thought, and I've been trying to figure out how to fix it ever since."

I'm watching him so closely. He is barely blinking. He is not pacing back and forth, which is what my body wants to do. He isn't lying to me. Or, at least, he believes what he says.

"You told him we were at the hotel," I say.

Mr. Hernández shakes his head, then winces. "I didn't. I swear. He told me that he'd gone to Flagstaff after the shooting, and I believed him. He was . . . he *is* out of his head, LuLu."

Truth.

"And you still didn't tell the police. Or me."

"No, I didn't. I thought . . . I thought I had things under control."

"You told him Fiona was dead."

"Yes, I needed him to think I was on his side."

I narrow my eyes. "You *were* on his side. And you didn't call the police for a wellness check on Fiona, did you?"

He shakes his head. I am opening my mouth to remind him—again—to say the words when he seems to remember on his own. "I pretended to call the police. As soon as I was alone, I called Jordan."

My throat thickens to know these details. "Fiona is still lying there on the floor?"

Mr. Hernández swallows and nods. I don't demand he uses words this time. I let my eyes fall closed. I send white light toward her home and then toward heaven.

I am so sorry, Fiona, I say to her in my mind. *You deserved better than this.*

After taking several seconds to compose myself, I speak again. "How did Jordan react to learning of Fiona's death?"

"Weird," Mr. Hernández said. "But, I mean, the whole day has been weird. He didn't say he already knew, but he didn't seem surprised, and then he said he'd call me back later and ended the call. The call you overhead was that promised callback. And, remember, I thought he was in Flagstaff."

Truth.

"He was making that call from, what, his truck in the parking lot?" I remember watching that little red car pull out of the parking space. There were dozens of trucks in the lot. Was one of them Jordan's? Had he been watching me through the window? It gives me the creeps to think about it.

"If you were listening to my side of that phone call, you know that I was losing patience. He must have been waiting for us to leave or something, and then when he heard me realize you'd been in the room and had then run out, he came inside. I swear I did not know he was at the hotel until I saw him, and I did not tell him that you and I had returned there, though he knew that the police had gotten you a room and, of course, knew that's where I've been living."

Truth.

"You've been lying to me since we first met," I say as much

to him as to myself. "You have deceived me from that first meeting." My voice sounds sad. I *feel* sad. And very alone. I cross my arms over my chest.

"I'm sorry," Mr. Hernández says. "I made a name for myself based on my ability to spot a lie and turn it into a confession. What you do, though, is different than that. It wasn't until you told me in the hospital that I fully believed it, but I was careful with what I said before then. Just in case what Jordan told me was true."

After the accident, I didn't want conflict, contention, or competition—the hallmarks of Catherine's life that I had found appalling after facing my own mortality. The accident changed me physically, with damaged areas in my brain that changed my personality, but also spiritually. Emotionally. I have crafted an easy and simple life because I want—more than anything—to have peace.

And I have it. Or, rather, I had it. Or maybe a truer truth is that I *thought* I had it.

Now, I am caught up in something that doesn't make sense, and I feel I've done nothing to deserve it. It makes me want to run until I can't run another step. Erase this life and start all over again.

I refocus on Mr. Hernández standing ten feet in front of me. The sky is deepening in anticipation of a sunset that's still a few hours away. The temperature has eased enough to notice, and a breeze swishes the skirt of my sundress.

"Who else knows about your ability to detect a lie?" Mr. Hernández asks. "Who have you told? Did Dane know?"

"It's not something I go around telling people; people think I'm weird enough as it is," I say, shaking my head, feeling exhaustion creep in. A cicada starts chirping to my left, and I close my eyes to focus on that single sound for a moment. "I can't think of anyone I've told here in Sedona other than you. If people know, it's sort of a worthless ability—as you have just proved. Because you knew, you worded things in such a way that I wouldn't realize you were lying."

"Because I wasn't lying," he says.

"Oh, yes, you were," I retort, opening my eyes so that I can glare at him. "Just because you didn't say lying words does not mean you were being truthful."

He slumps slightly but acknowledges that I'm right with a slight nod.

"You are not a good man."

He looks up at me and meets my eye. I'm expecting him to be angered by this, to defend himself.

"No," he says softly. Sadly. "I am not."

Truth.

I turn away from the sadness of those words and the sharp disappointment I feel but can't quite articulate. No one is rooting for me. No one is on my side. Except God. And my inner wisdom, which is a part of Him. And myself. I stare out over the red rock cliffs, bright with the summer sun so that the white striations in the stone are more obvious. I hate the feelings I'm feeling. I hate everything that's happened. I focus on a hawk slowly spiraling upward in the currents of the evening breeze, and I feel a swell of envy to be that free. To be that far above the splintered lives of the earth-bound humans that can't seem to help but mess things up for each other.

"I have no memory of Jordan before meeting him last year after he hired me to help Fiona," I say out loud, shaking my head. "Which means he must be part of the gap." The weeks of time I don't remember. The weeks of time I haven't *wanted* to remember.

"I did get a little more information today," Mr. Hernández

says. "I know that he met you before the accident. I don't know why or when exactly, but he says you blackmailed him." He shrugs and grimaces. He's confused too. "He says you were going to ruin him back then, but then you had the accident and seemed to have forgotten everything, and Dane told him not to worry about it."

"Dane's involved," I say. Even though I already know he must be, it still hollows out my chest to *know* it.

"Jordan and Dane grew up together; you figured that out today. Whatever threat you were to Jordan was a threat for Dane too. Jordan has been telling me all day that he'll explain what happened back then, but every time he's had the chance, he doesn't. And, like I said, he and Dane are in it together—though I don't think he knew Dane was coming into town. He was really flustered by that on the phone." He lets out a heavy breath. "I know Dane had told Jordan in the past that you're not a threat, but then Jordan said something about getting notified that you were in Sedona. He somehow got Fiona to help keep an eye on you. I'm assuming because he helped her financially."

"Notified?" I picture Mr. McFeely from *Mr. Rogers' Neighborhood* knocking on the door with information.

"I think it might be the articles that were published about the embezzlement charges," he fills in. "I found them when I did the research after our first meeting. They use your legal name—Catherine Dupree—and the timing lines up, assuming Jordan looked to hire you in the weeks after those articles were published. He could have easily set up a Google alert on your name and been notified when you showed up in the papers."

Could Jordan have not known I was back in Arizona before that? I imagine him being afraid of this threat I pose to him—whatever it is—and Dane talking him down, which I suppose I should be grateful for but can't quite muster the grace. I imagine Jordan going about his life, trying to trust Dane but setting an alert for my name to keep track of me, just in case. But nothing would show up because I wasn't . . . out there. Until I was charged with embezzlement and my name showed up in a newspaper stating I was a resident of Sedona. Jordan then goes to all the trouble of convincing his clinically depressed aunt to spy on me and hires me as her caretaker. It's ridiculous. What if Fiona lived in a different city? Would he have found someone else? How? More importantly, why?

It feels both impossible that it could have happened this way and also weirdly probable, and Mr. Hernández is right that the timeline matches. If he'd flagged my name, Jordan would have seen the alert in May of last year and convinced Fiona to help him by moving her to a more accessible home in time for her to get the knee surgery as reason to justify her needing me to take care of her.

What I wouldn't give to be able to ask her what she knew and when she knew it. Regret and grief meld together in my chest, and I imagine her still lying on her floor, hours after we discovered her there.

"And then, what?" I say out loud, not wanting to lose this conversation though I feel physically sick about Fiona. "He gets bored of the game and decides to just kill me?"

"I don't know why things changed, just that he was convinced you were going to destroy him now," Mr. Hernández says. "Maybe it was just the paranoia spiking? Maybe it has to do with his divorce being final a couple of months ago? But something changed. For some reason, he seems to have decided you had to be taken out of the picture."

I look back at the mountains. *Something changed.* I think

back to that day at the end of April when I arrived for my regular appointment with Fiona. Jordan's truck with the logo on the doors was parked in her driveway. I always park in front of her house because some people of her generation find it poor manners when people park in their driveway. I remember wondering if she was going to get after Jordan about that.

Jordan was on his knees on the east side of the sidewalk leading to her house, fixing a sprinkler head.

"Good morning," I had said, startling him.

I'd been wearing my yellow T-shirt dress and multicolored sandals. I had Kermit across my chest, as I do right now, and held a Diet Peach Snapple I planned to put in the fridge until it was time to leave. He'd turned to look at me and returned my greeting.

"I'm so glad that's getting fixed," I said, nodding to the slightly muddy patch of grass he was digging in. "It's been watering the sidewalk pretty well but missing the plants." I indicate the drying shrubbery to the left of the sidewalk. Even the hardy plants used in xeriscaping need some water.

"Yeah, I'm getting that figured out," he said, sort of laughing but sort of nervously. It didn't mean anything to me at the time. He sat back on his heels, still kneeling. "H-how are, um, things going?"

"Good," I said. "She hasn't fired me in six months."

He smiled, but it still looked nervous. I took it as a sign that he was better with his hands than he was with people. Sometimes I feel like I'm that way, too, but that day had been a good brain day. I'd felt up to the exchange.

I updated him on how the appointments were going. I cleaned her floors and bathrooms each week, and sometimes I would take her to the grocery store because she was becoming more and more anxious about driving. I told him she was doing well physically, though her knee still bothered her. I encouraged her to walk in the mornings before it got too hot, but I didn't think she ever did it. She was still complaining about being unable to sleep and had an appointment with an endocrinologist in two weeks. That had been my idea because I felt there was more that could be done about her diabetes than she was currently doing. It had surprised me when she'd agreed because she usually shot down those types of suggestions.

Jordan had listened and said very little, which had made me feel like I was prattling on too much. But I would rather say too much than too little.

"So, there's the update," I finished.

"Okay, thanks," Jordan said. He was standing now and wiped his muddy hands on the front of his jeans. He'd been wearing the same hat he'd had on in the stairwell today but turned backward since the front of Fiona's house had been in the shade that time of day. He looked past me.

"Did you get a new car?"

"LuLu," Mr. Hernández says, interrupting my memory. "I am so sorry about all of this, LuLu. If I could make it right, I would."

Truth. Too late.

"Not everything can be fixed," I say. It's a deep truth I have learned through heartache. I couldn't be well enough to live in Seattle after the accident. I couldn't recover the career I'd worked so hard for. I lost my daughter.

"Please let me help," he says.

"With what?" I ask.

Back in the memory of the day I chatted with Jordan at Fiona's, I turned to smile at George; I'd only had him a few weeks. "I am head over heels for him. I call him George Flemming III. It suits him, don't you think?"

I remember the look on Jordan's face. He had not been amused by the name, as some people had been. Not confused either. Surprised? Fiona had come to the door right then and informed me that I was two minutes late. I had given Jordan a final smile and headed inside. He'd come in to wash his hands and say goodbye to Fiona while I'd started on the primary bathroom. He hadn't specifically said goodbye to me, but I hadn't expected he would. He seemed like he was in a hurry.

I turn my attention away from the memory and face Mr. Hernández. "I will help with anything I can," he says. "I want to make this right. Let's go get that notebook, then meet with Dane together."

I consider this but not for long. "We can't work together after all this, Mr. Hernández, I can't trust you."

He pinches his lips together slightly. "In my own way, I *was* trying to help."

He believes this is true, that since his intention had been for some greater good it justifies all he's done. But it's not *my* good he's been focused on. Not *my* safety.

"You were looking out for yourself, Mr. Hernández. Jordan is looking out for himself, for reasons I still don't know. I guess I'm the only one who can look out for myself."

I don't know what I'm doing.

I should go to the police now.

I made so many mistakes today trying to do this without them. Yet, I learned important things too—things I wouldn't have learned if I hadn't stepped *way* beyond my comfort zone. I don't know how to balance all of that. Is everything turning out perfectly, or have I made an impossible mess?

I adjust Kermit on my shoulder and pull myself up straight as I turn back toward my car.

Mr. Hernández clears his throat. "Wait," he says, a hint of

desperation in his voice. "You were in contact with Dane for a while after the accident, right? Did you tell him, or someone who might have passed it on, that you can do this now? Maybe that's how Jordan knew. Maybe Dane told him."

"Now?" I ask, turning to look at him.

"Yeah, the lie detecting. It's something from the accident, right? I can help you figure it out."

"It's not part of the accident," I say, shaking my head, surprised at this assumption that the accident gave me some sort of special ability, like Matt Damon in the movie *Hereafter* when he woke up from his near-death experience as a medium. "I've always been able to spot a liar, Mr. Hernández. It's how Catherine became such a good one herself."

CHAPTER 19

We look at one another, and I see his expression change from surprise to confusion and then realization. "You've always been able to spot a lie?" he asks.

I nod, unsure why this is news to him. "I didn't always know what it was, but by the time I got to college, I had it figured out. It's not as cool as it seems, as you've proven." I wave toward him. "But it helped me get good at what I did, and, like I said, it made me—well, it made Catherine a very good liar."

"That means someone from your old life—your . . . Catherine life—could have known about the lie detecting," Mr. Hernández says.

"I didn't tell anyone then either."

"That you can remember," he says, watching me closely. "But you lost several weeks of your life before and after the accident, and Jordan knew it somehow."

"But Catherine didn't tell anyone," I explain. "She was all-for-Catherine all the time. To tell anyone would interfere with her ability to use it." But if the potential gain of something bigger than the ability to spot a lie put her in a position where she had to choose, wouldn't she have told?

"If she did tell Dane and Dane told Jordan," he says, "then it would explain how Jordan knew."

"Why would he tell Jordan?" I ask, frustrated by how confusing all this is. "Why would Catherine tell Dane?"

"You're sure you don't remember anything about the days before the accident? The trip to Tucson?"

"I don't remember it," I say, but that isn't entirely true. I remember turning up the air conditioner in an unfamiliar car. I remember two sets of documents, each held together by a black binder clip. They are in a . . . purse or leather bag—a bag like Lisa. Two sets? Have I remembered that before? Can I trust what I remember, and does it matter? I remember a road sign telling me that the Picacho Peak exit is coming up. Could I remember more if I tried?

The idea fills me with anxiety. I have to close my eyes and picture white light raining from the sky in order to keep breathing. After so many hours of keeping myself together, this rush of fear nearly knocks me off my feet, and with my eyes still closed, I start to tap the side of my right eye with my left hand. I don't *want* to remember the accident. I have made a concerted effort to live in the present. I start to tap below my eye. Except that my past has put my present and future at risk. Except that Jordan, for reasons I don't understand, wants me dead.

I wriggle my toes into the dirt, grateful I lost my flip-flops. I take a four-count breath and tap my chin. My eyes are still closed.

"So," Mr. Hernández says after a few seconds. "If the article made Jordan aware that you were in Arizona, then something else made him decide he needed to silence you." He seems determined to *help*.

Because the white light is transforming my anxiety into calm, I decide to let him. I open my eyes as I begin tapping my collarbone. He acts as though he doesn't notice the tapping. I do not care in the least what he thinks. I am managing myself, and based on the results of today, I've been doing a bang-bang job of it.

He continues. "We can be fairly sure he was getting reports from Fiona after each of your visits. What could she have told him that would have set him off?"

We have already been on this topic once, and I don't have anything new to add. Thinking of Fiona reminds me of the notebook, however, and I feel again how important it is for me to get it—the solution is in that room! And Fiona is still lying on the floor. I start tapping the top of my head.

"I was trying to get as much information as I could from Jordan in hopes of finding a compromise," Mr. Hernández says when I don't respond. "That's what I do—mediate conflicts."

Truth.

"With a man who had tried to kill me three times," I point out. I start tapping the side of my eye again.

He works his jaw, and I can see the defensiveness in his expression that he's trying to find the right words to explain.

"Did Jordan take the letter?" I ask. A different type of anxiety is pushing in—the "running out of time" type.

Mr. Hernández looks confused by my turn of topic, then his expression clears. "I didn't ask him."

Truth.

"Did you take the letter?"

"No."

Truth. He seems offended that I asked, which is almost funny.

"Has he been to Fiona's house since her death?"

"I didn't ask him that either. Like I told you, I didn't know he was still in Sedona until the stairwell."

Truth. I stop tapping and drop my hands to my side, feeling more awkward now that I've stopped.

"You knew when we found Fiona that there might be a connection to Jordan."

"Yes," he says.

Truth.

"Did you take Fiona's phone?" I ask.

"Yes, I took her phone when I searched . . . her. I don't know the code and can't get into it. It's at the hotel. Um, mine is too. I lost it in the stairs."

Truth.

Mr. Hernández and I look at each other across the trail.

"I won't trust you anymore, Mr. Hernández." I cannot *let* myself trust this man. I can't take that risk again. "We aren't a team anymore, never really were, I guess."

His jaw clenches. "You also can't do this alone, LuLu. You forget details. You are . . . malleable."

"So are you, apparently. Jordan has been managing you pretty well."

We continue to stare until I realize there's nothing left to say. I turn and start walking toward the parking lot. He reaches his good arm toward me as I pass him on the trail, but I slap it away, hard, which causes him to lose his balance and stumble backward, his whole face cringing as he grabs for his slinged arm again.

"You're going to leave me here?" he calls out once I'm a dozen feet ahead of him.

"Yep," I say over my shoulder as I turn the corner of red rock that separates the wilderness from the parking lot.

I pick up my pace until I'm full-on running for George, afraid with every step that Mr. Hernández is right behind me. When I pull open the driver's door and dare to look back, however, he's not there. I should have suggested he stay there and inhale some sage while pondering the decisions he'd made. But I don't think he'd have taken my advice.

Maybe he'll find a way to contact the police.

Maybe he'll find a way to contact Jordan and tell him everything we just discussed.

Maybe he knows more than he's told me.

It doesn't matter. His path is his choice now, free and clear of any connection to me, and my path is mine.

CHAPTER 20

I slide into George's bucket seat and drive about a block before I pull over in the shade of some pine trees. I tighten my grip on George's steering wheel and take a breath.

"George," I say with the gravitas of a conversation I do not want to have but cannot avoid any longer. "Are you the reason Jordan wants me dead?"

He doesn't answer me, of course, but something resonates in my chest. In reviewing my last encounter with Jordan at Fiona's that day—an exchange I have never thought about in detail since it happened—I keep going back to the expression on Jordan's face after I told him about George. Surprise. Fear?

The idea that Catherine was blackmailing Jordan before the accident is confusing but not surprising. Catherine was all about scheming. Like with any drug, an addict needs more over time to get the same high. Catherine's morality left plenty of room for her to add a new hijinks to her repertoire. As I accept this possibility, I close my eyes and pull the image of two stacks of paper with black binder clips to my mind. My breathing becomes shallow, and I zoom out for nearly a minute until I can control my breathing again. I can do this. The truth is already there. All these things already happened and not knowing has not protected me from the consequences.

I zoom back in and focus on the details of this image: One binder clip is bigger than the other, but the stacks of paper are the same thickness. They are in a big purse, or maybe a laptop bag. A zipper keeps them in the bag, but I'm taking them out. Catherine is taking them out. She lays them on a table.

What sort of table?

Not a dining room. Not a conference table. It's brown, fake wood. Formica? It's loud. There are a lot of people around. I smell . . . fried food. A . . . diner?

Why would she be laying out papers in a diner? I see her nails, painted a pale pink. The front pages of the document sets look the same, and I recognize them as legal documents. I zoom in further and read the name at the top of the first page out loud.

"George Flemming III." I feel a shiver go through me.

I open my eyes, pull my phone out of Kermit, and type in "George Flemming III Tucson Arizona." A moment later, I have an obituary for Mr. George Flemming III, an eighty-seven-year-old man who died at his home in Tucson six and a half years ago. I hadn't seen the name in a vision. It was a memory connected to those papers.

There's no mention of Jordan in the short obituary, which seems generic. Maybe it's something the funeral home drafted up. It looks as though Mr. Flemming had no children, no wife, no living siblings. According to the timeline Mr. Hernández shared with me, Jordan had started his company a few months after Mr. Flemming's death. Could he have left Jordan some money? What would that have to do with Catherine?

A paranoid Jordan might have thought I was taunting him

with the name, or that I knew—or remembered—more than he thought I did. Or maybe he just couldn't stand the stress of waiting for me to do whatever it was he was spying on me for.

What about my accident? I feel my thoughts pulling away, not wanting to look at this. But if Catherine and Jordan had a connection of some kind five years ago then was my accident really an accident? I almost want to laugh because it feels impossible. But crazy things have happened. Maybe they have been happening for longer than I could have guessed before today. Jordan told Mr. Hernández that I could send him to prison. Could that be because he had something to do with the accident?

I take a breath to keep me present and think about Fiona giving me that Snapple a month ago. I can't remember anything strange about that, aside from the fact that she'd never given me one before. She didn't have a weird expression; there wasn't a different tone in her voice. If she'd thought to chill it, I would have drunk it, and everything would be different.

But I didn't open it for a few weeks. And I did not die when I opened it last week.

What has happened has already happened.

It is what it is.

I open my eyes. "This is not your fault," I say to George as I shift into drive. "It's not mine either. I hope."

It's after six o'clock when I park a few houses down the street from Fiona's place. I've never thought much about her doorbell, which has a video feed to track who stops by, until today. Fiona has never mentioned the video feed coming to her phone. That's pretty advanced technology for any of my ladies. Does the video feed go to Jordan? In case it does, I need to be careful.

I let myself through the gate into the small backyard that's just pale dirt and up the back steps. The back door is locked, but there's a spare key hidden under the third paver to the east of the hose bib. I'd helped Fiona hide it there after another client had locked themselves out of their house and had to wait two hours for their daughter to bring the spare from Prescott.

I'm momentarily startled by the TV that was never turned off. It's playing *The Simpsons*, which seems so out of place. Fiona would hate *The Simpsons*. Seeing Fiona's body still on the floor, grayer and emptier, makes me catch my breath. I close my eyes to draw as much white light into the room as I possibly can. She's been lying here for hours. Hours when I'd taken some comfort in believing she was being taken care of. It isn't right.

It takes all the self-discipline I have not to cover her with an afghan.

Instead, I remain mindful of my mission and walk past her into the bedroom. The notebook is beside the bed, exactly where I'd left it. I tuck it under my arm, then grab a pencil from her kitchen drawer before exiting the house. I don't want to be there any longer than I have to. It's still hot as blazes, but her back porch faces east and is somewhat shaded this time of day.

I sit on her back stairs and open the notebook to the first blank page, turning it so I can see the indentations of whatever had been written on the page before it. The marks are faint, but they're there. I break the pencil, then smash one half against the deck to break the wood casing. I remove the shards of wood to get a two-inch section of graphite.

With light pressure, I rub the long side of the pencil lead over the indentations and watch as white words appear on the graying paper. I am careful to rub to each corner, filling the page to make sure I don't miss anything. When it's done, I set the lead aside, ignore the sweat rolling down my back and the sides of my face, and read Fiona's last note to me.

Dear LuLu,

If you do not already know, Jordan is behind the attempts on your life. He was willing to help me out if I would keep him informed. Looking back, I can't believe I agreed to do such a thing. The woman I used to be would never have done it.

He tried to shoot you this morning, though I did not know until it was over, and I cannot live with my part in this any longer. I do not know why he hates you so much. He's obsessed, and it scares me. I hope that you and God will forgive me for all I have done. I have nothing left to hope for but mercy.

God willing, I will be with Johnny again and finally heal the way you always hoped that I would. You're a good person, LuLu, and I am sorry for all I have done though I know that is not enough. I wish you a happy life.

Your friend,
Fiona A. Hernández

I run my fingers lightly over the words, the graphite blackening my fingertips, and send a prayer that she receives mercy. I think the God I believe in would accept the suffering she endured here as penance. I hope with all my heart that when she crossed to the other side, all she found was love. Johnny's open arms. Jesus's promise to take on her sins so that she doesn't have to suffer for them anymore.

I place the notebook on the deck, and a breeze ruffles the pages. I hold them down long enough to take a picture of the inverted grayscale letter with my phone, then let myself out of the gate. I dial 911 on my way back to my car.

I give my full name to the dispatcher and explain that Fiona Hernández is dead on the floor of her family room. I give her address and explain that the police should contact her nephews, Jordan Pender and Jaime Hernández, for additional details. Mr. Hernández, I remember to say, was at the Posse Grounds about fifteen minutes ago with a sling on his right arm that will identify him. I'm talking fast, but I know this call is being recorded. They'll be able to play it back as many times as they need to.

"I think it was suicide. There's a bottle of Diet Peach Snapple that I think had paraquat in it provided by Jordan Pender. I think she drank it on purpose."

"The police are en route," the dispatcher says in a remarkably calm voice, but I guess she literally takes this sort of call every day. How strange it would be for this to be normal. "Please stay where you are and remain on the line with me."

"I'm sorry," I say as I unlock George with my key fob when I'm still a house away from him. "I can't do either of those things. But tell Sergeant Rawlins that I will come to the police station as soon as I finish what I need to do. Also, there's a notebook on the back porch that has Mrs. Hernández's confession to her part in the attempts on my life and what I think is her suicide note. Thank you."

The dispatcher is in the middle of telling me that I *must* stay on the line when I end the call.

I arrive at Thai Spices at 6:48.

CHAPTER 21

I'm too anxious to wait in the car until seven o'clock, so I go inside and ask for a table.

The hostess, a young woman with a nose ring, glances at my feet, and I look down, almost surprised to remember that I'm barefoot. I look around for a "No shirt, no shoes, no service" sign but I don't see one.

"I'm meeting a man shortly, and I'm a very good tipper."

She smiles, instantly on board, and gives me a sly, knowing look as she gathers a couple of menus and leads me to the table.

"It's not a date," I feel compelled to explain when we arrive at the booth. "He's married."

Her smile fades.

"But it's not a date," I repeat as I sit. "I mean, we did date, but I was a different person then."

She's definitely looking at me strangely now.

"His wife knows," I add as she hands me a menu and sets the other one on the opposite side of the table.

"Would you like to order a drink now or wait for your server?" the girl says.

"Do you have Diet Peach Snapple?"

"Um, no."

"Oh, uh, okay. Water with lemon, then. And an order of fresh roll wraps." It is Thai Spices's version of fresh spring rolls, and they are delicious.

"I'll let your server know. Would you like to wait for your . . . uh, friend before we bring it?"

"No, you can bring it as soon as it's ready. And he's just an acquaintance these days."

She nods, gives me another awkward look, and leaves. I slump slightly in my seat as I push the menu away. I'm nervous about seeing Dane again, but also . . . excited? Is that the right word? It doesn't feel like the right word or the right feeling to be having. It's just been a long day with a lot of little details I might get answers to now. Maybe what I'm feeling is *ready* for those answers. Is ready a feeling?

Anticipation?

Relief?

"Hi."

I startle and look up, then scramble out of my seat so that I'm standing face to face with Dane Bohannan. As soon as I'm on my feet, I wonder why I stood. I'm not going to hug him; this isn't that kind of reunion. I put out my hand, and after a moment's hesitation, he takes it and gives it a firm shake. As soon as we release our handshake, I sit back down, aware that the hostess is watching us and relieved that our awkward greeting has likely convinced her that I'm not dating this married man.

Dane has put on weight since the last time I saw him, which was almost four years ago when he stopped by my

Seattle condo for a visit—the first and only time we've seen each other since the accident. I'd been in Seattle a few months by then and was still trying to be Catherine even though every day compounded the evidence that it wasn't working.

At the time of his visit, I had been struggling to remember where to find things in the condo and had started keeping all the cabinets open and leaving things out once I found them. My occupational therapist had called it object permanence, which was sort of an "out of sight, out of mind" sort of thing. If I couldn't see the Tylenol, I would forget I owned it and buy another bottle, or I would panic that I didn't have it on hand and call Mom, who would remind me where I kept it.

I had also spread out my clothes on the backs of furniture. Hence, my favorite Seattle Redhawks sweatshirt was draped over the mid-century armchair, every pair of shoes I owned were lined up along the left side of my living room, and all my pictures of Sophie were on display—taped to the wall if they weren't already framed. This quirk got better with time and as I got rid of things I didn't need, like all those Louboutin shoes and designer purses.

But Dane's visit happened before that particular issue had become manageable. He had stood in the cluttered living room of my high-end condo and looked around as though he was afraid to touch anything. I moved some clothing so he could sit on one end of the couch while I sat on the other. He gave me a bottle of what had been Catherine's favorite wine, though I couldn't drink it because alcohol interfered with my medications. No feelings of romance had been sparked by the visit, only the reminder that, once again, I wasn't Catherine and, once again, someone thought I should be. He stayed for maybe ten minutes, and I think I was as relieved for him to go as he was to get away.

The extra twenty pounds he's gained since then looks good on him, rounding out the features of his face and making him look more like a man and less like a college frat boy, which had very much been his persona back then. Very gym rat, "I drink green smoothies every day" vibes.

"You look great, uh, LuLu."

It seems he still struggles to see me as a different person than Catherine had been.

"Thank you," I say, then jump right in. "How did Jordan get so much money to start his company, and what does it have to do with George Flemming III?"

Dane's eyebrows go up, and he opens his mouth, only to close it as the waitress approaches the table with my wraps and water. She introduces herself as Maggie and although she is bubbly and friendly, I have a strong suspicion that she hates her job, which is a shame because this restaurant has the best spring rolls in town—she ought to be proud of that.

Dane orders chicken Pad Thai without opening the menu. And a Dr Pepper. The waitress takes the menus and, just like that, we're alone again, if you didn't count the other six tables with Friday night diners.

"You know about George," Dane says.

"No," I say. "I don't know anything. But you're here to tell me, right? You're here to tell me what Catherine did that has made Jordan Pender decide that the world would be a better place without me in it."

"Without you in it?" Dane repeats, his eyebrows lifting. "Has something . . . happened?"

I realize that I don't know what he knows, and he doesn't know what I know. "Someone has tried to kill me three times." Four if I count the stairwell. "I think it's Jordan. Is it?"

"Oh man," Dane says, putting a hand over his mouth. He

stares at me a few seconds, then straightens and lowers his hand. "He's tried to kill you?"

"Three times," I repeat. "I want to know why."

"Um, yeah," he says. "I guess you would. Um, man, I don't know where to start."

"The beginning would be best," I suggest. "And give me direct information. I don't have any more time to waste."

"Right," he says with a nod. The waitress returns with his drink, and he takes a long sip as though to fortify himself. He returns the glass to the table with a thunk that stutters my thoughts for just a moment. "Okay, well, then I'll just get right into it." He pauses for another breath, and I am here. Clear. Attentive. "George Flemming III was a client of mine, right out of law school. I was working here in Arizona for a small firm when I drew up his trust, but, um, he was a referral from, well, Jordan."

Truth. I continue to stare at him.

"Okay," I say. "What else?"

"Well, I drew up two trusts. The one he agreed to and signed, and a second one that changed his bequests."

"What does that have to do with me?" I ask.

"You found out," Dane says, meeting my eye.

"And I wanted you guys to come clean," I say hopefully.

He shakes his head slowly. "You wanted your share."

CHAPTER 22

Catherine

The drive from Phoenix to Tucson is perhaps the ugliest drive I've ever made in my life. Mile after mile of neutral colors that don't really seem like colors at all after a while, just blah. I listen to an economic update podcast and check Dane's location every fifteen minutes or so. I've had location tracking on his phone for a few weeks that he hasn't noticed yet. Sort of like he didn't notice me going through his computer to find out what it was he was hiding.

Once I had the details, I convinced him to bring me along—a business-meets-pleasure weekend away from the Seattle winter. He hadn't immediately liked the idea, but I have my ways. We flew in last night, and he headed to Tucson this morning to finalize the trust account he's been overseeing for nearly two years—*truth*—and meet up with his parents for dinner—*lie*—before he spent the night at their house—*truth*.

I told him I would be filling every minute he was gone

with my own remote work and couldn't wait to see him for lunch on Saturday afternoon. Instead, I only worked half the day, by which time the rental car I'd ordered had been delivered to the hotel. I printed out the copies of both trusts I'd found on his computer weeks ago, and here I am—about to ruin his day.

He *did* spend some time at the courthouse and a nearby bank, but halfway through my drive, he's on the move again before he parks at a sports bar called The Dugout. It's nearly seven o'clock, and since it's March, the sky is darkening.

I arrive almost forty-five minutes after he does and park a few spaces away from the rental car Dane and I picked up at the airport yesterday. I adjust my Yves Saint Laurent purse over my shoulder and keep my chin up. I'm not dressed up—joggers and an Athletica T-shirt—but the purse tells the world who I am, not that this is the sort of place where anyone will notice.

I stand in the doorway for a few seconds to let my eyes adjust to the darkened interior. It smells like wings and beer, exactly as I expected it would. I spot two men at a booth near the pool tables. One is wearing a baseball cap, the other—Dane—is wearing a suit. They are laughing over empty plates with the gleefulness of petty thieves. But there is nothing petty about what they've done. They've committed a felony.

I pull my shoulders back as I stride across the room.

When I stop at the end of their table, they startle, then freeze, and then Dane jumps from his seat.

"Thanks," I say as though he's being a gentleman. I slide onto the bench he's just vacated and set my purse beside me. I extend my hand across the table to Jordan, who is staring at me with wide eyes. "Catherine Dupree," I say when he finally takes my hand in a limp shake. "Jordan Pender, right?"

He looks at Dane, who is still standing and looking caught, which is exactly what's happened here, but not in the way Jordan suspects. He thinks Dane involved me by choice rather than ignorance and gross underestimation.

"I understand you've come into some money," I say as though not noticing the abject fear on both of their faces. I look up at Dane. "Sit."

He sits next to me on the edge of the bench.

I turn my attention back to Jordan. "As I said, I understand you've come into some money. Do you have a plan for it?"

"Uh . . . a plan?"

"Other than blowing your cover by spending it too fast, as you've already done."

His face turns red.

Dane clears his throat, but his voice squeaks when he speaks. "Um, Catherine, can I talk to you for a minute?"

"No, Dane," I say, turning to face him. "You had your chance to tell me about this yourself, and you didn't take it. You've been lying to me for weeks. This is the result of that miscalculation on your part." I look at Jordan in time to see him realize that Dane didn't set this up. "You guys are idiots and have put yourselves in a very vulnerable situation, especially you, Dane."

I turn back to him and hold him with my piercing stare. "Jordan's made nothing of his life, which gives him little to lose in a scam like this. You, however, have put your entire career and future on the line for him by filing a fraudulent trust and acting as trustee for the disbursements. And you're doing it for less than the amount of your outstanding student loans?" I shake my head and look back at Jordan.

"So, now we're going to do this my way." I settle against the back of the vinyl bench and pull out the two copies of the trust, the original, which left the bulk of Mr. Flemming's wealth to the Tucson Veterans Affairs Center, an organization that Mr. Flemming had been involved with for decades, and the fraudulent one, which distributed more than four million dollars' worth of assets to Jordan Pender, with a $400,000 payment to Dane for managing the legalities.

I've highlighted the particulars that they have likely glossed over—particulars about how to properly report the inheritance on their taxes, what portions are taxable, and the penalties for fraud.

"In exchange for my financial advice," I tell them after explaining how I'm here to help them stay out of jail, "I'll take 25 percent for keeping your secret and showing you how to grow this money instead of losing it, another 25 percent goes to Dane for putting his license on the line for this scam, and Jordan gets the other 50 percent, which I think is more than fair. I can help you with the bookkeeping to keep everything legitimate." I fix my glare on Jordan. "You're going to invest 80 percent of whatever you have left from your portion and do better living on the interest payments than you've done with your income to this point. In the process, you'll avoid a lot of taxes and, more importantly, a lot of questions. Right now, you have positioned yourself about as badly as you possibly could and a few questions from the wrong person could put you in prison. Do you understand what I'm saying?"

"Catherine," Dane says under his breath. "You . . . you've got this all wrong. We filed the original trust. The other one was just . . . a game. We didn't follow through."

"That's a lie, Dane," I say, narrowing my eyes at him. "I know you filed the fraudulent trust just like I knew you weren't meeting your parents for dinner and that you didn't graduate in the top 10 percent of your class. I know when you lie to me. It's best you know that going forward. This is what's happening, and we don't have time to waste on your lame attempts to get out of this."

I look back at Jordan, whose face has gone red. "I have an email ready to send to both the Arizona and Washington bars. It will include both versions of Mr. Flemming's trust and a tax record of the property you purchased with cash in Tucson six months ago, Mr. Pender. It might take a little while, but they *will* come after you, and you won't be able to wriggle out of it. You're both going to jail if I send that email."

We sit in complete silence for the time it takes for one pool player to sink the eight ball and four men to loudly trumpet their respective dismay and triumph.

"Or," I say, "we do it my way, the money is protected, you both stay out of jail and enjoy the windfall. Take your pick."

"Catherine—" Dane says under his breath, but he can't finish it.

Jordan cuts him off. "We'll work with you," he says. "But not for 25 percent. We've spent years working on this."

"Twenty-five percent or twenty-five years," I say, though he wouldn't really get that long. "Your choice. Keep in mind that without my intervention, you'd have been caught. I'm saving you both from yourselves for the bargain price of one million dollars."

Dane lets out a breath, and Jordan takes one. The silence between us stretches amid the noise of the bar. Finally, Jordan drops his shoulders and nods.

I suppress my victory smile as I move to extract the other documents I've brought that outline the tax codes I've referenced and the investments I'll be moving their money into.

I am so good at what I do.

CHAPTER 23

As Dane tells me this story, it feels like I'm there. Which I was, but I also wasn't. I can feel Catherine's triumph and superiority when she sets down both trusts on the diner table. I can feel the excitement she'd felt as she told these men how things would be. She'd outsmarted them. She felt . . . invincible. That was what it was always about for Catherine—seeking and gaining power. It's what fueled her.

I recall the smell of the wings and the feel of the cracked vinyl seat when I sat down across from Jordan—the first time we'd ever met.

I was there.

But I wasn't.

But I was.

When Dane finishes recounting, I stare at my half-eaten fresh roll. I can't look at him for fear I will see Catherine reflected at me. I am so embarrassed. Catherine hadn't been defensive of Mr. Flemming's last wishes; she hadn't tried to make anything right. She just wanted her cut and gloried in having figured out how to benefit from the deception Dane and Jordan had started.

"You did both trusts right out of law school," I conclude.

"Yes," Dane says, his voice humble. "I was working for a small firm in Tucson while I looked for something bigger and better. Jordan and I came up with the idea over drinks one night after he'd learned that Mr. Flemming was loaded with no one to give the money too. We thought we were pretty brilliant."

"How did you do it?"

"Just swapped out the pertinent pages. Everything else stayed the same. I held my breath when I filed it, but nothing was flagged. Four years later, when Mr. Flemming died, I performed my duties as trustee, which took almost two years to execute." He pauses, swallows, and shakes his head. "I'm not proud of this, LuLu. I am horrified too."

"But you weren't horrified when you finalized everything that weekend," I point out. "You were still pretty impressed with yourself."

"Yeah," he says with a sigh. "I was. We both were. You're actually the reason that changed for me." He glances at me then back at the table. "After you left the diner that night, Jordan was furious. Your new plan meant that he wouldn't get any additional capital. What he'd already received was all he would get, and that was long gone. That final portion he'd been counting on now that the trust was closed would go to you. He felt sure he wouldn't be able to keep his company going, or that you would demand more money down the road. I was just sick about everything. The fact that you'd figured it out fueled my fears of what I'd really put on the line. I hardly slept that night, and then when I called the next morning to see if we were still flying back to Seattle together, a nurse answered your phone, and I learned about the accident. The next few weeks were a haze for me. I was drenched in fear and regret and I started praying for the first time in years that you would be okay. And you were." He looks up and smiles again, a sort of pleading smile. "I vowed to change my life, and I did, LuLu. Because of you. Because of what it showed me about myself, and because God preserved you. I knew that if He could save you, He could save me too."

Truth.

"But you went back to the original plan you and Jordan had concocted. You took your $400,000, and Jordan took the rest."

Dane nods slowly, looking instantly penitent. "We sort of put everything on hold for a couple of months. The last of the money was in a trust account, ready to be transferred at any time. And then, you didn't remember anything about what had happened, and you were so . . . different. So, yeah, we went back to the original plan, though, admittedly, we both invested the money better and did the work to figure out the taxes in a way that better protected us."

He's giving me a compliment, but the idea that I helped them in any way does not give me any satisfaction.

It's hard to meet Dane's eyes, so I look around the restaurant as I process all of this. I feel so much judgment and disgust toward him and Catherine. I'm also grateful to know the truth.

"Did you try to run me off the road that night?" I ask.

"No," he says strongly, shaking his head.

Truth.

"Did Jordan?"

He pauses, purses his lips together, and then says, "I don't know."

Truth.

"Have you asked him?"

He pauses again and shakes his head.

"Use your words," I say, even though my own faith in my abilities feels thin. It's not enough to know if people are lying or not. There is so much more to trust than telling the truth, though that's a good start, I suppose.

"Honestly, it never occurred to me until these last few weeks, and each time I think it, I tell myself it's impossible. Jordan's got some problems, but I've never known him to be violent with anyone. We were close back then. We were each other's secret keepers, and I think he'd have told me if he'd caused your accident—I really do."

Truth. He holds my eyes as though to confirm his honesty.

"Do the police reports give any indication that another car caused the accident?" he asks. "I didn't think they did, but I never read through the reports or anything."

Truth.

"I haven't read them either," I admit. "But I probably will once this stuff is taken care of. For the first time since the accident, I want to know the truth about what happened to me."

"I can see how that would be important. I'm so sorry, LuLu. I'm sorry that all of this happened, and I'm sorry that you're still having to deal with it. It isn't fair."

Truth. Despite myself, I feel comforted by his sympathy. It's validating to have what I've been through acknowledged.

"So, I guess my accident was just a lucky break for you guys."

"I never saw it that way," Dane hurries to say.

Truth.

He continues. "I never thought Jordan was behind it, but I felt responsible for you being on the road that night. It really shook me up. As time went on, I came to hate the man I was. I wanted to be a new creature and was in the depths of my despair when God found me."

Truth. I'm happy that he found redemption and a better path; I understand that sort of journey.

"But you kept the $400,000," I remind him.

"Yes," he says, nodding. "I know. It's . . . uh, complicated."

"Not really," I say, but I leave it there because it doesn't matter. The truth is going to come out now, and the piper will have to be paid up. I have no idea how the fraud will be unwound but have confidence that it will be. Somehow.

I search my brain for anything else I want to ask Dane.

"What happened after the accident? With you and Jordan?"

"Right," Dane says, nodding. "I went to the Yakima office, and Jordan continued to build his company. Things seemed to be going well. He and his wife had another baby, and business was good. I really wanted everything we had done to be behind me, and we just sort of naturally grew apart. But every few months, he would call me for an update on how you were doing and download all this anxiety about what would happen if you remembered everything. I would call you to check in so that I could let him know that you weren't a threat. That would calm him down for a while."

Truth.

I swallow my embarrassment that what I had thought was Dane's concern about how I was doing was actually him monitoring that I was still addlebrained enough not to pose a threat. "But then you stopped talking to me."

He fiddles with his napkin. The waitress had brought his Pad Thai during his storytelling, but he hasn't touched it. I guess neither of us has an appetite anymore.

"My discontent with the state of my soul led me to Jesus," Dane says, folding his napkin into a triangle. Triangles are a symbol of change. I wonder if he knows this. "I met Tiera at church, and my heart was even further changed through her influence. She is a remarkably good woman. You had moved to Arizona, which I knew would be upsetting to Jordan, but he wasn't checking in with me as much, and so I let things be and didn't tell him. Jordan called one day after several months of no contact, wanting an update, but I told him it was time to let it go and find peace. He didn't take it well and hung up on me. It was a couple of weeks after that when you next texted me. I didn't respond, but you wouldn't give up and just kept texting and texting and texting. I'm not proud of how I handled it, but I felt it was best that all three of us just went our separate ways."

"And you haven't had contact with Jordan since then? You didn't tell him I was in Arizona?"

"I never told him," Dane says, shaking his head. "And I didn't know he knew you were here. When six months had gone by without contact from him or you, I figured that was that. We had all moved on, and things were okay."

Truth.

"So what happened a few weeks ago? You said something happened that worried you."

"Yeah, he called me late this one night. I think he'd been drinking. He was ranting about how he's lost everything, and something about George's car and his aunt Fiona spying. He was furious at me for not telling him you'd moved to Arizona—I thought he'd just found out." His words go up at the end like a question, and I realize that he doesn't know Jordan set up Fiona 007 more than a year ago. There's something empowering about knowing more than he does.

"And then he said that this had to end," Dane continued.

"That he couldn't take it anymore, and then he hung up. I honestly didn't know what he was talking about. I figured what had to end was our friendship, but I sorta thought that had already run its course. I chalked it up to a drink-induced rage, but then I learned through a mutual friend about his divorce and that he'd left Tucson. I reached out to him a few times after that in hopes of offering him some support, but he wouldn't reply. Then, a couple of days ago, I sent him Lamentations 3:58." He pauses, watching me as though he expects me to know it. I'm a God-fearing woman, but I haven't memorized the Old Testament.

"I can't say I know that one by heart," I say.

He brightens at this and makes a point to hold my gaze while he repeats it from memory, "You, Lord, took up my case; you redeemed my life."

Of all the scriptures he could have shared to give comfort, he chose that one? Well, to each his ownership, I guess. "And did he respond?"

Dane visibly deflates. "Yes, he texted to tell me that he was done talking to me, that he was going to end this." He pulls his phone out of his pocket and toggles around for a few seconds before he holds it out to me as proof.

I see Jordan's name at the top of the screen and then a few texts sent from Dane over the period of a couple of weeks asking how Jordan was doing and requesting that Jordan call. Then there's the scripture he just recited and a final message in green from Jordan:

She will ruin me. I have to end this.

A shiver runs through me as I look from Dane's phone to his face. "And you didn't tell me."

Just like Mr. Hernández.

Is my life so worthless?

"I sat with it longer than I should have, I know," Dane said, nodding as he puts his phone away. "This was the first I realized that *you* were his focus, and it was a big shift in my understanding of what was going on with him. Yesterday, I finally told Tiera about it. She immediately booked me a flight to Phoenix. I had to tell you in person to make sure you would believe me, and I couldn't wait any longer."

"And you knew I could spot a lie because I'd told you at the diner that night in Tucson."

"Yes."

Truth.

"But you also knew that I can't spot a lie on the phone?"

His cheeks flush. "Because I lied to you all the time during our conversations when you were in the facility here in Sedona and you never picked up on it. I thought maybe the accident had made it where you couldn't do it anymore—you were so different—but then that time I met you in Seattle, you offered to order a pizza, and I told you I had to go because I had an appointment. You looked at me a few seconds and then told me you knew that wasn't true. You said, 'I understand. I'm not what people expect anymore. I'm glad you stopped by.' It was sad, but it also showed you could still spot the lying in person. That's why I knew I had to meet with you in person today. I wanted you to know I was sincere."

Truth.

I sit against the back of the booth and stare at the table again. I'm not sure how to process this, so I decide not to. I can process later. Right now, I need to keep learning whatever I can.

"You never told Jordan I was in Sedona—you're sure of that."

"I never told him," Dane said. "I purposely withheld that for fear that it would upset him."

Truth.

"All I wanted was for us to move on with our lives," he continues. "I don't know how he found out you were here or what his aunt had to do with anything—there's a lot of missing pieces for me—but I needed to tell you what I knew. You deserved to have the truth. At least the truth I could give you. Better late than never, right?" He smiles and does one of his little laughs.

Truth. I can appreciate that he did finally tell me, but his self-satisfaction with having done the *right thing* rubs me wrong.

I line up my silverware on the table.

"Can I ask what's happened?" Dane says after the silence has become uncomfortable. "You said Jordan's trying to *kill* you?"

I give the summary of the last week, and Dane's eyes go wide. "Oh, my heck," he says when I finish. "I had no idea."

"Actually, you did," I said. "He told you he had to end things."

Dane's cheeks flush. "And you don't know what set him off?"

"I got a new car and named him George Flemming III."

Dane stares at me and sits back against the bench seat. "So, you *have* remembered things. That's exactly what Jordan was afraid of."

"I haven't remembered a lot," I say, and I haven't remembered anything with meaning. George's name was only a name I gave my car. But Jordan wouldn't have known that.

I feel so icky about all of this. Dane's lies. Catherine's behavior. Jordan's obsessive paranoia that I would mess up his life. Which, I guess, turned out to be true. I *am* going to mess up his life because he's not going to get away with this any longer. There are other things to ask, but I decide that I have enough for now. I know why I crossed paths with Jordan Pender all those years ago, and I know why he's crossing my path again—and why he wants me dead. I have enough pieces now to go to the police and let them take over.

"Will you come with me to the police?" I ask Dane as I put Kermit back over my head, preparing to leave.

He looks at me and shifts in his seat. "I'd like to suggest one more thing before you do that."

I pull my eyebrows together and stare at him.

"Let's give Jordan a chance to explain all of this," Dane says quickly.

I sit up straighter. "You think I should talk to the man who's been trying to kill me?"

Dane puts up both hands as though in surrender, and I remember this gesture from when we dated—it's unnecessarily dramatic. "Hear me out," he says, then returns his hands to the table. "If we can convince Jordan that you aren't a threat, I think we can find a way to move forward without police involvement."

Truth.

"No," I say immediately, shaking my head and remembering all the times today that I wanted to involve the police and didn't. For all sorts of reasons. But *this* reason—that the God-fearing Dane is suggesting—is the most confusing. He knows what he did all those years ago was wrong, and yet he still thinks he can outrun it—out "righteous" it. He isn't seeking accountability. He just wants to sweep this under the rug. Again.

Another thought comes on the tails of that one. Did Dane

wait those few days because he hoped that Jordan would succeed in silencing me? It was his wife who booked the flight once he admitted what Jordan had said. Not Dane. Does Tiera know he's still willing to risk my life to protect his fraud?

"Jordan is dangerous, and Fiona is dead," I say leaning forward. "We are out of our depth, Dane, and need to do the best-right thing. I am inviting you to come with me to the police so you can earn whatever mercy might be there by taking accountability, but I am prepared to go myself. I will not be making any deals with you or with Jordan Pender."

I can see an argument forming in his mind as he swallows and tightens his jaw. I pause two seconds, but realize I have no space for another man trying to talk me out of doing the right thing—especially a man who didn't do anything once he knew I was in danger.

I stand up from the table and though I think of things I can say and ways I can explain myself, I just turn and walk away from him the same way I walked away from Mr. Hernández at Posse Grounds. If he's not ready—after all that's happened—to do the right thing, I am not going to convince him.

"LuLu," he calls out, but I don't look back.

I stop at the hostess stand and put three $20 bills on the podium. The hostess looks at me with confusion.

"Twenty to cover my spring rolls, twenty to the very nice waitress, and twenty to you for letting me sit without shoes."

I smile and resist trying to explain anything more than I already have. I'm done explaining myself. I'm done with this day altogether. I am going to trust my inner wisdom that is telling me to let the police take things from here.

I don't look back to see if Dane stays at the table. I'm done with him too.

I walk across the parking lot to George, trying to avoid the worst of the rocks. I have that extra pair of flip-flops at the hotel, but do I want to go back there? Will the police take me less seriously if I show up without shoes?

The sun is setting over the red rock formations on the west side of the city, deepening the shadows. It's my favorite time of day, but everything inside me feels too tight to enjoy it, which is really sad. But, I remind myself, there will be another sunset tomorrow, and I will enjoy that one twice as much.

I am pulling open the car door when my arm is grabbed from behind and twisted behind my back, sending a sharp pain through my shoulders. A hand comes over my mouth to suppress the scream crawling up my throat as sheer panic engulfs me.

"I'm sorry," I hear Dane's voice say as I am shoved into George's back seat. He's not the one wrestling me into the car. Instead, Dane is sliding into the driver's seat. It's someone else with their knee in my back. I can't breathe as George's doors snap closed. It's all happened in a matter of seconds. When I twist my body enough to see what's happening, Jordan Pender's face appears above me and a gun is pointed at my head.

"I don't need a reason," Jordan says, clicking something on the gun while still managing to press his other hand against my mouth. Did he turn off the safety?

We stare at each other. The man who, despite all *he's* done, thinks I am the reason his life is so miserable.

"I'm sorry, LuLu," Dane says as he backs out of the parking stall and starts to drive. "I really didn't want it to go like this, but we have to talk things out."

For what it's worth, he's telling the truth.

CHAPTER 24

I close my eyes to stay connected to myself through the drive. My whole body is reverberating from the overwhelming amounts of fear and shock coursing through me. I'm shivering even though I never shiver in Arizona. Jordan is poised on the back seat. I'm wedged along the floorboards with a half dozen bottles of Diet Peach Snapple, an assortment of books, that dang Amazon return, and the floral comforter that's half under me and half above me on the other side of the seat. Dane is driving.

I am praying and breathing and picturing rainbows of light. I claw my thoughts for an affirmation that will help me calm down, and then I find it: *Right now, in this moment, I'm okay.*

I don't think about the moments to come. I can't think about them. But it's true that right now, I'm okay. I'm not dead. I'm not even very hurt. Just scared, and that's completely reasonable under these circumstances.

Jordan is giving directions that I can't follow. Dane is saying nothing, and I hope he's feeling the hypocrisy of who he believes himself to be and what his actions are saying about his true character.

I'm okay.

I'm okay.

I'm okay.

Right now, in this moment, I am okay.

Jordan finally removes his hand from my mouth and sits up on the back seat of my car. There must no longer be a threat if I scream. I open my eyes and stare at him while trying to take in what details I can to help me figure out where we are. We're not in the city anymore. I can tell it's a dirt road beneath George's tires, and all I can see is darkening sky through the windows.

"Here is good," Jordan says to Dane.

George comes a stop, doors open, and I am roughly pulled from the car and stood up. I stumble to get my balance, cringing when I step on a sharp rock with my bare feet. The sun has disappeared, and twilight is setting in as I take in my surroundings cast in shadows: cleared desert, something being built to one side, pallets of building materials to another. There's a truck parked a short distance away with Jordan's logo on the door. And absolutely nothing else.

I think about screaming again just in case there's someone close enough to hear it, but I am still shaking and feeling mentally numb.

This must be the land Jordan had bought for his Sedona location, the one Mr. Hernández has been helping him with. Did he decide to expand to Sedona before or after he realized I was here?

"LuLu, I'm so sorry it came to this," Dane says, his tone pleading and his hands out as though surrendering to me, the same gesture he used in the restaurant. "I really think that once you hear what we have to say, you'll see things a little different. This can still be fixed."

I stare at him and send pink light to my brain to stick my thoughts back together. After nearly ten seconds, I shake my head. "No," I say flatly. "It can't be fixed, and now you have kidnapping to add to the list of things a judge is not going to take lightly. You're as unstable as he is." I wave toward Jordan, who has yet to say anything as he stands a few yards away, his gun still trained on me.

"Just hold back your judgment for a minute," Dane says with such a patronizing tone that I would slap him silly if not for Jordan's gun. "We want to make this worth your while too."

Truth.

I realize before he says it that they are about to offer *me* money. My mind goes back to the scene I created when Dane told me the story of what happened in the sports bar. What Catherine had wanted then was money, and they think they can fix it with money now? I almost want to laugh. Do they really think they can negotiate with me after all this?

"Jordan called me on my way to Sedona tonight. I hadn't talked to him since those text messages I showed you at the restaurant, and I didn't know how far things had gone." He glares at Jordan for a moment, but then looks back at me. "We determined that between the two of us, we can put together a substantial amount we hope can make up for everything—$500,000 to be exact." The hint of smugness in his voice makes my toes curl into the dirt at my feet. "It's clean money, thanks to Catherine's advice all those years ago. I know it doesn't make up for all that's happened this week, but it's our hope that you'll take a comfortable life in exchange for all of us going our separate ways and never speaking of this again. I swear to you, LuLu, that we have learned so much from this and will never do anything like this ever again. We will be upstanding citizens for the rest of our lives." He ends with one of his trademark laughs.

I say nothing because there are so many thoughts going through my head that I have no idea where to start. I might not be able to read the address on a mailbox, but I know how to manage the assets Catherine stockpiled during her short but very successful career. Money is not a motivation for me. Being able to live with myself and my choices, however, is essential.

"What do you think, LuLu?" Dane says like a used-car salesman. "Is this something we can work with? Can we reach a meeting of minds?"

"No," I say flatly. "I'm not here to negotiate my integrity with one man who's been trying to kill me and another one who is a rotten dirty liar."

Dane's expression falls. "LuLu, Jordan is prepared to—"

"Enough," Jordan says, cutting Dane off. "I told you this wouldn't work."

Dane turns to face his friend, a hint of panic creasing his forehead. "No, we're going to work this out, Jordan, just like I suggested on the phone. LuLu gets it, don't you, LuLu?" He glances back at me with a pleading look. "You're on board with finding a way to work this out, right?"

I remain silent and look between the two men as an unexpected calm begins to settle in my chest, where every emotion *except* calm had been duking it out since the restaurant parking lot. I keep my focus right here and right now, and it isn't even that hard to do. I have a sudden memory of the original *Karate Kid* movie and how he thought he was learning to paint a fence and wax a car when he was really creating the muscle memory he needed for karate. Maybe all my mind hacks had been like that—consciously summoning pink light so that when it mattered, I could keep my thoughts together without it.

"She's not on board," Jordan says as I tune back in. "She's going to ruin me, just like I said." He straightens his arm and points the gun toward my head.

I stare him down, unblinking, unflinching, and unafraid. He stares back.

"Wait!" Dane says, waving his hands back and forth as he steps closer to Jordan. "Dude, we're not doing this. We're going to reach an agreement. She's going to see things our way."

"No, I'm not," I say, still staring at Jordan, who is starting to sweat from something that has nothing to do with the temperature and everything to do with his guilt.

"LuLu," Dane begs, turning back to me with genuine fear in his eyes.

I can see his thoughts playing out—he'd agreed to bring me out here because he truly thought that my moral character was as flexible as his. As flexible as Catherine's had been.

"Stop," Jordan says, then he waves the gun toward Dane. "Get next to her, Dane. Start walking." He waves to his left, where a dirt road leads out to the desert.

"Jordan," Dane says in shock.

"Go!" Jordan yells.

Dane puts his hands up again as he steps gallantly in front of me. "What is going on here? You and I are in this together, man."

"Shut up!" Jordan bellows, causing Dane to fall back a step as his eyes go wide with understanding of just how messed up Jordan really is. "It's over, Dane. I'm not going to put up with loose ends anymore! Get moving—we have somewhere to be."

Dane pales, and his arms start to lower. "But I—"

"Stop talking!" Jordan screams, and I swear the whole desert goes silent. "Walk!"

I turn toward the road and start walking on what seems to

be the tire tread of something big and heavy. Dane, stunned, follows me, with Jordan bringing up the rear.

It is what it is.

What's happened has happened.

Right now, in this moment, I am okay.

I move my feet and keep my breathing even as I look ahead. The outline of something starts to come into focus in the distance—a bulldozer? Is that what the things with the big bucket-shovels are called?

I focus on breathing and affirming and try not to marvel at how oddly calm I feel.

"Jordan, there is nothing you've lost that can't be restored," Dane says over his shoulder.

I keep my gaze on the ground in front of me. If I could think of something to say, I would say it, but there seems no reason to talk right now. A paranoid and desperate man is in charge, and until I feel like I have something to offer, my best option is to stay silent and take in as much of my environment and situation as I can.

We're getting farther away from George. Farther away from a chance to escape. I realize for the first time that I don't have my purse over my shoulder anymore. Did Jordan somehow get Kermit off me when he wrestled me into the car? Impressive if he did, but also highly inconvenient for me because it would be really helpful to shout, "Hey, Siri, call 911!"

The random rocks and cactus spines hiding in the tire tracks make me wince with almost every step. Sedona isn't a barren desert; it hosts a lot of trees and shrubs, some of them big enough to shade, say, a driveway, and others that add color to the red dirt. This part of the desert, however, is more sparse than even the area around my house, and I find this hopeful. I can see what's around me. I know my directions.

"Things are not so broken that they can't be repaired," Dane continues, his voice shaky.

"You can't bring my wife back to me," Jordan says from behind us. "And I . . . I've got to preserve what George gave me. It's all I've got."

"Gave you?" I say, though Jordan shows no notice of having heard me. I'm at the front of this little caravan, picking my steps as carefully as I can and feeling surprisingly calm. He hasn't killed me yet—not with poison, not with fire, not with a bullet. Based on results, I will survive whatever this is too.

Everything works out . . . I can't quite make the "perfectly for me" part stick, so I just repeat the first part. *Everything works out.* One way or another, everything always does.

"I know, man," Dane says, affecting that light tone again as he talks over his shoulder. "You do deserve a good life. You went way more than the extra mile with George all those years. I know that. And LuLu doesn't want to take anything away from you. We can work this out and move forward one step at a time."

Dane is preaching redemption *and* continuation of their scam at the same time. On what spiritual plane does that make any sense?

I'm watching the ground right in front of me to better avoid the hurty things embedded in the tracks but stop abruptly when I look ahead far enough to make out a gaping hole dug into the red-brown dirt in front of the bulldozer. I can't see the bottom because of the shadow the hulking machine casts, blocking the rising full moon.

"You're planning to bury us out here." My tone is even and controlled. The poison didn't work, my house didn't blow up, and the shot he fired in broad daylight missed. And so, this time, he made sure he could get the job done and bury the evidence. Escalating aggression.

"What?" Dane asks in a squeaky voice from behind me.

I step aside so I'm not blocking the hole from his view and watch his face blanch.

He faces Jordan without any of his lightheartedness. I'm pretty sure Dane is putting together the same thing I am: This hole wasn't dug within the last half an hour, and it's got plenty of room for two. Whatever Jordan had agreed to with Dane in that phone call, he had already put together a plan of his own.

"Dude, are you seriously turning on *me*? After all I've done for you?"

"It's too late for compromises," Jordan says, shaking the hand holding the gun. "You'll both destroy everything I've built, and it's all I have left."

"We won't," Dane says at the same time that I say, "Owning up to what you've done is the only option left to you!"

"LuLu," Dane growls at me, his hands up like he's part of an old-fashioned stickup. "You're not helping."

"You defrauded an old man," I yell across Dane to make sure that Jordan hears me as words finally start forming in my head. "The only mercy left for you is justice. It's the only way you'll find peace in your soul ever again. Fiona is dead, and you can't—"

"Aunt Fee made that decision!" Jordan shouts back at me, spittle spraying from his lips. "She told me what she was going to do, and I told her not to—that we could talk about things. When I got there, she'd already drunk the bottle. There was nothing I could do!"

"Did you take the letter?"

"Of course I took the letter!" he snaps back. "But I didn't kill her."

"No, you just created a situation where she lost all faith in life and herself. And then left her there on the floor."

Jordan presses his lips together, and his nostrils flare.

"You don't need me to ruin your life, Jordan. You've laid that track all by yourself." Well, with Dane's help.

"Stop talking, LuLu," Dane says, his voice low and flat though he's still facing Jordan. "Please. You're making everything worse."

I continue staring at Jordan, whose jaw is clenched and eyes wild as I respond to Dane. "It was never me that haunted him, Dane, and if he's going to kill me and leave me in a hole in the desert, I want my words to ring in his ears for the rest of his life, which will continue to be miserable, by the way."

Jordan and I stare at each other across Dane's shoulder, the night sounds getting louder as the sky continues to darken, casting the desert into a sepia photograph around us. His jaw moves, but apparently, he's the one without words right now, which suits me just fine since I suddenly have lots of them.

"Admitting what you've done won't be easy for either of you, I get that, but being at peace with yourself from the inside out is the only remedy for what you're feeling, Jordan. I swear to you that it is."

"You think *finding myself* will make up for spending the rest of my life in a prison cell?"

"I do," I say with a nod, though I take note of his reference to life in prison, something that his fraud would not quite justify. I stay on topic. "I found myself through metal plates and a brain that doesn't always do what I want. I had to walk away from the life I had and accept the limitations and potential of who I am now, and I created a life where I can wake up with joy to have another day. Finding peace can happen anywhere, for anyone, in any circumstance, but it takes an inside view to find it."

"*And* you can still find salvation," Dane says, finding his preacher's voice again and, apparently, deciding to jump on my train now. "There is a way back from even this, Jordan, and, like LuLu said, you can't know what a clear conscience feels like because it's been so long since you've had one. It's worth any price you have to pay to be right with God. You *can* find peace."

I believe that, too, though I'm not sure Dane's conscience is as clear as he proclaims it to be. I also understand that the journey back from the decisions he's made are difficult to "choose" for yourself—I didn't choose it. A new life chose me five years ago, and yet right now, I'm facing consequences of choices I can't remember making, but I'm still responsible. I can change my name and build a new life, but I can't outrun who I was any more than these men can. That's the justice part of mercy. It's the only way.

"Peace," Jordan spits out like a lemon seed. "There's no such thing."

Truth; he believes it. I bet he can't remember the last time he felt peace. Before the decision to falsify George's trust, I bet. Ten years at least. A decade of suffering will cloud anyone's vision, and despite everything, I feel sad for him. He's missed so much.

"There *is* peace," Dane says as he steps toward Jordan, squaring himself against the middle of the hole behind him. He still has his hands up. "I've found it, Jordan. After what happened to Catherine—uh, LuLu—that night, I couldn't find peace either. I was haunted by what we'd done. I knew I couldn't undo the fraudulent trust without sending both of us to jail, but I had to find peace somehow. I found myself a church in Yakima and made a promise to God that I would devote the rest of my life to Him. Jesus can wash that blood from your hands, brother, and from your soul. It won't be easy, but it *will* be worth it. When you and I talked this week, my wife and I prayed about what to do and decided that I needed to come clean to LuLu. I needed to tell her the truth so she could be set free by it. That's why I'm here, Jordan. You deserve to be set free too. And we'll help you. We'll be there with you through your own Gethsemane. Won't we, LuLu?"

"No," I say, because it's the truth. "I won't be there for that. He's been trying to kill me for weeks, and Sophie's going to be here in a few days."

Sophie.

I feel the hole yawning larger behind me, portending a future that does not include me seeing my daughter again. Lights start popping in my peripheral vision as fear rears up from the calmness in my chest. I can't think about her right now and force myself to picture a roving spotlight from the surface of the moon above me, training its perfect circle of light on the three of us. Just us. I can't think about anything outside of this small section of earth right now. I can't risk the distraction at a time where clarity is so essential to my survival.

Dane lets out a breath while I take one in. I hold it, and then let it out slowly.

"My forgiveness does not replace his accountability," I say, "and you'll both have to face the reality of what you did to Mr. Flemming. My forgiveness can't protect you from—"

"Enough," Jordan says, shaking his head as he speaks and leveling the gun at my chest. "This is why this is the only solution."

"Do whatever you need to do," Dane says calmly. "Then you and I can talk things through, Jordan. You know you trust me."

I shake my head at Dane's inflated sense of self-preservation, and I'm betting Jesus is shaking His head too.

Jordan stares at me, then suddenly moves the gun a few

inches to the left. Dane and I realize in the same moment what is about to happen.

Dane opens his mouth, but no words come out.

My inner wisdom issues a command: *Run.*

I turn into the desert a split second before Jordan pulls the trigger and Dane screams.

CHAPTER 25

The sharpness of the gunshot sends my mind skittering but, thankfully, my feet keep going. This morning's gunshot that had been meant for me also flashes through my mind, and the intense dizziness I feel makes me want to fall to the ground and curl up in a ball. But my feet seem to know what to do even if my thoughts are fracturing.

"Stay present," I say to myself, running without any sense of direction at first.

I tune into my senses to bring all my thoughts back together. The only sound in my ears is my breath as I dodge sagebrush and prickly pear on what looks like an old dirt road slowly falling prey to the desert. I can smell the sage as I run past it, and I can taste the dryness of my mouth. As soon as I tune into the sense of touch, I feel the pings of rocks and cacti needles beneath my bare feet. The pain helps bring my mind back to the now, and I send a prayer of gratitude for all the work I've done all these years that has made this mental cohesion possible.

The spotlight of the moon I had imagined earlier seems

to stay a few steps ahead of me, and I'm able to see the places of clear ground between the places of "plants that would really hurt to step on." I twist my skirt into one hand to keep it from snagging on the bushes and realize that I am running in a direction I know. Not the coordinates, but I'm running toward a vortex of energy. Airport Mesa, I think. I'm not sure how I know this since I'm in a section of the desert I haven't explored before, but I know. I'm miles from the vortex, of course, but every step gets me closer, just as everything I've done today has gotten me closer to the answers I now have.

Right now, in this moment, I am okay. And I'm moving forward.

However, night hiking a few times a week and an occasional Kundalini yoga class is insufficient training for a sprint like this, which means I need a plan other than running all the way to the vortex. There's an outcropping of rock ahead with some taller cedar trees grouped around it, and I veer toward it, leaving the road for more precarious desert in the process. Something pierces the center of my left foot and stays, pounding deeper with every step.

When I am behind the rock, I put my back against the stone and place one hand to my heaving chest as I pull whatever I stepped on out of my foot. It doesn't come out completely, and I suppress a groan of pain from the attempt as lights pop in my peripheral vision.

It is what it is.

What's happened has happened.

I take a deep breath and hold it, listening to the desert and, specifically, footsteps coming after me. Maybe Jordan didn't see what direction I went . . . but we're in the middle of the desert, the moon is full in the sky, and this outcropping is the only cover I could see. He could have tracked me from half a mile away.

Then I hear him crashing through the brush toward me, and my racing heart sinks.

I push away the panic that springs up and inhale quickly to get more oxygen to the cells of my body that are screaming for it.

"Jordan!" I yell, then breathe again.

The crashing stops; he's breathing hard too. I can't gauge how far away from me he is. I turn around so that my voice will bounce off the rock, which I hope will make it harder for him to determine where I am though, obviously, I'm behind the rock formation and trees. It's the only place to hide.

"I can't keep running," I say.

"Then come out so we can put an end to this!"

"Well, I can't do that either." Breathe. Picture white light. Picture that dance recital photo. "My daughter is coming for the summer in a few days. I intend to be here for that."

He grunts. Is that grunt closer?

"Where are your kids?" I ask between breaths.

Silence.

For a moment.

I picture pink light to keep me strong and focused and a blue wall of light between Jordan and me so that his frenetic energy doesn't throw me off.

"My kids are in Phoenix with their mother and her fiancé." His tone is bitter.

Truth.

"That must be hard. I'm so sorry she left you because . . . what you did is . . . destroying the man you were. You realize that, right?" My words come out between my gasps for air.

"She doesn't know anything about it."

Truth.

I'm still breathing hard, but at least I can say more than a few words at a time. "She doesn't have to know the details to know that *you* changed. It's karma, Jordan. . . . A person cannot act in such contrast to right without it catching up. Doing what you can to make things right . . . will put you on the road to finding a life worth waking up to every day. That's what I've done. It's not easy, but it works."

Jordan's derisive laugh is closer. I am still facing the rock, but I change my position so I'm at more of an angle. I take some steps backward, looking over my shoulder to make sure I don't stumble into a cactus.

"And if I am unwilling to take your word for that?" he asks.

"Then you will continue to suffer." I shake my head. "The way I did."

"Ha," Jordan says. Closer still.

I look over my shoulder and back up a few more feet, which puts me at a poor angle to the rock I'm using for cover. But then, I really *can't* keep running, and I have more truth to tell if these end up being my last words.

"When you sat down at that sports bar, you weren't suffering, Catherine," Jordan says. "You were relishing the power."

Power.

Mr. Hernández's hypothesis is that murder is always about power. I am a threat to the power Jordan has left. So was Dane. *Oh gosh, Dane.* Is he dead?

I take a deep breath and picture a flamingo parachuting from the sky with those old aviator goggles on.

My fears for Dane go with the flamingo, allowing me to stay engaged in this conversation. "I bet I was relishing that," I say, agreeing with his assessment of who I was back then. "I had isolated myself from people and become so focused on success—on power—that I stopped seeing the good in anything other than accomplishment. People became stepping stones or stumbling blocks, and I didn't even care. I am *so* glad not to be her anymore, Jordan. You don't have to remain this version of yourself either. You can re-create your life and be someone you can respect."

He says nothing, but I hear a footstep in the soft sand. Which means he's *right* here. A few steps away on the other side of the rock. I move closer to the rock now, pressing myself into a curve but knowing it won't hide me. The moon is illuminating the light colors of my dress, making me literally glow against the red sandstone and black-green of the trees that are too thin and too short to hide me completely. My feet are throbbing from all the things I ran through. I still haven't quite caught my breath. There are miles of desert on every side of me.

But the energy of Airport Mesa to my right is throbbing in my chest. I bend down and pick up two handfuls of dirt for the simple security of having something to hold on to—a bit of Mother Earth—and I feel less alone.

I love my life, and I don't want it to end, but not everything that happens to us is of our choosing, and opportunity does not favor the passive.

I step away from the rock and out of the bit of shadow it provided. A desert breeze washes over my skin, finally cool and invigorating. I inhale the scents and sounds of the desert I have come to love, imagining the particles fusing with my spirit. This is not a terrible place to die. Better than on the side of an interstate highway. Better than in a life flight helicopter.

Sophie, I think in my mind and let my heart ache a little. But at least she had the chance to know a mother who paints rocks and makes blue pancakes. At least she has memories of night hikes and painting a wall her favorite color. And she knows that I am madly in love with her. I am so glad for those things.

The desert sounds get louder, and then a butterfly unexpectedly lifts from a shrub only a few feet away. It flitters in front of me, then goes up, then comes back. I am breathless as I watch its delicate wings carry it forward. I can't tell the colors, but there are spots of white that are illuminated by the full moon. I let out a breath I've been holding and clench the dirt more tightly in my hands as I watch the butterfly and remember God's hand in my life. The butterfly lifts over the edge of the rock, and I stare at the spot of its disappearance for another moment. There are all sorts of power, and I feel infused by the gift of that butterfly's flight.

Jordan suddenly steps around the rock from his side, only four or five feet away from me, the gun pointed at my chest. His expression is tormented, almost crying, almost raging. His chest is still heaving as he sucks in breaths. The calm enhanced by those butterfly wings stays with me, and I feel it settle in like a fresh sheet over a bed.

We stare at each other across the space between us.

His teeth are tightly clenched. He radiates tension, and it occurs to me that if his wife didn't know and Dane took his calls less and less over time, Jordan has had only himself to process all that's happened for all these years. Only himself to validate his justification. Only himself to convince.

"How did you know George?" I ask, buying time but also wanting to know this man at the center of so much sorrow. "Was he a neighbor?"

"He was a customer," Jordan says, hesitant but with an unmistakable eagerness I think surprises him. George changed Jordan's life, but he likely never talks about him.

"And a friend," I say.

"Yeah," Jordan says, nodding his head.

"How did you meet him?"

Jordan pauses but must decide there's nothing to lose in talking about this. "He called for lawn service. There aren't that many lawns in Tucson, but he was determined to keep his."

"And then what happened?"

He pauses again but can't seem to help himself. "I start mowing for him every week, and he pays me in hundred-dollar bills. He needs his fence re-stretched and then carpet removed from a spare bedroom and his roof patched. He had no family, no friends. I brought my kids sometimes, and he taught them about the birds he liked to feed in his yard." His expression has softened, but it hardens again and his eyes narrow. "I had worked my tail off for years trying to get my landscaping business to catch, but I didn't have the right equipment, or I had to buy my chemicals in bulk. I kept having to work other jobs to bring in a paycheck, which would take away from my business all over again. He'd have wanted my kids to have the sort of life I couldn't give them."

"Or," I say when it seems as though he'd finished his explanation, "he might have feared all that money would corrupt you. Maybe he'd determined that enhancing VA services for the men and women who sacrificed their lives for the good of others would be a better use of his fortune than putting such a burden on one man's soul. After all, he had to pay in hundred-dollar bills to have a friend."

Jordan's face tightens even more, and he squares the gun at my chest again.

"Did you kill him?" I ask. "It was four years after the fraudulent will that he finally died." While Jordan's actions haven't been those of a hardened criminal—until today—they have been more than I would expect from someone only trying to hide a financial crime.

"He was going to have to go to a care center anyway," Jordan defends. "He was having more and more problems at home. I was there almost every day taking care of one thing or another. He was miserable."

I bite back the lecture on there being no justification for taking someone's life from them. He knows this. Even in his paranoia and obsession, he knows what he's done is horrible. It's been eating away at him ever since.

"Did you run me off the road that night?" I ask him, my voice calm.

He moves his jaw, but the fact that he is debating how to answer is answer enough. Surprisingly, this isn't shocking or upsetting. Rather, I am relieved to know the truth. He'd kill his own friend for the money, and then shoot his accomplice. It's not so surprising that he'd also get rid of the woman who threatened to reveal him. He will kill me tonight if he has the chance. He has no reason not to.

"You did," I say, and I sound surprised even though I'm not. "You tried to kill me."

"You should have died," he finally says.

"Yes, I should have," I acknowledge. Everyone said so during my recovery. "But the police ruled it an accident."

"Driver caused," he says in a flat tone, not revealing how he got away with it. "That much was true. You should never have come to Tucson that night. You should have kept your nose out of it."

"You shouldn't have stolen that money from Mr. Flemming," I say with a shrug as though we are talking of casual things. "Or lied to your wife, or implicated your aunt, or tried to silence me, or shot your friend a few minutes ago. And you aren't going to get away with any of it. The police have a copy of Fiona's confession by now, and Mr. Hernández has likely been picked up as well, and, if he's smart—which he is—he's telling them everything he knows to save his own skin. Your road is a dead end, Jordan."

I see the reality penetrate his compulsive brain. His mouth falls slightly open. His face goes slack. Finally, he understands. I can only imagine what that feels like—a burning, probably, an emptying out of all the energy left in his body.

I take a step toward him like they do in movies when the bad guy faces his true self and the good guy takes the gun easily from his hand. I'm not going to hug Jordan when I take the gun, though. That sometimes happens in the movies, too, but I'm not feeling authentic about that.

That throbbing of the Airport Mesa gets stronger. I can feel it in my feet.

He suddenly straightens and raises the gun toward me again. "I just need all of this to be behind me. I can make a fresh start once I know that this is over. What's done is done."

"But it's not done," I say, surprised that he still isn't seeing the whole picture that I think I've done a really good job of explaining. "You'll have to go after Dane's wife next. He said he told her everything. And then his pastor. What about the people who know the name of my car and might make the connection? Are you going to kill all of them?"

He stares at me, and I wince—I hope I didn't give him any ideas.

"You cannot run from what you've done any more, Jordan, and the past does not stay in the past only because you want it to. It is a universal law of impossibility that people can do what you've done and not suffer for it somehow. You've already been suffering a long time. The only solution is to come clean and make things as right as you can."

"I can't accept those terms."

"You no longer control the terms, Jordan. The only choice you have any power over is how to heal from the inside out. It's the only decision left."

Speaking of power—the throbbing energy of the vortex has become a virtual churning. Does that mean I'm about to die? Is that what happens when you're in your final moments of life? But then I look over my shoulder and see an actual helicopter moving toward us, a searchlight sweeping across the desert.

I turn back to face Jordan as he looks at the sky behind me.

Run, my inner wisdom bids me. *One more time.*

I throw both handfuls of red dirt I've been holding into Jordan's wide eyes and run again.

The throbbing of the helicopter reverberates in my bones, and I move as quickly as I can. I separate the thrumming of the helicopter from the pull of the energy that was not my imagination. My feet are in bad shape, and I'm not on that partial road anymore, which means the ground is even more precarious, but I keep going. I can take one more step toward the life I want—the life I've made—and then another step. Toward Sophie. Toward a future.

Over my ragged breathing and my pounding feet and the thum, thum, thum of the helicopter, the sound of a gunshot rings out from behind me. My thoughts scatter like mice as I fall to the ground with a scream. Something sharp pierces my shoulder in a dozen places. I curl into a ball while thoughts of freeways and piano music and creamed eggs in the air fryer ping about my brain like a pinball game—a hundred different thought centers firing at the same time. I imagine pink light, white light, bright white daisies, and a beautiful, brown-skinned man smiling at me as he offers me a chocolatey cookie that is also good for me.

The sand is still warm from the heat of the day. I manage to take a breath. And then another one.

My thoughts rein in, and a stillness snuggles into the chaos as I take a third breath into lungs that still work. I flex my throbbing toes, roll my shoulders, release my knees, and straighten one leg at a time before pushing myself into a sitting position and looking back to where the searchlight of the helicopter has focused on a section of ground thirty yards away from me, next to the outcropping of rock that had hidden me just long enough. I can't see what's on the ground that the people hovering in the helicopter can see. But I understand.

That gunshot had no longer been meant for me.

CHAPTER 26

The only other time I've been in a helicopter was when I was life flighted to the trauma center in Tucson that saved my life. I don't remember it. *This* helicopter ride, I will never forget. I cry most of the way, overwhelmed by all that's happened, with relief that I am still alive, with fear for Dane, who I've been told is in an ambulance headed to Valley Verde Hospital, and with pure sorrow for the misery Jordan's life had become and the pain this will mean for his children and ex-wife.

A police officer I have never met greets me at the helicopter pad at the airport and hands me some tissues as she helps me into a police car that takes me to the station. Sergeant Rawlins is at the main doors when we pull in and leads me inside, limping, then toward a conference room. My feet burn as though I have walked on coals. Except I actually walked on coals at a mindfulness retreat once, and it wasn't anything like this.

"Send an EMT in here," Sergeant Rawlins says to another

officer as we pass her. The young woman nods and disappears to complete her task.

Mr. Hernández stands when I step into the conference room. I don't meet his eyes until I'm sitting. Then I look at him across the space between us, unable to think of a single thing to say. He has a new sling on his bad arm and has cleaned himself up. I wonder how long he's been here.

"We picked him up at the Posse Grounds," Sergeant Rawlins says from where he's standing in the doorway. "Mr. Hernández has assisted us in putting together a rough timeline of what's happened and put us on to both your meeting with Mr. Bohannon and Mr. Pender's property. He's been very helpful."

"He *can* be a very helpful guy," I say. Is he a good guy or a bad guy? Is he doing the best he knows how, or only doing what makes the most sense for his particular situation? "When he chooses to be."

"I chose to be this time," he says evenly, without malice. "You're welcome."

I narrow my eyes at him, still no closer to having him figured out.

"Officer Courbis will help you write up your official statement, Mr. Hernández," Sergeant Rawlins says as a female detective joins him in the doorway. "I need to discuss some things with Ms. Dupree."

After another second of eye contact with me, Mr. Hernández follows the detective. Before the door closes, another officer slips into the room with a hefty backpack bearing a red cross. It takes nearly ten minutes for the EMT to clean up my feet, using tweezers to remove a piece of glass from my foot and a few cactus spines from both my feet and my shoulder. He treats the cuts, puts something numbing on them, and wraps both of my feet with gauze. If I unfocus my eyes, it looks like I'm wearing thick white socks. Not much of a fashion statement, but my feet feel so much better. My whole body is gritty from the desert sand, and I really want a shower. A warm one.

"You'll want to have those looked at in the morning," the EMT says as he zips his pack closed. "Leave this dressing on until then."

"Thank you," I say, realizing that I will have no choice but to explain to Sophie what happened to my feet. Which means I might as well tell her everything. I feel peace about this. How could I not tell her what has happened today?

Today. One day. Holy moly.

The EMT leaves the room, and when the door closes behind him, I face Sergeant Rawlins, who sits on the other side of the desk, steeples his fingers, and stares at me for a few seconds.

"Before we get started, Ms. Dupree, I would like to apologize for not having taken you seriously when you came in earlier this week. I'm sorry for all that's happened since then and assure you I will be better for having missed this."

Truth.

"Thank you for that, but it's okay," I say, because it is. "I am used to being underestimated." Today has proven to me that I am far more capable than I thought. I still want a simple, predictable, and low-conflict life, but that isn't because it's all I can manage. It's because that's the life I want to live. Because of the particular way things have worked out, I get to do that.

"Is Dane . . . dead?"

"Mr. Bohannon?" Sergeant Rawlins clarifies.

I nod.

"No, the bullet hit him in the shoulder but passed clean through. He'll feel it for a long time, and he'll need surgery on his ankle that was broken in the fall into that pit, but I think he's going to be okay."

I nod, hoping that all of this will strengthen his testimony of justice and mercy but not diminish his faith. "And Mr. Pender?"

Sergeant Rawlins holds my eyes but says nothing. I nod and look into my lap as I take a breath. I imagine Jordan's former wife getting the phone call that the father of her children is dead. As the truth comes out, she'll realize why the man she'd fallen in love with had changed so much over the course of their marriage. How will she tell his children? What will Jordan's choices mean for her family going forward? My heart aches for them, and I send a burst of white light toward the woman and children I do not know. May God hold them through their pain and help them find their way through it.

"If you're ready," Sergeant Rawlins says, bringing my thoughts back to the present. "I'd like to start at the beginning."

"Which one?" I ask.

He raises his eyebrows in surprise. He doesn't realize there are multiple beginnings to choose from.

I take a breath. "I used to be a woman named Catherine."

CHAPTER 27

An hour later, Sergeant Rawlins leads me to the foyer. One of the female officers loans me a pair of orange, open-toed, foam sandals from her locker. They look ridiculous on me as there is no orange in my sundress for the color to coordinate with, but they are comfortable and I hobble less in them, though I'm certainly not walking normally.

"You'll look into Bart Roberts's death?" I ask as we leave. I remembered to tell him about it, and he took some notes. I want to make sure that Maryanne the Murdering Mistress doesn't get away with what she's done.

"Yes," Sergeant Rawlins says. "We'll be opening a separate investigation."

Mr. Hernández stands from where he's been waiting and smiles somewhat sheepishly.

I smile back, equally reserved. Has he been waiting for me?

Sergeant Rawlins instructs us both that he'll have more questions for us after they've finished processing the different crime scenes and tells us not to go far from home so that we'll be available when the police need us. We agree to his terms, and then we are left relatively alone. There's a lot going on in the station, but no one is paying much attention to us standing here in the foyer.

"Um, can you drive me back to the Arroyo?" he asks, looking at my feet.

"George has been arrested, or, rather, impounded as evidence," I explain.

"Can you drive at all?"

I look back at my feet. "I can walk, so I think driving will be okay."

"You can use my car until Tuesday, if that helps," Mr. Hernández says. "The police helped me pick it up on our way here, but I still can't drive." He lifts his broken wing. His nose is still swollen, and he'll likely have an impressive black eye by tomorrow.

"That would be a big help to use your car. Thank you."

We walk out of the police station together, but silent. It is almost midnight, and my brain feels numb, but also . . . intact. I feel like I did a good job of recounting things to Sergeant Rawlins, and my mind feels pretty clear. I'm proud of myself.

It is seventy-five degrees outside, and I can only just make out the outline of the red rock mountains standing like sentries around the city. We don't speak for the duration of the walk to Mr. Hernández's unnamed car and the drive to the hotel.

"Are you going to stay at the Arroyo tonight?" he asks when I turn into the parking lot several minutes later.

"No," I say, though I hadn't thought about it until right now. The realization that I can go home fills me with a sparkle of joy. "I'm going home."

"Will you lock your doors?" He smiles as though he's making a joke, but it sounds like a reprimand disguised as a jest.

"It's actually a good thing I left my doors unlocked," I tell him. "If not for the candle, Jordan would have tried another method and that one might have achieved his intention."

"Maybe," he says, but I can tell he isn't convinced.

I *will* be locking my doors from now on. I just don't want him to take satisfaction in my decisions, which is childish on my part but, whatever. It's been a long day. I feel how I feel.

The hotel parking lot is crowded, and I pull into an open space a long way from the front doors. We passed the area I'd been parked in before—Mr. Hernández's blood will still be on the pavement over there. And in the stairwell. It makes me shiver.

"Are you coming inside to get your things?"

I shake my head with another instantly made decision. Sergeant Rawlins gave Kermit back to me, which has my phone and wallet. There isn't anything else I need to be comfortable once I'm tucked inside my favorite place in the world.

Maybe I'll cry some more when I'm alone.

Maybe I'll journal about this.

Maybe I'll watch reruns of *Moonlighting* and make a batch of Body Toddys until two o'clock in the morning. I am free to live this night however I choose to. That's an astounding gift I will not take for granted.

"I'll get my things tomorrow. Checkout is at eleven, right?" Even if I stay up late, I'll have plenty of time.

"I think so." He doesn't move to get out of the vehicle, and I hear him draw in a long breath.

I tuck a strand of hair behind my ear, cognizant of him watching me from the passenger seat with his very focused look. Why isn't he getting out?

"Well, anyway, um, thanks," I say. "And thanks for loaning me your car."

"You're welcome."

"I hope you can get your shoulder fixed soon."

"Me too. It's been quite a day."

We continue to sit there.

"LuLu," he finally says.

I turn to look at him.

"Do you ever eat at restaurants?" he asks.

"Not really," I say, scrunching up my face at the memory of how loud Thai Spices was. The fresh roll wraps, however, were delicious, even though I'd lost my appetite after those first two bites. I bet I could learn how to make spring rolls with cocktail shrimp and pre-prepped ingredients. I bet Sophie would love them.

He pauses a minute, then nods. "Um, do you ever . . . uh, hike?"

"Sometimes," I say. "Usually only at night in the summer. It's too hot during the day." I look at my bright white and orange feet. "I don't think I'll be hiking for a while, though."

"Right, um . . ." He clears his throat. "When will I see you again?"

"Probably Tuesday after I get George back, although if you need a ride somewhere before then, just let me know and I'm happy to drive you."

"I mean, other than that. I'd like to get to know you . . . differently than we've been able to so far."

I pull my eyebrows together as I try to make sense of what he means and turn in my seat so I'm facing him directly. "Get to know me differently?"

He laughs under his breath and shakes his head. "I would like to get to know you in a way we haven't been able to do so far. Let you get to know me at my best, instead of . . . what this has been."

"Why? We solved the case. I don't need an attorney anymore."

"You don't make this easy," he says, laughing again but with vulnerability in his voice.

This? What is *this*? And then I understand and feel my eyebrows rise. "Oh, wait, do you like me? Like, I mean, *like* me? Really? Are you asking me on a date?"

He lets out a breath, and his face darkens with a blush beneath the parking lot light shining in through the windows of his car. I would not have thought him capable of blushing. "Honestly, LuLu, I don't know what exactly I feel—it's been a really intense day. But I don't want things to end like this between us."

Truth.

I feel myself smile as the thrill of being chosen washes through me. It's been a long time since I've felt it, and I let myself indulge. For all my independence and security in this new life, I would love to have a true partner who could accept me, quirks and all. Someone to wake up with. Someone to love and hold and be with. That possibility starts with investing time, and I relish the validation of Mr. Hernández wanting me to fill some of his hours.

But I don't indulge the feeling for very long because this man—despite the good that he did, eventually—also spent days seeing my life as nothing more than a puzzle to solve. Days where Jordan could have killed me. Days that put people I care about in danger. Mr. Hernández monitored everything he said to make sure he didn't tip me off to his deceit. He lost his temper, treated me like a child, and is going to make me pay for his new glasses. He could have ended this before Fiona only saw one way out, and he didn't. He weighed his options and chose his interests over everyone else's.

People aren't all good or all bad, and these last few days can't define Mr. Hernández entirely. It isn't that I'm in unrighteous judgment, I don't think, but I still have no interest in a relationship with a man who has shown that he manipulates situations toward his own self-interest and does the right thing mostly when he's run out of other options.

I take a deep breath and give him a new smile, softer, sadder, but honest.

"Thank you for that, Mr. Hernández," I say. "And thank you for helping me get out of that stairwell and for helping the police find me tonight. I appreciate those things very much."

His expression closes, back to that stoically neutral expression I recognize from those first few visits to his office. "But," he says for me, his tone more reprimanding than disappointed, which further validates my decision. He wants me to please *him* with my answer.

"But," I repeat, "I don't think you and I could create a trustworthy connection after all that's happened." I almost add an apology but then stop myself. I don't owe him an apology for feeling like I do. I owe *myself* authenticity, and that is the side of the fence I am on right now. "I would like to be friends, though," I say, knowing that sounds silly. We were never really friends. "And thank you for asking me out; that was validating."

"Validating," he huffs as he places his left hand on the door handle.

He chose me, and it's amazing to feel choice-worthy, but I get to choose too.

I take a deep breath as he pushes open his door. "Does this change your mind about loaning me your car?"

His back is facing me as he puts his feet on the pavement. He has to think about this, which is all the answer I need.

"I'll arrange for a rental tomorrow," I say. Offering his car was part of an agenda, and without my agreeing to do things his way, he no longer feels generous. I get it. "Thank you for letting me use it tonight. I'll take good care of it."

He gets out of the car without saying another word, slams the door, and starts limping to the hotel. I guess I could have dropped him off at the front, but I hadn't yet decided I was going home. I watch him until he reaches the front door safely, then shift his car into reverse. Within a minute, I am back on Main Street driving toward home in this almost silent car, which is very comfortable, but it's no George Flemming III. I focus on that feeling of Mr. Hernández wanting to spend time with me. That feeling, fleeting though it was due to the circumstances, is breathing life into a possibility I have maybe worked too hard to keep tucked away. But, what if . . .

I keep driving and thinking until I turn onto Sanborn Drive and smile because there are still lights on inside Handy Manny Candy's house when I reach it. That means he must not work with his framing crew tomorrow, which makes sense since tomorrow is Saturday. I wouldn't have woken him if his house was dark, but the fact that he's still up feels exactly right. Exactly perfect.

As I limp toward his front door, I take in details I didn't notice the first time I was here today. His yard is tidily xeriscaped, with a large patch of prickly pear off to the side of his porch and a pot of daisies that won't last much longer as the summer heat increases. Manny can't know that daisies are my favorite flower, but the universe does. It makes me smile.

The porch light goes on almost as though he were watching for me. I take a breath and relish the thrill coursing through my body as I see him framed in the backlit window, looking out to see who's bothering him at 11:47 on a Friday night. I reach the base of the stairs at the same time he opens the front door of his house and steps onto the porch that's crumbling around the edges.

He's wearing the same khaki cargo shorts and gray T-shirt that strains against his biceps. Gracious, he's a beautiful man. And smart. And kind. And honest. And very handy around the house.

"Luh-loo?" Manny asks from where he stands.

"Hi," I say, giving a silly wave.

"What's happened?" he says, frowning at my bandaged feet.

"Oh," I say, embarrassed. "I had a little incident in the desert tonight, but I'm okay."

"Do you want to come in? Sit down?"

"Uh, yes, actually. I would like that."

He comes down to take my arm so that he can help me up the steps. He's never touched me before, and the sensation is thrilling. Inside, he lets go of my arm and hurries into the kitchen to pull a chair out from the table. The air smells like chocolate and peanut butter—a grandmother's house.

"Sit," he says. "Your timing is perfect. The cookies are almost cooled enough to eat."

I sit in the proffered chair and feel a lightness in my chest which validates my coming here. "You're making No-Bake Cookies at eleven o'clock at night?"

"When I'm feeling bad, I clean and cook. You should see my bathrooms right now." He whistles under his breath. "After your visit, I felt bad about Ms. Fiona and the fact that I did not stay for lunch. Also, I'm very close to having the most perfect, yet health conscious, No-Bake Cookie recipe ever. Pretty sure."

I smile as he rinses a washcloth and begins to wipe the traces of cocoa powder and oats off the counter. The only thing about this interaction that doesn't fit my fantasy is that he's wearing a shirt. It feels inappropriate to ask him to remove it.

"Did you find what you needed?" The lilt of his accent sounds like a lullaby. He looks up as he rinses the washcloth again. "Are you okay?"

"I did find what I needed," I say. "I'm . . . okay." Things aren't perfect, and there is a good deal of sorting to do, but everything is going to be okay. I'm okay.

He's gorgeous.

We look at one another across the kitchen bar that separates us, and I notice a butterfly magnet on his fridge holding a picture of his kids. It further empowers me, and I meet his curious gaze again.

"I really like you, Manny," I blurt out like a complete idiot. I feel my cheeks heat up, but I don't pull back. I can be impulsive and direct and a little . . . off, but the only way to know if he can accept me is to be me in the first place. "I, um, I . . . would like to spend time with you, get to know you better. Let you get to know me better too. Would you be open to that? It's okay if you aren't, I completely understand but . . . would you want to, um, see me outside of handyman projects and sidewalk interrogations?"

His soft smile widens, and he comes around the counter. He crosses his arms over his chest and leans his hips against the counter. Oh, my heck. I can't even . . .

"You came here to ask me that after the difficult day you have had?"

I nod, feeling silly again but also accepting the silliness. Relationships require a lot of a person—trust, time, vulnerability. I'm willing to invest if he is. "The days I get to see you are my favorite days, Manny," I admit. "I would like more of those. Please. I mean, if you want to . . . too."

His smile splits wide open, and I see on his face the feeling I had not too long ago—of being chosen. If he chooses me back, I think we could make something beautiful. Easy. Exactly right for both of us.

Or maybe we could just have a nice time together for a while. I could be okay with that if it's all it was meant to be. It would still prove me capable and courageous enough to try—and I didn't even need pink light to give me the strength to do it.

"I *would* like that," he says. "I'll have my kids off and on for the summer starting next week, and I'm still three days with the crew. I might not have a lot of extra time."

"I have Sophie for the summer too," I say, a little embarrassed that I didn't lead with that. Forgetting to mention my child is something Catherine would do, but I forgive myself immediately. I am not like that anymore. Not even close.

"Well, then, maybe we can take things slowly and see where it goes."

"That would be really nice," I say, wishing I'd thought to put on my lip gloss. Or even look in a mirror before coming here. I've been running through the desert. I'm probably a wreck. And the fact that he's taken no notice says something beautiful too.

He looks over his shoulder before turning back to me. "You'll stay for a cookie? The versions you've tried were still a work in progress, and the consistency wasn't exactly right. I think I've got it now—equal amounts of honey and coconut oil are the key." He half turns toward the door. "Would you like one?"

"Now?"

He shrugs. "There's no time like the present, though my curfew is one o'clock because I have a nine a.m. appointment with Carla tomorrow. She is considering turning off her pilot lights in the summer and wants me to shut off her gas so she can try for the weekend. I wonder where she got that idea." He smiles that smile that fills his whole face.

"That's funny, because I had a lovely warm shower this afternoon at the hotel the police arranged for me that had me thinking of turning my gas back on." There *is* no time like the present. In fact, the present is the only time that really exists.

The past is finished, and its only power is to be learned from.

The future, as I've learned, is impossible to predict, and its only power is to be a hope.

But in the present, I can always do my best to be my best.

One day at a time, one step in front of the last. Life is meant to be lived, and I am ready to live it with a bit more joyful momentum.

I am LuLu, and LuLu is great.

A FEW OF LULU'S FAVORITE THINGS

Four-Count Breathing

- Inhale for the count of four.
- Hold your breath for the count of four.
- Exhale for the count of four.
- Hold your lungs empty for the count of four.
- Repeat.

Conscious breathing exercises help reset your parasympathetic nervous system, a network of nerves that assist the body to relax and conserve energy. Resetting this system helps your mind and body feel safe and calm after periods of stress. Practice up to eight counts per step to find what count works best for you. As with anything else, practice improves performance and response.

LuLu's Affirmations

- I am (insert your name), and (insert your name) is great.
- Everything works out (perfectly for me).
- The solution is already in the room.
- What has happened has already happened.
- It is what it is.
- Right now, in this moment, I am okay.

Rachel's Knoll

Rachel's Knoll is a sanctuary within Seven Canyons Golf Club, preserved by a legal legacy thanks to Rachel Lunt, who fell in love with Sedona years ago and wanted to create a

park for meditation and relaxation that would remain accessible to the public. You can find directions by Googling "Rachel's Knoll Sedona" and looking for the most up-to-date reference.

DIY Linen Spray

    3 tablespoons witch hazel
    2 tablespoons distilled water
    40 drops quality essential oils

1. Use a small funnel to combine witch hazel and distilled water in a 4-ounce glass spray bottle.
2. Add 40 drops total of your favorite essential oils.
3. Shake spray bottle to combine before each use.
4. Store out of direct sunlight for up to a year.

Notes

    Oils can break down some plastics, so always use glass containers with essential oils. Look for oils marked "100% pure essential oil" to ensure the highest quality.

Some favorite oil combinations:

- lavender and marjoram (calming)
- lemon and rosemary (energizing)
- bergamot and grapefruit (uplifting)

Creamed Eggs

    1 teaspoon butter, cold
    1 egg
    1 teaspoon fresh herbs of your choice (consider sage, chives, thyme, or basil)
    salt and pepper
    1 tablespoon heavy cream

1. Spray an oven-safe 6-ounce ramekin (or muffin-tin cup) with nonstick spray.
2. Add ingredients to ramekin in the order listed. Do not mix together.
3. Bake at 400 degrees F. for 12 minutes, or until slightly browned on top.
4. Remove from oven and let cool five minutes.
5. Serve directly from the ramekin or scoop egg onto a plate or serve over toast or grits.

Notes
- Dry herbs work, but they aren't as flavorful as fresh herbs.
- Garlic and onion powder or salt can be used instead of regular salt and pepper. Be careful not to over-season, especially if using salted butter.
- If cooking in an air fryer: Bake at 360 degrees F. for 12 minutes.

Gloria's Poppyseed Cake

Cake
- 3 cups flour
- 2¼ cups white sugar
- 1½ teaspoons salt
- 1½ teaspoons baking powder
- 1½ teaspoons vanilla extract
- 2 teaspoons almond extract
- 1½ teaspoons butter flavoring
- 1½ tablespoons poppy seeds
- 3 eggs
- 1½ cups milk
- 1 cup plus 2 tablespoons oil

Glaze
- ¼ cup orange juice
- ½ teaspoon almond extract
- ½ teaspoon butter flavoring
- ½ teaspoon vanilla extract
- ¾ cup sugar

1. Grease a Bundt pan or two loaf pans.
2. To make the cake: In a large bowl, mix all cake ingredients together.
3. Pour batter into greased Bundt pan and bake at 350 degrees F. for 50 minutes. (If using two loaf pans, bake for 40 minutes. Make sure the centers of the loaves are firm.)
4. Allow cakes to cool in pan(s) for 10 minutes, then turn out onto a cooling rack.
5. To make the glaze: In a small bowl, mix all glaze ingredients together and stir until sugar is dissolved.
6. Using a pastry brush, liberally glaze top and sides of warm cake.

Notes
- Use flavor emulsions instead of extracts; emulsions do not "bake out" like some extracts do.
- Loaves freeze well. Cool completely then wrap in plastic wrap and seal in a gallon-size zip-top freezer bag. Freeze for up to 3 months.

Manny's No-Bake Cookies

1 cup creamy or crunchy peanut butter
½ cup refined coconut oil
½ cup honey
1 teaspoon vanilla
1 teaspoon cinnamon
4 tablespoons cocoa powder
2½ cups quick or regular oats

1. Set a sheet of wax paper on the counter.
2. In a saucepan over medium heat, combine peanut butter, coconut oil, and honey. Stir consistently until melted and combined.
3. Add vanilla, cinnamon, and cocoa powder. Stir until thoroughly combined.
4. Add oats and stir for two minutes to soften slightly.
5. Use a ¼-cup scoop to drop cookies onto wax paper. Allow to cool completely.
6. Makes 9 large cookies.

Notes
- Cookies can be stored, covered, on the counter for a few days or in the refrigerator for up to two weeks.
- Cookies are dairy free and gluten free.

ACKNOWLEDGMENTS

I have many people to thank for this book coming together—first, the team at Shadow Mountain Publishing, and, specifically, Chris Schoebinger (Publisher), who asked me one day why I didn't have anything on the "to be published" list. His question led to conversations that led to a new contract that put me back on the publication track. I will forever be grateful that he asked the question that led to everything else.

I am excited to be working with the Shadow Mountain team again. Big thanks to Heidi Gordon (Product Director) and Lisa Mangum (Managing Editor), whose arms were wide open to welcome me back, and Callie Hansen (Product Manager), who was the first of the team to read the full manuscript. Thanks to Rachael Ward (typesetter) and Holly Robinson (designer) as well as the entire sales and marketing team: Amy Parker, Lehi Quiroz, Troy Butcher, Haley Haskins, and Bri Cornell.

Thank you, Lane Heymont, my agent with Tobias Literary Agency, who has stuck by me through some thin years.

ACKNOWLEDGMENTS

Your guidance and faith has been more validating than you can know. I have needed the steady integrity I found in you.

Nancy Campbell Allen (*Protecting Her Heart*, Shadow Mountain, 2024), Jennifer Moore (*Discovering Dahlia*, Covenant Communications, 2025), Brittany Larsen (*Britta & the Beach Boy*, Brittany Larsen Books, 2024), and Becca Wilhite (*Whispers of Shadowbrook House*, Shadow Mountain, 2025) are my patient critique group members who have given me a writing foundation when I struggled to find my own.

Brittany Larsen, specifically, read the full manuscript and gave me great feedback, as did Kaylee Baldwin (*Rosie and the Beast Next Door*, Sweetly Us Press, 2024), who helped me with specific Arizona references.

Patty Bartholomew, a brilliant financial adviser for Harold Dance Investments in Logan, Utah, helped me get my terminology and processes right for the financial know-how I needed. If I messed anything up, it's because I changed things after she advised me correctly.

Ashley Rahlf of Cokeley Body Co. was incredibly helpful in recommending which DIY home product recipes were safe to share recipes for, and which could be dangerous if not handled correctly. Her expertise changed the course of the story.

Jennifer Moore shared her grandmother's legacy of "Rachel's Knoll," which I visited with my friend Tracy Rawlins, the model in the photo on page 291, during a research weekend in Sedona. It's a very cool place to visit.

Thank you to my Aunt Melinda (Rich), who allowed me to use her famous and well-loved Poppyseed Cake recipe, my dear friend, Tiffany Dominguez, for making me Creamed Eggs and allowing me to use them in this book, and my new daughter-in-law, Kayla Limb, who allowed me to use her No-Bake Cookie recipe. I am grateful to have such smart, talented, and generous women in my life—thank you!

Many thanks to the readers who continue to share with me how much they love my books and ask me what I'm working on now. On the nights when I worried that my best books were behind me, these comments helped me keep faith in myself and remember what I want my future to be. Thank you for lifting me up, cheering me on, and recommending my books to the people in your life. Word of mouth makes all the difference.

Much love to my children, who love me for reasons other than my words and encourage me to keep going and keep being. They are the great loves of my life, and I cannot imagine my life without them. Watching them "become" is my greatest joy. I am so proud to be their mother.

Thank you to my sweet husband, Doug, who made space for me and my children in his heart and his home. He has given me new faith and perspective within this life we are building one day, one trip, one laugh, one hunt, one embrace, one home project, one meal, and one book at a time. Thank you also to Doug's family, who have loved me and given me a new role as "Grandma Josi." It has been a joy and a pleasure to find my place with each one of them.

Lastly, thank you to my Father in Heaven who, in the valley of shadows, told me, "When it's time to make a decision, you'll know." While I would prefer advance notice, blinking lights with arrows, and a loudspeaker, I am learning to better recognize His whispers and trust His timing. When I did need to make those important decisions, I knew what I needed to do—just as He said I would. Thanks for not giving up on me even though on my darkest nights I considered giving up on You. I have seen Your hand, outstretched still. Thank you, thank you, thank you.

DISCUSSION QUESTIONS

1. What are your feelings about earth energies such as minerals and vortexes as described in this book?
2. Do you have a geographic location that invigorates you?
3. How do you feel about LuLu's decision to move to Sedona, even though it meant leaving her daughter in Seattle?
4. Have you ever had to make a decision that was best for you but required great sacrifice? How have you found peace with that in your own life?
5. Have you, or someone close to you, experienced a brain trauma or a severe concussion? How were you affected by this injury?
6. Do you, or someone close to you, struggle with anxiety? Did any of LuLu's "tricks" resonate with you? Do you have other methods of working through your own anxiety?
7. Do you have experience with affirmations? If so, do you have a favorite affirmation?
8. If you've read other books by Josi S. Kilpack, how does LuLu's story compare?

Enjoy this sneak peek
of the next

LULU DUPREE MYSTERY

CHAPTER 1

The horrible terrible has happened.

The thing I have worried about since we ran out of indoor projects and I instituted a two-hour limit on Sophie's phone. Which she has already used up today video-chatting with friends back in Seattle, scrolling through social media, and posting a silly photo of us with a filter that made us look like aliens. I find those filtered photos a little disturbing, but I keep that to myself. I'm working hard to be a cool mom. I so much want her to have a good time.

"I'm bored," Sophie says again, and the blood further drains from my head.

Everything works out, I affirm to myself as I take a deep breath and prepare my response. *I can do this.*

Sophie arrived two weeks after my "Terror in the Desert," which is what I have titled my *Dateline* episode, should the producers ever approach me. She was supposed to have come sooner, but her dad and I agreed that it would be best to delay it. I couldn't put weight on my feet for the first week due to the injuries I sustained during the Terror. I'm doing better now, but I still can't spend much time on my feet, and the only shoes that are comfortable are Crocs, which look ridiculous with my sundresses. I've even had groceries delivered, which I never thought would be my thing. It's gone okay except for the quality of the tomatoes the shopper chooses for me each time. Surely there are better options than the rock-hard orange ones I have received three times now. The first batch is just now ripe enough to eat.

Sophie and I have been pretty homebound, and we've used our downtime to make items to restock the boutiques that sell my DIY household products: Body Toddys—skin-softening sponges infused with sugar scrub, two batches of fall-scented soap that are now curing on the baker's rack I keep in the kitchen pantry, and two dozen Good LuLu soy-based, organic candles with essential oils—none of them mulberry-plum scented, thank you very much.

We painted some rocks from the yard—I can't hike yet to collect better specimens—and we've baked enough cookies and quiches that we are officially sick of both. As we ran out of homebound activities, Sophie spent more and more time on her phone. In fact, the only thing she's been willing to set her phone aside for is to hear more about my narrow escapes from death. Maybe it's because of those true-crime podcasts she has been listening to more than I would like.

Her level of interest makes me uncomfortable, if I'm honest, so I have become more casual in my responses—"Oh, you want more details about the bad choices I made years ago that made me a target of a very disturbed man? Maybe later. Let's watch something uplifting. How about *The Hunger Games*?"

We've watched the entire series twice already. And the YouTube videos where they dub bad lipreading dialogue to the scenes—hilarious. "Do something, Fruity!" People are so clever.

Sophie doesn't seem to grasp the depth of what happened to me over the course of those two days, which might be for the best. For my part, I've had nightmares about large gaping holes and running over cut glass, trying to save Fiona, who I do not save. It's not someone else's story revised for time and recorded for informative entertainment of the masses; it's my life. And while the intensity is in the past, the situation is not. The police have been by twice since Sophie's arrival and called several times to clarify details. Dane's wife even called me last night to hear my version of events. He's home in Yakima now, and they have some work to do as a couple as they come to terms with his part in things, I guess. Each time someone pops in for information, Sophie hovers and absorbs and when they leave, she has a dozen new questions.

And now she's bored, and I don't know what to do.

I take a four-count breath, hold it, and release it to invite calmness.

"Well, what sounds like fun?" I reply in a falsely chipper tone.

Sophie sighs dramatically and lifts both shoulders before letting them drop. "I don't know," she says with a heavy whine in her tone. "Can we go swimming?"

"*You* can go swimming," I say. "I need another few weeks before I can immerse my feet, but I could drive you and sit in one of the loungy-chair things."

I haven't driven since she got here, but I'm sure I could manage it. Sophie took an Uber from the Sedona airport, and Manny—the most handsome man in the world and sort of my boyfriend—brought us dinner twice. His two teenage sons came with him the first time, which was very loud, but the second time was just him because his kids were back with their mom in Mesa. He's supposed to get two months of visitation in the summer, but his kids have jobs and sports and church camp, which means that while he gets them for longer stays in the summer, it's not for the whole stretch. He rolls with it and enjoys what time he gets.

Sophie sighs again, and even though I know she's thirteen and thirteen-year-olds are managing a lot of feelings and hormones and whatnot, my anxiety increases. When she turns fourteen in a few months, she gets to choose which parent she lives with. I want her to choose me, but I haven't worked up the courage to ask her yet. That we've already argued about her phone, and she's bored after only a week and a half makes me so scared that she'll want to stay in Seattle. I want her to love it here, but what if she doesn't?

I am LuLu, and LuLu is great!

I relax the muscles of my body and force some optimism into my brain. Of course she'll choose to move to Sedona once the choice is hers. I'm her mother, and she loves and misses me. We say that to each other all the time.

"The public pool at Posse Grounds is open until 5:00, I think." I'm already toggling to the information on my phone while picturing a chorus line of flamingos in high heels to keep my thoughts from continuing down the path of worry over what Sophie will choose. Visualizing flamingos in silly situations and costumes is a mind-hack my therapist, Dr. Cindy, helped me develop a few years ago to keep my thoughts from spinning out as they are sometimes wont to do.

"I don't want to swim by myself." Sophie makes a face, and I take another four-count breath. I shouldn't take things so personally, but I do.

"Well, you're not going to meet any new kids here at home."

"I *know*," she says. She turns away from me but not before I see her roll her eyes. It makes my breath catch in my throat. She's rolling her eyes at *me*?

I push myself up from the couch as though remembering something I need to do in the kitchen. I am not going to let her see my dismay. I'm making too big a deal of this.

It takes a few seconds on my feet to get my balance. Though the bottoms of my feet are healing well and I'm only wearing socks now, not bandages, some of the injuries were deep. A few cactus spines had broken off in each foot, and a piece of glass had gone halfway through my left foot, requiring minor surgery to remove. I'm able to walk around more and more every day, but I'm still limited, and my feet throb after I've been on them for even a few minutes.

"I don't want to meet other kids," she says, flopping onto the couch while I walk—almost hobble—into the kitchen. "I just want to do something fun. I'm *so* bored."

Truth. I would know if she were lying about that; it's something I've always been able to read in people. But that inner sense isn't helpful in this instance. For one thing, why would she lie about that? For another thing, I'm already feeling responsible for her happiness or lack thereof and *knowing* that she really feels bored does me no good whatsoever. Ignorance about what your teenagers really think of you might be actual bliss. I will never know.

And we've come full spiral back to the fact that she's bored. "What are your ideas, then?" I open the fridge, looking for a way to eat the feelings of insecurity rising inside me. But we're running low on options. I'm completely out of cheese, case in point.

Sophie comes into the kitchen and sits backward on a kitchen chair. I swear she's taller than she was when she came out in April, and she has braid extensions now that reach almost halfway down her back. Forrest—her dad and the genetic contributor to her dark hair, eyes, and skin—wouldn't let her get braids until middle school, which starts in a couple of months. The braids make her look older, which I don't like at all. Can't she stay little for a while longer? And have a bit less sassafras?

"Can we drive past the house where the lady died?" she asks, looking at me hopefully.

The excitement in her voice catches me like a snagged fingernail. "No."

"Can we go see the big hole that guy dug to bury you? Do you think they filled it in?"

"We're not going out there either." The mere reminder of that hole meant to be my grave makes my skin clammy. I close the fridge and move to the pantry. We have graham crackers and chocolate chips—perfect eat-my-feelings fodder—but believe it or not, I'm sweeted out. That rarely happens to me, but we've made cookies every day for the last two weeks. I'm seriously craving cheese. If I put in a grocery order now, would it be deliverable today? I usually do the order the night before, but the extra lead time hasn't paid off in ripe tomatoes.

"Can we go to that hotel and see if there are bloodstains in the stairwell where that guy attacked you?"

"Absolutely not."

Sophie groans just as the doorbell rings. I check my phone on the counter to see if anyone has texted to tell me they are stopping by, but I don't have any new messages. The police never give me a warning, and my stomach sinks at the possibility of another interrogation.

I might be more reluctant to answer if the doorbell wasn't offering salvation from the moody judgments of my wonderfully smart and beautiful daughter, who I absolutely adore and don't know what to do with.

I limp to the door and open it, aware of Sophie coming up behind me. I can literally feel her eagerness like a bubble of energy around her. Has she always been this curious or is it the proximity to my dramatic escape drawing it from her?

My eyes travel down from the adult height I expected to the intense look of a thin girl with straight, blonde hair in need of a good brushing that just touches her shoulders. Her gray eyes meet mine behind glasses with bright blue frames. When she smiles, her freckled cheeks round out, and she reveals a gap between her front teeth. Her T-shirt has a big red heart on the front with the word *Calculus* in the center, and her cutoff shorts reveal knobby pale knees.

"Hi!" she says and waves even though we're standing three feet apart on opposite sides of the threshold. "I'm Abi, with an *i*. A-b-i. Not with a *y*, and it's not short for Abigail."

"Um, hi, Abi," I respond, grateful for this unexpected shift in the energy. "I'm LuLu. Both *L*'s are capitalized, and it's not short for anything either." I wave behind me to Sophie. "This is my daughter, Sophie—short for Sophia."

"But it's not actually shorter," Sophie volunteers. I can hear caution in her voice but also intrigue about this stranger who's presenting herself as though she belongs here. "Same number of letters, just less 'old lady.'"

Abi's big smile gets even bigger, and I wonder how old she is. Maybe eight, if I judged by looks and frame alone, but her demeanor is more mature than that, and her shirt says she loves calculus.

"Does anyone call you 'Soph'?" Abi asks.

"My dad, sometimes," Sophie answers.

I didn't know this, and it makes me feel left out.

"Grandpa calls me 'Abs' sometimes, which is funny, 'cause I don't have any."

Sophie laughs.

Don't have any . . . abs? *Oh, there's the joke.*

"Is there something we can help you with, Abi?" I ask, looking behind her though I can see that she's here alone. Where did she come from? There are four homes at the end of Yellow Sky Way, though it isn't really a cul-de-sac, just the end of a road, and it's not the time of year for Girl Scout Cookies.

Jerry lives almost across from me, though there's a solid fifty yards between our front doors, and it's not a direct line. Gwyneth Nardoni lives to my right; she never waves or smiles or thanks me for the Christmas gifts I leave on her porch. The only reason I know her whole name is because her mail gets misdelivered here sometimes. The first few times I tried to take her mail to her, she didn't answer the door, so I just put it in her mailbox now. Once there was a letter to Gwyneth Smith, but I assumed it was the same person. The big cottonwood tree on the west side of my driveway mostly blocks the view of her house if I'm inside, and I rarely see her unless one or both of us are coming and going. The fourth and farthest house from me—on the other side of Gwyneth's—is a second home for a couple from Colorado. They won't be back until November.

"I hope you *can* help," Abi says, but she's not looking at me. She's looking at Sophie, her gray eyes sparkling. "Do you want to help me solve a murder?"

ABOUT THE AUTHOR

Josi is the award-winning author of several novels across a spectrum of genres and a contributor to many anthologies. In addition to her writing, she enjoys reading, cooking, watching the same movies over and over again, her work as a real estate agent, and naps when she can fit them in.

She is the mother of four, stepmom to three, stepgrandma to six, and lives in Northern Utah with her husband, Doug, their two hounds, and five chickens. You can learn more about Josi and her books at www.josiskilpack.com.

Facebook: authorjosiskilpack
Instagram: @authorjosiskilpack